ONCE, A LONG TIME AGO

ONCE,
A LONG TIME AGO

Kay G. Jay

ELM HILL

A Division of
HarperCollins Christian Publishing

www.elmhillbooks.com

Once, A Long Time Ago

Published in Nashville, Tennessee, by Elm Hill, an imprint of Thomas Nelson. Elm Hill and Thomas Nelson are registered trademarks of HarperCollins Christian Publishing, Inc.

Elm Hill titles may be purchased in bulk for educational, business, fund-raising, or sales promotional use. For information, please e-mail SpecialMarkets@ ThomasNelson.com.

Publisher's Note: This novel is a work of fiction. Names, characters, places, and incidents are either products of the author's imagination or used fictitiously. All characters are fictional, and any similarity to people living or dead is purely coincidental.

Library of Congress Cataloging-in-Publication Data

Library of Congress Control Number: 2019932199

ISBN 978-1-400325221 (Paperback)
ISBN 978-1-400325238 (eBook)

DEDICATION

This book is dedicated to my husband, Chuck Johnson.
He is my one true love and my hero -
a warrior in his own right.

CHAPTER ONE

The boy was calling for him. There was desperation and fear in the voice. His boots pounding on the concrete floor echoed off the block walls as he followed the sound. The small voice was begging now. He burst into the room, his weapon at the ready and stopped dead in his tracks. He would never have recognized the bruised and bloody face of the child, but the eyes were his. He lunged at the man holding the boy in his grip.

"Angelo, what have you done!" He was stopped short by the glint of the knife blade against the boy's pulsing jugular.

"Not so fast, Danny Boy. He sold you out." The boy struggled convulsively to free himself.

"No Danny. You know I would not do that." His words were made thick by swollen lips.

"It's all right. Don't be afraid." Their eyes met. The boy's trust was unwavering. No one had ever cared about him before. He was a street kid, but from the very first, Danny had looked him in the eye and had really seen him.

"Oh for God's sake, who needs this worthless snitch?"

Before Danny could react, Angelo slashed the young boy's throat and shoved him forward. He bled out quickly as Danny held him, blood pumping into a pool around them. His eyes never left Danny's. He died still believing Danny would save him.

*   *   *

The anguished cry made the hair stand up on the back of Kenann's neck. Without stopping to think, she leapt to her feet. Turning in circles, she dislodged the wooden lid of a packing crate onto her bare foot. With pain now added to fear's adrenaline, she held the injured member with one hand and hopped into the hallway facing the other apartment door. The colonial style house had been divided into two large apartments. It was the only possible location of the distress. She intended to knock and inquire if everything was all right, when still hopping, she caught her toe on the edge of the large Persian rug in the center of the foyer. She slammed head and shoulder first into the door. It burst open at the force of her impact. She sailed into the room, airborne for several feet. She landed with an audible grunt and finally slid to a stop across the hardwood floor.

The ensuing silence was deafening. As her eyes adjusted to the dim light, she encountered bare toes and muscular calves. She raised her head and uttered an involuntary gasp. She covered her face with both hands. She heard movement and when she peaked between her fingers, she saw a towel where flesh had been.

"What are the chances of me turning around and crawling back out of here?"

"None."

"That's what I figured." She sighed and accepted the hand extended down to her. As she came up to her full height, she was aware of his chest in front of her. The moon shifted from behind a cloud and bathed the room in soft light. His dark hair ruffled from sleep and the hands on his hips gave him a roguish appearance. Her mind went involuntarily to pirates. Light colored eyes made more intense by the tanned skin studied her. She felt herself begin to stammer.

"I heard someone cry out, so I came to check and well, then I sort of tripped in the hallway and ..." she held out her hand.

"Hi, I'm Kenann James, your new neighbor. I drove in just this evening. I didn't see anyone over here when I unloaded my things."

He found himself shaking the extended hand. He was edgy from the recurrence of the painful dream and the shock of having someone shoot into his living room like a cannon ball. She seemed harmless enough in her baggy shorts and T-shirt, her brown curly hair flowing wildly about her face.

"Do you always come to the rescue so boldly?" His deep voice echoed quietly in the room.

She turned to look at his front door standing ajar and the rug curled up at his feet. Despite her earlier trepidation, she burst out laughing. She put her hand to her mouth to stem the tide without success.

"That *was* quite an entrance, wasn't it?" she managed between giggles.

The musical quality of her laughter stirred him.

"One I'm sure I won't forget for a while. I'll nominate you for captain at the next neighborhood watch meeting."

She knew he was mocking her, but she didn't mind. It *was* funny.

"Hey, no problem. Everything okay with you?"

"Uh huh." He ran his hand through his already disheveled hair. She couldn't help but admire the movement of hard muscle in his bare upper arm and chest. She wanted to ask him more questions but made herself refrain. He did not seem the type to pour out his heart to a total stranger.

"Well I promise, the next time I'll knock." She made her way back across the hallway and turned to open her door before saying goodnight. Instead she leaned her forehead on the door and groaned.

"Locked out?" He was leaning in his doorway across the hall looking completely at ease wrapped in a towel.

"Yes," she said disgustedly and kicked the door like a petulant child.

"Hang on." He came back with two short sturdy metal pieces and had her door open in swift time.

"Thanks. I think. Do you do this sort of thing often?"

It was her turn to enjoy the sound of his laughter. "No. It's one of my many talents now retired."

He cut further conversation short by saying goodnight. She closed the door pondering her enigmatic neighbor and headed for her couch.

Unpacking could wait. As she curled up under a favorite afghan, sinking into the soft cushions, she realized she didn't even know his name.

She dreamed of dark-haired pirates.

* * *

The name was Daniel Joseph MacKenzie, an orphan, from Oklahoma. Because of his naturally dark skin and general aquiline features he had been told that one of his parents had probably been Native American. His light-colored eyes pointed to the other parent being of European descent. He had been left in the proverbial basket on the door step. It was a church affiliated orphanage on Mackenzie Ave. Locals referred to them as the "MacKenzie kids." Those without names, who had not been adopted by the age of majority, were given that as their legal name. The staff provided the children with names from the Bible. They fed, clothed and educated him but he experienced his first real sense of family in the United States Marine Corp.

* * *

Kenann James had been named after both her parents. Ken and Ann James had been high spirited adventure seeking nomads. He was a photographer for National Geographic. A tall lanky man with the dark hair of the Welsh, he had an easygoing manner and his grin could charm even the most suspicious indigenous tribesman. Ann was a freelance illustrator. She had the soft-spoken ethereal manner of an artist. With her long mane of honey colored curls, she always reminded Kenann of a woodland nymph. Ann had adored Ken and was delighted to follow him anywhere the next assignment took them. Kenann (pronounced Kee` nan) had been born in Nepal, weaned in Brussels and home-schooled all around the world. She always figured she developed her desire to become a Social Worker by witnessing man's inhumanity to man on a global scale. She learned to pack light and move fast. She called home anywhere she laid her head but "going home" meant Granny James in West Virginia. The notification of her parent's death came from the National Geographic Society in her last week of graduate school. She had been told her parents were missing in the jungles of Borneo as their light aircraft had not arrived at their destination. Extensive search and rescue efforts had been unsuccessful, and the Society was presuming them dead. With shame, her first thought had been Adam, her father's pilot and bodyguard and her surrogate father. Her parents indulged her. Adam loved her.

Devastated, Kenann went home to Granny. She was a little bit of a woman with a freckled face and snapping green eyes. The long braid of her youth still hung down her back. Its red color was now mixed with silver giving it the color of peaches. She loved her farm along the Ohio River, but as most Irish do, dreamed of her homeland along the seacoast of Waterford. She had left her beloved Ireland for work in London where she met Justin James, a Welshman from Llangochlen, at one of the military clubs. He was so tall and handsome, not unlike the son they created together. Their little family immigrated to the United States for work in the mines. He continued to dazzle and delight her until the day he dropped to his knees in her flower garden, dying of a massive heart attack before his fiftieth birthday.

Upon learning of her parent's deaths, her instructors waived the finals due to her excellent record. She packed up all her belongings and returned home to West Virginia. Without bodies to bury, they erected a monument on the family farm. Granny's church family swamped them with food and helped with chores for days following the memorial service. Granny finally put her foot down and told them it was high time they helped someone else.

Kenann studied these people with an eye of an anthropologist recording the habits of an agrarian African tribe. She was fascinated by the various subcultures and unspoken mores that governed the Appalachian community. She pumped Granny for information and shared her observations over evening meals. Granny cocked her head to the side one evening and laughed with the hint of Ireland in her voice.

"Girl, one of these days you're gonna have to stop observing life and start living it!"

Kenann loved being with Granny. She created a warm cocoon of love and security around her. Nothing had changed on the farm since her childhood visits. The smells coming from the kitchen brought back such fond memories of being pampered by fresh baked treats. The smells from the barn hadn't changed either and even that held its own sense of serenity and continuity. No matter what happened in the outside world, stalls had to be mucked out, animals tended, gardens planted and harvested in due season.

Granny had adored her son and his beautiful wife and wept bitterly as she stood before the monument resting beside the one of her husband's. Yet, her serenity had never wavered. Kenann observed this phenomenon with a critical eye.

Granny told her when she asked, "Honey, God gives, and God takes way. Blessed be the Name of the Lord."

Kenann had bitten back a bitter reply. She would not share her hateful thoughts about what she wished God would do with his giving and taking. No, she did not voice her thoughts as she faithfully attended worship services and Bible Study with Granny every time the doors were open. And they were open entirely too often for her taste, but Granny asked very little of anyone and Kenann knew this pleased her grandmother. It was one small way she could repay her.

Kenann began receiving e-mails and texts from her friends from grad school. They had all gotten jobs in their chosen fields. Kenann began to grow restless. Granny knew the signs. When Kenann's dearest friend, Judy, called to tell her about a job in her medical complex for a master's level Social Worker, Granny knew it was time to push a little. Judy had gotten her master's in nursing at the same time Kenann had gotten her master's degree in Social Work. Judy was now working out of a doctor's office in a large medical complex attached to the hospital. The Counseling Center was looking for an MSW and was willing to provide the required two-year clinical supervision for advanced licensure. It was perfect.

Granny got into the computer and printed off the vita Kenann had developed and sent it off to Judy, who supplied a cover letter. Kenann knew exactly who to blame when the call came requesting an interview, but she couldn't be angry. She was too excited and gladly flew back to Memphis for the interview. Before she returned to West Virginia to get her belongings she had not only been hired for this dream job, but also had found a terrific duplex apartment housed in a small colonial style house in a nice section of Memphis. Granny was especially pleased to learn it was directly across the street from a church building.

"You missed your calling, Granny. You and Jude should have hired out to maneuver corporate takeovers."

"Are you sorry to be going?"

"You know I'm not. And you also know I wouldn't have done this on my own. Thanks." She hugged Granny tight.

"So, go and start living a little." Granny swatted Kenann's behind. "Take a few risks, kiddo. Make a few mistakes, okay?"

"What kind of advice is that from a respectable grandmother to her granddaughter? Besides I've seen more in my few years than most people see in a lifetime."

"I'm talking about your heart. You moved around so much you learned to keep a part of yourself closed so you wouldn't get hurt when you left. That became a way of life for you - the closing up - I mean. The only way we can really know ourselves is to be deeply involved with others. Get dirty. Make a fool of yourself. Open yourself up to being hurt. You've never lived until you felt like you were going to die."

"Granny, what's got into you?"

"Let's just say I see things for you and I don't want you to miss it because you won't grab it when it comes by."

"You're not going fey on me again, are you?"

"Oh, you laugh all you want. One of these days you'll believe ole Granny and what she knows. Now get in that beat-up old Subaru and go to Memphis before I take a switch to you."

*   *   *

Kenann stepped out of the shower and looked at the clock. She thought renting an apartment across the street from a church building would increase the probability of getting there on time. Guess not. At least she was going, even if her heart really wasn't in it. She was still more than a little mad at God. She tossed on a summer shift and sandals and looked in the mirror to study her square face framed in naturally curly shoulder length hair. The caramel colored highlights were a natural gift from her mother. Large hazel eyes stared back at her. She harbored no illusions about her looks and spent little time on something she accepted as simply pleasant. She had earned herself a few bruises with her acrobatics the night before. She could only hope her new neighbor thought the whole escapade had been part of his disturbing nightmare.

She slipped into the back pew as the congregation stood to sing the opening song. She found the page to the familiar hymn and looked up singing the chorus. Her horrified gasp was audible in the natural pause in the lyric and all eyes turned to stare at her in concern.

The man standing on the raised platform at the front of the auditorium, raised his songbook a couple of times to encourage her to resume breathing and to drop the horror-stricken look. She came to herself and smiled reassuringly to the kindly concerned faces around her. The crowd resumed eyes forward. She then turned her narrow-eyed attention to the man on the podium who was trying desperately not to smile.

It became clear soon enough that the source of her discomfort was the *minister* of this congregation. She could have crawled out the door and would have done just that during his sermon, had he not lifted an accusing eyebrow as she rose to leave. She recognized a challenge when she saw one and dropped back into the seat, folding her arms in a perfect pout. As the congregation stood singing the closing hymn, he came down the aisle stopping at her pew. She stiffened when he took her elbow giving him the perfect leverage to propel her bodily into the aisle and lead her out into the foyer.

"This is intolerable!" she hissed.

"Why?"

"Why didn't you tell me?"

"Are you saying I should have clutched my delicate members and proclaimed, I am a man of God!"

She snorted at this image. "Oh, all right, but you cannot tell anyone what happened."

"And invite commentary on my manhood? You have my solemn promise. Now, make nice." He turned her to face the crowd coming through the doors from the auditorium.

CHAPTER TWO

"Okay, why did everyone laugh when I mentioned the great deal I got on that apartment?" They were eating lunch at a nearby café. Daniel MacKenzie, (Kenann had finally learned his name) looked uncomfortable.

"What?!" She pressed.

"Okay, you met Mrs. Gage, right?"

"Yeah, short, energetic lady - frosted hair. So?"

"She owns most of the old homes in this neighborhood. She has more money than sense and rents them out for a steal."

"I'm still waiting for the funny part."

"Well, she has a penchant for reading novels of high intrigue and matchmaking, so she places her tenants like chess pieces and then tries to manipulate the game."

"You're joking right?"

"Nope. She's harmless for the most part. People like to go to her fancy dinner parties for the food and fun and a few have even found their soul mates. She's happy. They're happy. But she can be a pain in the rear to a confirmed bachelor like me. I thought she had given up on me long ago."

His implication did not immediately sink in with Kenann. When it did, she burst out laughing.

"No way. You don't mean she has me picked out for *you*?" and burst into another round of mirth.

"Well, I don't think it's *that* funny."

"No offense, Danny Mac," in perfect imitation of the southern drawl most of the congregation had used that morning. "You're too pretty for me."

He made a pained expression, but she went on before he could speak.

"Oh, I know it's just the packaging, but you turn heads. I'm strictly Middle America plain Jane. But even though I'm plain on the outside, I am pure grade gold on the inside. I can't say what you're packing yet."

He raised an eyebrow and she laughed. "Oh, you know what I mean. This is your lucky day, my friend. I am the most uncomplicated person you will ever meet. I develop no lasting attachments to anything. I have no cumbersome obsessions. And I promise not to fall in love with you or scorn you for unrequited passion. Meet your new best friend."

She thrust her hand across the table with a beguiling smile. He laughed despite himself and forgot all the things he had intended to say in refute.

They finished their meal in casual conversation. They were walking down the tree-lined street back to the house and their respective apartments when Kenann heard her name squealed in a familiar voice. She immediately began running toward the tall leggy blond racing to meet her. They collided on the sidewalk and jumped up and down in syncopation.

"Hey, Jude."

"I can't believe you're here. Really, really here." They were totally oblivious to the man approaching them pondering the mysteries of female behavior.

"When did you get here?"

"Last night."

"Why didn't you call me?"

"You said you had to go to some nursing conference in Mountain Home this weekend."

"I did but you could have called my answering machine. Oh, Kenann, I can't believe you are going to live here." They began to jump and squeal again.

"Ladies?"

They stumbled to a stop holding each other from toppling over. "Oh, Danny Mac, sorry, this is my very best friend and partner in many crimes, Judy Crawford."

Judy was beautiful in the way of models and actresses. Fine boned face, chin length golden hair and all legs.

"Guilty." They grinned at each other over shared memories.

"And I am Kenann's neighbor." They turned their attention back to him once again. Judy's face sobered slightly in cool appraisal. She obviously reserved her warmth for friends.

"He's the preacher here." Kenann offered, tossing her head toward the church building across the street. "Oh, man, wait till I tell you how we met."

"Hey, I thought we agreed not to tell." Danny Mac objected.

"No, we agreed *you* would never tell. Besides, Jude doesn't count."

"Well, please be generous."

Kenann snorted and swatted his shoulder. He smiled at her and their eyes held for a moment at the shared memory. He stepped back continuing to smile and looked at Judy.

"Nice to have met you, Miss Crawford."

She nodded in response and watched him go up the steps into the house. Then she and Judy turned to each other and began jumping and squealing.

Kenann said, "Let's go see my great front porch." The brick two-story house had a small front yard enclosed by a black wrought iron fence with a central stone path up the middle to the porch step. Flowerbeds flanked the walk. Large columns supported the tall porch roof. Two huge oak trees in the front yard shrouded the entire house. The white porch swing and rattan furniture with colorful pillows complimented the white shutters on the windows.

"These are great digs, Kenann. I know the rent. What gives?"

She described the circumstances surrounding the great deal. "So, you got chosen for tall, dark and handsome there?"

"I told you Mrs. Gage was nuts."

"Do you get evicted if you don't hit it off?"

Kenann laughed heartily. "I sure hope not. Let me tell you, he is a lot different than I thought last night. He was actually a little scary. Today, I find out he is mild mannered preacher boy. Come on. Let me give you the grand tour. Mrs. Gage furnished it with these great early American pieces after I paid the security deposit."

The large central hall that rose to the height of both stories duly impressed Judy. A grand staircase lifted to a landing at the back wall framed by an impressive stained-glass window overlooking the extended portion of the first floor and the back yard. From the landing, separate stairs led up to the second floor on either side. Adjacent balconies overlooked the hall below. A huge tapestry hung on the wall above the front door and a chandelier was suspended from the ceiling above their heads.

"Whoa."

"Pretty neat, huh?"

"Awesome."

She swung open the heavy oak double doors into her apartment and stepped aside for Judy to view the lovely fireplace across the room. A plush couch and chairs formed a cozy sitting area in front of the fireplace. To their left and at the front of the house was a large bay window with a padded window seat. To their right was a small but elegant dining area with mahogany table and chairs, side board and china cabinet. Swinging café doors led into a well-equipped kitchen and half bath. The back wall of the kitchen was made up of tall, narrow windows looking out onto another porch and large yard surrounded by a tall wooden privacy fence. A line of huge trees formed the boundary at the back of the yard. A wrought iron circular staircase led up to the second-floor bedroom, bath and office space.

"It's perfect, Kenann." They had finished the tour of the second floor and Judy fell across Kenann's queen size bed.

"It is, isn't it?"

"You still have a week before you have to start your new job, don't you?"

"Yep."

"Lucky dog. What are you going to do?"

"Oh, I don't know. Settle in, shop, read."

"Fix your best friend dinner," she added.

"Moocher."

"Hey, I've eaten your cooking. I consider myself a martyr," and was rewarded with a pillow bounced off the side of her head.

"Finish telling me the story about meeting tall, dark and handsome."

"His name is Danny Mac."

"Whatever."

Kenann obliged and had Judy's undivided attention until the end. Judy sat staring for a few seconds and then fell back in a whoop of laughter across the bed.

"Oh, Kenann, it's like having Lucille Ball for my best friend."

"I guess that makes you Ethel."

The pillow barely missed Kenann's head.

*   *   *

The phone was ringing when Danny Mac entered his apartment. He took a deep breath and put on his face.

"Hello?"

"You seemed a little distracted today, son." It was one of the elders, Jake Taylor, and the main reason Danny Mac was now a preacher. Jake was larger than life, a grizzled man who instilled fear into the men who served under him in the Marine Corp but could now shepherd his flock of Christians with tender care. When Danny Mac's life had seemed empty and beyond repair, he remembered Jake's quiet serenity in the midst of their fiercest battles and had come to him for answers. He had never been sorry.

Danny Mac chuckled and told him about his meeting his new neighbor, omitting some of the more delicate parts, and of her stunned surprise to find he was the preacher.

Jake laughed. "That explains the look on her face when she saw you. Well, that may be part of it but it's not all. Something has been bothering you for days."

"What do you mean, Jake?"

"How long have I known you son?"

"Two lifetimes."

"Exactly, and I know every shadow that crosses your face. Some of those I helped put there."

"It was your job, Jake."

"And it was yours. So, don't let it torture you now. Are you dreaming again?'

"Some, I guess. But it's not the dreams themselves that have me bugged. It's Angelo."

"He's dead. He's part of the past. Leave it there."

"I want to. I have no desire to ever think that name again, Sir." In his fervor Danny Mac reverted to his military etiquette. "I can't seem to shake the feeling. You know we never found his body?"

"Are you suggesting he is still alive?"

"All I know is the hair stands up on the back of my neck at the strangest times and the first thing I think of is him."

"I hope to God you're wrong, son."

"So, do I, Sir," he looked out the window, "So do I."

*   *   *

Kenann had looked forward to sleeping in the next morning after a late night of unpacking. She was extremely vexed by the sound of a bouncing basketball echoing off the hardwood floor of the foyer below her bedroom. Then the loud voices started.

"Yo, Danny Mac, time for our rematch. Hey, wake up!" She heard Danny Mac come out on the balcony of his bedroom across the way from hers.

"Give me a break, Blade. It's 7 in the morning and it's my day off. I want to sleep."

"You promised. It's great outside. Come on, old man, you can take you a little nap later after I whip your butt."

"Who you calling an old man? Who kicked your butt last time dude?" Danny Mac challenged the grinning bi-racial child bouncing the basketball below him.

"If you guys don't shut-up I'm gonna kick *both* your butts." Kenann had stepped onto her balcony in her robe. She hadn't bothered to smooth her hair from sleep.

"Way to go Blade. You woke up Medusa." Before he knew what was happening, she ran down the stairs and was heading up the other side to his balcony growling the whole way.

Blade called encouragement. "Run, man, she looks serious."

Instinct had him retreating back into his bedroom with Kenann in hot pursuit. She chased him back down the inside stairs and caught up with him in the foyer where, laughing, Blade grabbed him before Danny Mac could run out the front door. She was able to land a hearty punch on his shoulder before turning with great dignity to sashay up the center staircase to her bedroom.

"If you gentlemen will excuse me, I will begin my toilette."

"Whoa, Dude. Who was that?" Blade whispered after she had closed the door behind her.

"I think it's my new best friend." He stood staring up at the closed door.

Chapter Three

Kenann came out to the church parking lot cum basketball court with coffee for her and Danny Mac – juice for Blade.

"Who's winning?" They both were eager for a break and joined her at the picnic table on the church lawn. "Hope you like it black?" handing the coffee to Danny Mac.

"Just like he likes his women," Blade interjected. They both turned to look at him.

"Well, isn't that what you white folks always say?" Kenann and Danny Mac exchanged glances and burst out laughing. Danny Mac put the young boy in a headlock.

"What am I going to do with you?

"Give me lots of money?"

"Dream on, Alice."

"You say the weirdest things, man."

"Oh, come on. You know. Alice in Wonderland - the fairy tale? Dream on?"

"That's a white folks fairy tale. If you're gonna hang with me, you gotta learn my language."

"Okay, tonight at 5:00. You can tutor me."

"No way, man, that's a trick."

"You know what your principal said. If you can pass some basic skills tests before school starts this fall, he will promote you to your next grade. Otherwise you have to take fifth grade over again."

"Come on, man, summer just started. I don't want to study now."

"No study no basketball, my friend."

"That's cool. I can hang with other guys and play ball."

"Okay. See you around, Blade." The boy sat for a few seconds undecided what to do. He looked to Kenann for help. She merely looked back with what she hoped was an expression of friendly neutrality.

"That's blackmail." Blade stuck out his chin.

"Yep."

Blade heaved a great sigh. "Oh, alright. I'll be back at 5:00. Does my mom know?"

"Yep."

"It's a conspiracy."

Danny Mac chuckled. "Anyone who knows about conspiracies needs to pass the fifth grade. See you tonight."

Blade left grinning. He was cool with the whole tutoring thing. It just meant more time with Danny Mac. Ever since his Dad died, Danny Mac had been there for him. Danny Mac was awesome. But he couldn't make it look too easy.

"Sorry for the Medusa crack." Danny Mac looked at her sideways when they were alone.

"Hey, never apologize for a getting in a good jab. I should come with a warning label in the mornings." She grinned, and Danny Mac was enchanted once again by her openness and total lack of pretense. They sat in companionable silence enjoying the warmth of the sun on their backs.

Danny Mac broke the silence. "What's on your agenda for the day?"

"Oh, I don't know. Get some groceries, I guess. I promised to fix Judy dinner. You want to come over and eat with us?"

"I wasn't really hinting for a good home cooked meal."

"Good, because you won't be getting one. My cooking has been known to defy the natural laws of science. But I can guarantee stimulating conversation and all the antacids you desire."

"I wouldn't miss it."

Danny Mac's eyes never left Kenann's as he said, "Brace yourself."

"Excuse me?" Her heart fluttered in her chest.

She was answered by squealing tires at her back. She whirled around in time to see a small red sports car slide to a stop a few feet from them. A short, well-built woman in a white flowing pant suit, leapt from behind the driver's seat with amazing agility for someone wearing ridiculously high heels.

"What a glorious picture you make." Her voice was deep and melodious, rich with an Eastern European accent. Danny Mac was always reminded of old black and white movies when she spoke.

"Good morning, Mrs. Gage. You're out early."

"I've got a home to refurbish into a honeymoon cottage. Jim and Karen are getting married you know. Isn't it wonderful? Young lovers. They are the nectar of my life." Kenann heard the sigh in the words if not in her voice. You had to love this woman.

"Of course, you will both attend the reception I am having a week from Saturday at my house." It was not a question.

"I trust you are settling in Kenann, dear? Anything you need, you call me, yes? Must run." She blew them a kiss trotting lightly back to her car and was off in a squeal of tires.

Kenann spoke first. "Whoa!"

"Yeah, she fills up her space and yours too."

"But she was so quiet when I inquired about the apartment."

"She was sizing you up for me."

*   *   *

Kenann kept her promise to cook or arrange takeout meals that week for Judy who worked late almost every night. Sometimes Danny Mac joined them in between his church duties. He seemed to thrive on it though. When he wasn't helping old ladies cross the street, he was studying. Granny would love this guy, Kenann thought.

Danny Mac could sense how guarded Judy was with him, so he never stayed long when she was there. But he did make an effort to eat lunch with Kenann most days that week. There developed between them a companionable easiness. No demands. No expectations. Their comfortable relationship spilled over to Judy and by the end of the week she had started to thaw in his presence. Blade also began dropping by for hot chocolate before he went over for his tutoring session with Danny Mac. Danny Mac lodged a complaint. He saw Kenann first. Blade actually giggled.

On Friday night, Kenann, Judy and Danny Mac had enjoyed a simple, if rather bland, meal of Kenann's creation, before heading to the front porch for some coffee. Danny Mac had just put his feet up on the railing to enjoy the evening breeze, when he leapt to his feet. In two long strides he was down the steps and almost to the front gate to meet the man whom Danny Mac had obviously spotted getting out of his car at the curb.

"What do you want?" Danny Mac resembled a snarling dog going nose to nose with the lanky man in the dark tailored suit. The man merely responded with a benign smile.

"Is that any way to treat the man who saved your life?"

"Bull. If I had known I would have to pay for it the rest of my life I'd have taken the bloody bullet like a man and been done with it. Go away!" Judy and Kenann were staring in fascination at this exchange. The stranger made no move to leave.

"Did Carter send you?"

"Yes."

Danny Mac emitted a low growl before the man could finish.

"It is not what you think. I need to talk to you." He took Danny Mac by the arm in order to focus him completely. "It's important."

Danny Mac wavered and then sighed resignedly. "It had better be. Come on. You've got ten minutes," and led him across the street to the church building and his private office. Danny Mac had obviously forgotten the women gaping at them from the porch, but Andrew O'Hanlon had been all too aware of them. He flashed them a dazzling smile over his shoulder and with a jaunty nod of his auburn head, was propelled by the upper arm into the building.

Kenann looked at Judy. "I've never seen him act like that." She paused, "I think I like it."

CHAPTER FOUR

Danny stormed into his office and then whirled on Andy with force. "Start talking."

"Can I at least sit down?"

"No." Danny Mac felt deep in his soul that Andy's appearance was threatening to take away the life he had so preciously created. He had nothing against Andy. They had watched each other's back many times in the past and he knew in a crunch there was no one better. But he wanted nothing more to do with the circle Andy traveled in.

"Please, Danny, I'm not here to recruit you back into the business. I'm here as your friend."

"Then why did Carter send you?"

"He came upon some information and passed it to me. For your ears only."

"To bait me back in?"

"No Danny. To warn you." He didn't know how else to say it. "Angelo is back."

The impact of those words slammed into Danny Mac with paralyzing effect. He stood very still for several seconds and then eased down onto the corner of his desk. Andy took the opportunity to sit as well. He hadn't slept in thirty-six hours and was starting to sag.

Danny Mac finally spoke. "Have you verified?"

"It's iron clad and this file goes pretty deep. As in clear to the White House."

"What does Angelo have to do with business on that level?"

"It looks like our buddy Angelo has feathered his nest quite well since we left him for dead in that warehouse in Kuwait."

"Okay, I'll admit I am stunned at this news, but I fail to see what this really has to do with me. So, he is some hired gun now. I'm out of all that."

"Don't you think Angelo would take you out in a heartbeat if he found you?"

"Well that's the operative phrase - if he found me. He has obviously been in circulation somewhere since Kuwait and I've never heard from him. Regardless, it's my problem not yours or Carters."

"There's more." Andy dreaded this part because he knew what it would do to Danny. "He's getting specific. That's how he came to Carter's attention." Andy took a deep breath and just told him. "Danny, he killed Bhina and Saulie a few days ago."

Danny's only visible reaction was the jaw muscle that jerked in the side of his face and an imperceptible glint that surfaced in his eyes.

Andy continued. "He entered the states yesterday, so we've got to assume he is coming for you. Killing Bhina and Saulie was the most expedient way to find you and maybe to send you a message. Carter is sticking his neck out by not sharing what he knows about this piece of evidence. If the big boys find out about your connection, they'll be on you like white on rice. Carter wants you back but not like this."

"How did they know it was Angelo who killed them?"

"He left some DNA behind."

"It doesn't sound like Angelo has gotten any smarter."

Andy snorted.

Danny Mac continued, "My concern is not so much about Angelo but the people he works for. Angelo was working for someone when he killed Ramalla. That is where the real danger lies. I should talk to Jake."

"Danny, you can't involve anyone else in this. We're talking National

Security here. You know how it's been since 9/11. Carter and I could both be brought up on obstruction charges as it is."

Danny Mac stood up to pace. Andy had seen this behavior before and knew to give Danny his time and space. He had been the most respected squad leader, the keenest strategist before a raid and the one everyone wanted at their back when the fight got nasty. To see him pacing back and forth in the office of a church building and to know he was now a preacher, blew his mind. Danny had also been the deadliest assassin in their special ops unit.

"I won't run."

"We never thought you would."

"If he makes contact, how do I reach you?"

"Well, for the time-being I'll be on your couch."

"I don't need a babysitter, Andy. Go home."

"Can't. I'm under orders."

"I'm happy for you. I'm not. Not anymore."

"You can't have it both ways, Danny. He's coming. And you know it. Our guys want the people he is working for, so they want him alive. If we can deliver him wrapped up in a bow, everybody wins. But we've only got one chance. If we blow it, Carter turns you over and they pull you back in to help take down this cell."

They sat staring at each other.

"Give me a few, Andy."

"Sure, no problem, can I go entertain the lovely ladies across the street?"

"Yeah, but be cool, okay?"

"I was born cool."

He laid a hand briefly on Danny Mac's shoulder as he walked past him to the door. As soon as Danny Mac heard the door close behind him, he was on his knees.

"Father, help me. I need your wisdom and your guidance. You know who and what I used to be. Deliver me from this evil and keep those around me safe. Stop Angelo before he hurts anyone else. Oh God," his voice broke, "Have mercy on Bhina and Saulie. Use me, Father, and allow me to glorify you and not the desires of my sinful nature for revenge or hatred. Fill me with your Spirit, Lord. An extra measure please."

Danny Mac could see Andy's tall frame leaning languidly against the pillar of the front porch. He was comfortable in his own skin, moved with the grace of a dancer and had the Irish gift of gab to go with it. It didn't matter if he had the ear of a Senator or was talking to the kitchen maid, you saw the same old Andy. He could also see the faces of the women sitting across from him. Kenann was laughing and shaking her head at something he had said. Her eyes actually twinkled when she smiled, Danny Mac mused. Judy on the other hand was observing Andy like a bug she'd love to squash. Danny Mac was secretly pleased to see someone immune to Andy's boyish charm.

He stepped up onto the porch avoiding Kenann's thoughtful gaze.

"So, I see you have met my hero, Andy O'Hanlon." Kenann continued to look pensive. She had noticed the change in their demeanor. Both men were working very hard to hide something. Danny Mac looked at her and winked. She smiled back and tried to hide her curiosity. *Danny Mac has some secrets.*

"He's been entertaining us with some good stories." Kenann said.

"None about me, I hope?" Danny Mac responded.

Andy said incredulously. "Now, why would I bore these ladies with stories of you when I have a wealth of one's about me?" Kenann laughed. Judy rolled her eyes. Andy looked triumphant. Danny Mac marveled how a person's whole life could change in an instant.

*   *   *

When Judy had gone with Kenann to her apartment, Danny Mac and Andy continued their discussion about Angelo. "Who's he working for?"

"Apparently it's a group with ties currently in Egypt. But they move around. They're not Taliban or Al Qaeda, though they've made some overtures to those camps. That's why it has been so hard to pin them down. They don't fit any known profile yet. But we're getting intelligence information out of Alexandra that something big is cooking there. There's been a lot of chatter about the European financial market."

"How long have the guys in Washington known about Angelo?"

"Don't know. He's not a major player so they may have been aware of him on some level for a long time without much interest. Killing Bhina and Saulie, kicked the interest level way up. Their cover had not been blown. Someone had to have inside knowledge of their connection to us. When Carter saw the DNA report and attached photo, it was the first time he knew Angelo was alive. He is really sticking his neck out holding back on what he knows about Angelo and the rivalry between you two."

"Our guys haven't even made the connection that he started out working for the UN Security forces in Kuwait. The only thing saving our butts from a potential firing squad is they aren't really interested in Angelo. They could tell he was small potatoes. They want who he's working for. I still can't believe he is alive. That man was as dead as anyone I've ever seen after you got done with him for killing that Arab kid."

"His name was Ramalla."

Andy nodded. "Well, all I know is Angelo was beaten beyond recognition and that kid was dead."

Danny Mac's eyes narrowed in pain as he recalled what he was capable of doing with his bare hands. "All I could think was that kid trusted me. He had no family, no home, no one to even bury him."

"He had you, Danny."

"All the good I did him. I knew Angelo hated me, but I never dreamed he'd use Ramalla to get to me. When his body disappeared while we were burying Ramalla, I figured his new-found friends took him to bury. Looks like they nursed him back to health instead."

"I'll bet he'd love nothing better than to take you apart piece by piece."

"There was never any love lost between us."

"Carter believes it was hatred for you that drove Angelo to turn. No matter what he did you were always one step ahead. One step better. His juvenile ego couldn't handle it, so he went where there wasn't so much competition. Killing Ramalla was just another way to make you bleed. Whatever his reasons are now, he's coming, friend, and we've only got one chance."

"Let's make it count."

"Now you're talking."

*   *   *

Kenann put on a pot of flavored coffee. Judy sat at the kitchen table. Kenann was the first to voice what was on both their minds.

"What was that all about?"

"Kenann, how much do you know about Tall and Dark?"

"His name is Danny!" She turned and stared at Judy.

"Whatever."

With a snarl of exasperation, she set cups on the table. "Judy, sometimes you can be so cold."

"We'll analyze me later."

"Okay, I know nothing. He's drop-dead gorgeous and he preaches across the street."

"Has he ever been in the military?"

"I don't know. Why?"

"He smells like a grunt."

"Excuse me?"

"A Marine. He walks and acts like a Marine."

"Well, he's not a Marine now."

"There is no such thing as *was* a Marine, sweetie. These guys are hiding something."

"We're all hiding something."

"You got a secret life I don't know about?"

"Funny. You know what I mean. We've all got baggage. So, they have a history together. Big deal."

"Are you falling for him?"

"No," she nearly shouted. "No," she lowered her voice. "I promised him I would be his friend. Period. So, what if he has a secret. Let it be. If he wants to share it, that's up to him. It doesn't have anything to do with me." Kenann knew she was as curious as Judy, but she felt a need to protect Danny Mac for some reason - even from Judy and her critical comments. She saw something in him that she connected to on an elemental level. An abiding sense of aloneness. Her parents had loved her, but they adored each other. No one existed when they were together. They traveled so much she never made any close friends, so she learned to go inward for companionship. And soon she didn't know how to come out. She merely sent out who was needed at the time - the funny clown or the brainy intellectual. Her nurturing friend was the most popular in college because she listened well. But Kenann, the real one, just stayed down there deep and looked out on the world like a little lost girl most of the time. That little coping mechanism managed to make her feel safe, even if it did border on a little schizophrenic at times. She had no desire to change.

And somewhere along the line she knew Danny Mac had done that too. He seemed like he was so out-going but she connected with that part of him that he kept deep inside. The only difference was, Kenann felt Danny Mac was a little afraid of who he had in there.

CHAPTER FIVE

The first three days at Kenann's job were a whirlwind of names, faces and reading policies. She had met the licensed counselor who had agreed to provide her clinical supervision weekly. But she had yet to see her first client and was sulking in the employee lounge over a cup of coffee when one of the partners walked in. Unconsciously she sat up straighter. Mr. Kesselring smiled to himself.

"Are you settling in, Kenann?"

"Yes sir."

"You seemed a little preoccupied just then." He wanted to say despondent but thought better of it.

"Oh, I guess I'm just adjusting. I was overworked and underpaid in grad school. Here, I'm overpaid and under worked." She looked up suddenly ready to apologize when she saw him smile.

"Oh, we'll get our pound of flesh out of you soon enough, Kenann. We just want you to start on a good foundation. Come with me. I want to show you something."

She grabbed her purse. She had spent her time between the office library and the lounge and had no place to keep personal belongings. He took her down one of the carpeted hallways on the third floor and stopped before a closed door.

"After you." He motioned her to enter. She opened the door into a small but warmly decorated corner office with soft lighting. She was drawn to the small narrow window by the desk chair that had a great view of the gardens in the park across the street. She turned with a questioning look on her face.

"It's yours Kenann."

Her pleasure was immediate. "Oh my. Oh my." She repeated.

"Now tell Jenny at the front desk what you'll need tomorrow to get settled. You see your first client at 9:00 am Monday morning. Here's her intake file."

Without thinking, Kenann grabbed Mr. Kesselring's forearms and squeezed. "Really?" She released him quickly and stepped back. "This is great, sir."

"You're a welcome addition to our office, Kenann."

After he had closed the door behind him, she did a little victory dance in the middle of the room.

Kenann wanted to share her good news so she ran up the front steps yelling Danny Mac's name. The front door burst open in seconds of hearing her cry. He relaxed the minute he saw her jubilant face. She leaped into his arms and he twirled her around in a friendly hug.

"What gives James?"

She took his hands and led him back into the house closing the door. To those who watched, it appeared Danny Mac had just welcomed his lover home.

*   *   *

Andy had set up communications at Danny Mac's dining room table. He had other irons in the fire back in Washington he needed to monitor. He was talking into his cell phone via a head set and clicking on the keyboard of his laptop at the same time.

"Gotta go." He shut down the phone and laptop with one smooth motion as Kenann and Danny Mac came into the apartment.

"What's got you so jazzed, girlfriend?" Andy smiled at her with what had become genuine affection.

"You are looking at a woman with her very own office and a client to see on Monday. I have arrived in Memphis, boys!"

She twirled around and 'the boys' stood smiling at her like proud brothers.

"Let's celebrate." Andy rubbed his hands together. "Let's see. I saw a liquor store a few blocks over and I'll even spring for the pizza and pretzels."

"Nice try, ace. Pizza and cokes, all around."

"Can't blame me for trying. You used to be so much fun."

"I still am but now I get to remember it."

Andy headed for the door. Danny Mac grabbed his arm. "Let's order in."

Andy stopped and nodded. "Yeah, that's a better idea." He picked up the phone book on the end table. "Everybody like anchovies?"

"I'll order the pizza." Kenann took the book out of Andy's hands.

"Well, then I'll fix the drinks. Cokes for all." He sneered as he headed for the kitchen. "Make mine a diet." Kenann yelled to his back. He raised a hand to acknowledge.

"Where has Judy been?" Danny Mac asked.

"Don't tell me you've succumbed to the spell too?"

"Excuse me?"

"Oh, come on, beautiful shapely blond?"

"I told you I'm a confirmed bachelor."

"Mightier men than you have fallen." She paused. "And died where they lay, I might add."

He responded by pushing her head back with his palm in what was becoming a signature move between them. "Seriously, she was here every night the first week you were here. You all have a fight?"

Kenann laughed. "Oh, believe me, you'll know it when we do." She smiled at the memories of some of their more spirited encounters. "She's doing an evening rotation over at the VA Hospital this week on their psych unit. She does it every couple of months."

"That sounds like fun."

"She's tough. People call her the Iron Maiden behind her back."

Kenann made the connection with the pizza delivery and ordered like the pro she was on take out.

"If it's behind her back how do you know people call her that?"

"I started it."

He laughed. "You're brave."

"It started out as a joke between us, but it caught on. No one dares call her that to her face."

"Except you."

"Except me." Kenann smiled.

Andy came back in with cokes in hand. "It's more like the Ice Maiden if you ask me."

"Oh, O"Hanlon, you just can't stand it because someone finally has the good taste to ignore you."

"And you, my friend, have always been jealous."

Just then a fist pounded on the door. Danny Mac shoved Kenann behind him and Andy went for his gun. Danny Mac raised his hand for Andy to hold off but not before Kenann saw what was strapped under Andy's jacket.

"Jake, is that you?"

"Sure is."

"Come in, sir." The door swung open to reveal a man filling the entire doorway.

Before Andy could react otherwise, he snapped to attention and saluted.

"By jingo, I love it when that happens." In an instant he took in the informal command center at the table without appearing to notice anything.

"How are you doing Andy?"

"Fine, Sir. Good to see you, Sir. How are you, Sir?"

"We aren't in uniform anymore, son." Chock one up for Judy, Kenann thought. "Call me Jake."

Jake used his big hand to pat him on the shoulder as he passed him and whispered, "At ease."

Danny Mac took pity on Andy and intervened. "Would you like a coke, Jake?"

"I believe I would, if it's not too much trouble. Kenann, how are you getting along?" She had stood quietly during this exchange absorbing the fact Andy was armed.

"Oh, I'm fine, sir."

"Now don't you start."

She laughed. "Okay, Jake. We were about to celebrate my new office and caseload of one."

"Can a lonely old widower crash your party?"

Andy had retreated into the kitchen with Danny Mac. "How do you do it? I mean like hang out with the old man?"

"He's my friend."

"That's just creepy. Does he like sleep and eat?"

Danny Mac laughed, "Yep."

"I never saw him do either one the whole time we served under him."

"He always made sure we were taken care of first. He's still doing that but now it's with the church."

"This is too weird."

"Kenann saw your gun."

"I know. But one of us has to carry since you refuse."

"I told you about that."

"I know. I know. I wish Angelo would show himself. I'm getting edgy sitting here waiting on him."

"Maybe that's our problem. We're not making ourselves vulnerable enough."

"We agreed. We stick together."

"It's not Angelo's style to kill me outright. He'll want to play with me first. That will buy us some time. Let's give him an opening."

"Like what?"

"I don't know. I'm making this up as I go along."

Jake and Kenann were sitting knee to knee on the couch swapping stories of their mutual mishaps in other cultures. In some Slavic countries it is considered rude to show someone the sole of your shoe (comparable to raising the middle finger). Jake roared with laughter as Kenann recounted her bewilderment to the reactions of passersby in front of her hotel in Moscow. Her parents had left her there for a few minutes and told her to stay out of trouble. So, she sat down in one of the chairs and propped her feet up like she had seen her Daddy do countless times on the porch rail back home at Granny's. She practically caused an international incident before their Intourist guide could smooth things over. Her parents had wagged their heads indulgently. She always managed to find herself knee deep in trouble without ever trying.

Danny Mac handed Jake his drink when another knock sounded at the door. This time it was a petite soft sound. Kenann raised her eyebrow at Danny Mac. He knew she was questioning whether they would jump to alert again. This was going to be a problem. When he opened the door, he was delighted to see his eccentric but entertaining landlady.

"Why Mrs. Gage, come in. You're just in time to join our impromptu party. Kenann order more pizza, please. Are you a coke drinker or would you prefer a diet?"

"Why this is lovely, my dear. A diet if you please."

But first he linked his arm through hers. She always invited chivalry in Danny Mac.

"Mrs. Gage, this is a friend of mine visiting from the East Coast. Andy, this is Mrs. Gage." She extended her free hand. Andy did not disappoint them. He made a sweeping bow and kissed the back of her hand. She gave her signature deep and throaty laugh with always the hint of mystery.

"I can see you and I will get along just fine."

They turned, and Jake stood to greet them. Danny Mac felt something pass between Jake and Mrs. Gage as palpable as a tremor.

"Have you met?"

There was a slight pause. Jake seemed puzzled when he spoke, "No,

I don't believe so. Have we?" His big hands swallowed up Mrs. Gage's in greeting.

"Not in this life," was her enigmatic answer. Everyone seemed to be holding their breath as they continued to stand enrapt in each other. Mrs. Gage took command as smoothly as if she had called this small gathering together of her own choosing. She disengaged herself from Danny Mac's arm and Jake's massive hands and stepped apart in a flowing motion of silk and exotic scent.

"I have come to ensure guests for my party Saturday night. And now I have been rewarded with these two delicious men."

Was Jake blushing? Andy speechless? As if on cue there came a knock at the door. Danny Mac smoothly disguised that he was checking discreetly before opening the door to Judy. She looked more remote than usual and gave Danny Mac a piercing and accusing look.

"Is Kenann here?" Kenann, missing what had passed between Judy and Danny Mac, waved from the background.

"Here I am Judy. Join the party."

"No, I'll just head home."

"Don't be silly, Judy. Come in. Please." He reached out to touch her shoulder. She pulled away and stepped in. Kenann took up introductions. "Mrs. Gage, this is my best friend, Judy Crawford."

Sensing the unsettled spirit emanating from Judy, Mrs. Gage abandoned her expansive manner and approached Judy warmly and with an enveloping demeanor. She made direct eye contact and spoke quietly to her. When she touched her arm, Judy visibly relaxed and rewarded the room with one of her rare but devastating smiles. Andy was mesmerized by the transformation. He retreated to the sanctuary of the kitchen to get Mrs. Gage her drink.

With Judy settled into the armchair by the window, Mrs. Gage once again took command.

"My little soirée is in honor of another successful union of soul mates. Mr. Taylor you must bring your wife."

"I'm a widower, ma'am."

"Does that also mean you are currently unattached?"

"Yes, ma'am it does." Jake had regained some of his confidence.

"Well, since I too am widowed, I would be honored if you would be my escort for the evening."

Jake looked like a kid at Christmas. "I would be pleased, ma'am."

"Judy and Andy?" She looked at each in turn. "You both must come." Judy lost all sense of calm. Andy smiled broadly and was about to accept when Danny Mac said, "I'm afraid Andy won't be in town for the party." Jake noted the body language of both men.

"How disappointing. But Judy, you will come, yes?"

"I have to work a double this Saturday but thank you, Mrs. Gage. Maybe next time."

"Of course, dear."

The pizza arrived, and conversations continued as everyone filled their plates and found spots to settle and eat. Danny Mac followed Judy into the kitchen when she took Mrs. Gage's glass in for a refill.

"Judy, what's troubling you?"

"You tell me."

"Help me out here. I want to understand."

"So, do I. What is it about religion that draws hypocrites?"

"Have you heard something about me?"

"Oh plenty."

"At the VA Hospital?"

"Bingo."

"Judy, a person can change."

"Not that much."

"With God's help, anything is possible."

"Save it for the pulpit. You are some kind of whacked out hero to those guys on the psych unit - a real killing machine. Who *are* you?"

"I'm a sinner who found the grace of God."

Her profanity shocked him. He reached out again to touch her shoulder in an act of kindness. She slapped his face as Kenann walked through the door.

"Keep your hands off me." Judy hissed and ran out the back door of the apartment. Kenann was too stunned to move or speak. She felt a pain stab sharply into her chest.

"Kenann." Danny Mac didn't know what to say. He watched raw emotion pass over her face before she pulled it back and put on a mask to conceal it. She took in a deep breath and held it for a few seconds. She turned on her heels to leave. Danny Mac let her go. Maybe it was best if she pulled away from him. They had practically been joined at the hip since she arrived two weeks ago, and he had grown far too content having her there. He would only be trouble for her. He refused to acknowledge the feelings tearing at him beneath the surface. Things like longing and need were locked away with all those other things he used to be and do.

Everyone headed home shortly after that. Kenann was as remote as Judy ever hoped to be as she left. Danny Mac pretended not to notice as he saw everyone to the door. He assured Mrs. Gage that he and Kenann would be there promptly at 8:00 Saturday night. As soon as the door latched Andy whirled him around and got in his face.

"What gives, pal? If I wasn't chained to this house like a rabid dog, I could have gone after her. Why did Judy whack you? Yeah, we all heard it." Andy looked like he wanted to take his own shot at Danny Mac.

"I don't know."

"Guess." He spat out.

"She heard something about me at the VA Hospital. Gonzalez is in right now. I'm sure he's regaling his therapy group with war stories."

"So?"

"She can't reconcile who I was with who I am now."

"Neither can I but I've never whacked you over it."

"I don't know, Andy. She's raw about something. I haven't known her long enough for her to hate me that much. Usually takes a little longer."

Andy grinned despite himself. "Well, whatever it is, it just spilled over on Kenann. That girl looked like the Giza Sphinx when she came out of that kitchen."

"I know but I've got to figure that's a blessing."

"Yeah? How?"

"I need to put some distance between me and Kenann. I'm like a walking target right now and I won't have another person hurt again because of me."

"You mean because of Angelo."

"Same difference."

"Big difference, buddy."

"Either way I'm the catalyst that gets people hurt." He saw Bhina and Saulie's faces alive with laughter on his last visit to Kuwait. His face was impassive and as hard as stone when he spoke.

"I want this over." He stared beyond Andy for several seconds. "He'll make his move soon."

Andy didn't question how he knew. Danny's gut was famous.

"I'll make myself an open target tomorrow at the church building. I'll walk alone to Mrs. Gage's party on Saturday."

"What about Kenann?"

"I'll trump up something and have Jake take her to the party. And you, my friend, will be skulking nearby."

"Skulking's good."

"Have you got the ring ready with the hypodermic tranquilizer to take him down?"

"That's if you get close enough."

"Oh, he'll want to get a piece of me before he tries to kill me. We'll get really close, don't worry."

"What if he's not alone?"

"That's your department. But we agreed. Tranqs-no bullets or I bail."

"Personally, I think you've gone soft on me, but you are right, dead men don't talk."

"And dead men don't get second chances."

CHAPTER SIX

Kenann decided to give Judy some cooling off time before she talked to her. She needed her own time. The wall of raw emotion she slammed into when she walked in on Danny Mac and Judy had taken her breath. It left her feeling edgy and vulnerable. She did what she always did when she felt threatened emotionally. She put on her 'face' and retreated inward where she could fortify her emotions behind a wall of carefully constructed reserve.

The next morning started out gray and rainy but it couldn't dampen Kenann's enthusiasm about getting her office set up and going over the case file for Monday. She had been noticing the same car pull out behind her for the last two days. It was always the same. They never turned off. They kept the same distance between them and pulled into the curb across from her office. No one ever got out. It was really starting to tick her off.

Today she got out of her car and stood under her umbrella staring directly at the mystery car. She was edgy enough over Danny Mac to want to take it out on someone and marched determinedly toward the car. She would find out who the freak was that seemed to be following her and drag him out of the car if she had to. The windows both front and back were opaque, preventing her from seeing inside. She hesitated as she felt a prickle of fear. The car seemed to be waiting expectantly for her to come closer. She slowly stepped off the curb to cross the street. She halted and turned when she heard Judy calling from the second-floor walkway on their office complex. Kenann looked back and watched the car slowly drive away.

"Who was that?" Judy asked when Kenann joined her on the covered walkway.

"I don't know. Probably some nut case trying to decide if they want to make an appointment." She paused, "You okay?"

Judy sighed softly. "Yeah, I'm sorry I ran out last night like that. Kenann, Danny Mac is not who you think he is. And this Andy is bad news too."

"Judy, how can you say that? You don't really know either of them or their history."

"I know part of it and its ugly. They're killers, Kenann."

"Oh Judy, for goodness sake, that's a real stretch even for you. I know they were in the Marines. Mr. Taylor was their commander. Andy practically wet down his leg when he showed up last night. But that's like calling the Vietnam vets baby killers. Get a grip."

"They were trained assassins and Danny Mac was the best of their best. They act like he's some kind of war god."

"How do you know this?"

Judy only looked at her.

"Never mind, I get it. Judy, those guys are on the psych unit for a reason."

"Danny Mac didn't deny it."

"Okay, so he was some bad dude in the Marines."

"It was more than that."

"Whatever. That was then. This is now. Men come home from the military all the time and resume normal lives."

"You think he can just turn all that off? As a freaking preacher no less. It's a joke."

"Judy, do you hate him because he's a Marine or because he's a preacher," she paused and said more gently, "Or because he's a man."

Judy's head was lowered. When she looked up her eyes were glistening with tears.

"Don't go there, Kenann. If you can't guarantee all the pieces will go back in the box, don't take them out."

"Judy, I want to help you."

"I've got to get back to work." She squeezed Kenann's hand and went into the clinic behind them. It was always work for Judy. As long as she was working, she didn't have to face whatever demons were dogging her heels.

*   *   *

As Friday morning dawned, Danny Mac was going over his sermon at the dining room table. When he heard muffled groans from the living room, he whirled to his feet. He chuckled as he righted his chair. He recognized the once familiar sounds of Andy trying to greet the day. He poured another cup of coffee and walked over to the series of lumps on the couch. He lifted one end and found toes, so he approached it from the other end. He wafted the coffee cup near the opening of the cover and like the cobra rising to the sound of the flute the head began to move and weave until it was upright and staring through hooded eyelids. One hand fumbled out from the folds of the blanket and encircled the wrist holding the coffee. The other hand made its way around the cup. Not trusting himself, Andy leaned forward and took a first sip of the life-giving drink.

"What time is it?" he croaked.

"Almost 6:00."

"Why didn't you wake me for my watch?"

"Oh, I was working on my sermon for Sunday anyway."

Andy looked puzzled and then realization dawned. "Oh yeah, I forgot. Do you actually dig this church stuff?"

"Yep, you want in too?"

"No way. You're not getting me into no Bible banging cult!"

Danny Mac patted Andy on the head. He knew he hated that. Laughing he went back to get his own cup of coffee from the table.

"Jake's already called me this morning."

"I thought you said the old man slept."

"I didn't say how much. He knows something is up."

"How?"

Danny Mac arched one eyebrow. Andy grinned. "Yeah he's got eyes in the back of his head. Hey, you suppose that's why some the guys called him a 'mother'?"

Danny Mac snorted. "I don't think so."

"What did you tell him?"

"It was useless to try to snow him. I just told him you were working on something and were staying with me a few days under cover."

"It's the truth."

"I try to make it a habit."

"Okay, since we are playing truth or dare..."

"Who said we –"

"Shut up. Have you got the hots for Judy?"

"No, Andy I don't."

"What about Kenann?"

Danny Mac hesitated. That alone scared him. "What about her?"

"You're stalling."

"She is my friend."

"I'm asking what *you* feel."

"What is this? Dear Abby. Drop it."

"Ooh, we seemed to have touched on a tender spot."

Danny Mac's mouth was poised to tell Andy what he could do to himself before he stopped. The realization that he could so easily slip into the old behavior pained him deeply. Andy saw his expression.

"Hey, I'm just messing with you man. She's a great kid."

Danny Mac sighed. "That's the operative word, Andy. She's a kid."

"She's the same age as Judy."

"Oh, there's light years between those two." Glad to change the subject, "I'm going up to take a shower. You're on watch."

Danny Mac came down a few minutes later towel drying his dark hair. "I'm going over to the office. You keep watch from here. If anything goes down, don't move in."

"What do you want me to do?"

"Let him play out his hand. We need to see what kind of manpower he has. Besides, I'm wired with that minuscule transmitter you brought. Trust me."

"It's not you I'm worried about."

*   *   *

Much to Danny Mac's dismay, nothing happened. He called Jake that afternoon to ask if he would take Kenann to Mrs. Gage's party and had to leave the message on his answering machine. What he didn't know was Jake had spent the day in his car watching the church building from a discreet distance. He figured the boys wouldn't object to a little help if and when the trouble started. They were both on high alert no matter how casual they tried to act.

Kenann went shopping after work and was late getting in. She had made a habit of running over to Danny Mac's side of the house for a few minutes after work just to say hi. Tonight, she slipped in quietly with her packages. She was putting the last few bricks in her emotional wall and needed time for the mortar to set. She made her weekly call to Granny who immediately asked her what was wrong.

"I'm just tired, Granny." She changed the subject to Mrs. Gage's party. "I bought this great dress tonight. Black and slinky."

"Good for you girl."

"I also found these great dangly earrings and sexy high heels."

"Wear your hair up."

"Why?"

"Just trust your ole Granny on this."

"Oh, alright. Hey, I see my first client Monday."

"Are you excited?"

"Nervous. I spent the day pouring over the case file and being grilled by my clinical supervisor."

"You'll do fine, honey. Are you sure everything is alright?"

"I'm fine, Granny. What's got you so edgy?" The image of the black car came to Kenann unbidden.

"I'm just uneasy. I'm probably just missing you, honey. You kick up your heels and have a great time at the party tomorrow night."

"I plan on it. I'll call you Sunday night and give you all the juicy details." They hung up with words of love. They both were only too conscious how quickly one of them could be gone.

*   *   *

Danny Mac spent the next morning again alone in his office. He was getting edgy and he began to pray.

"Lord, I don't see any way I can walk away from this. Father, protect the innocent. Keep me from the shedding of blood. And if there is any way to soften Angelo's heart, I pray that You will. It is hard for me to fathom that you love him." He sucked in a chest full of air and expelled it before he could bring himself to pray, "Help me to love this enemy too."

Kenann took Granny's advice and pulled her thick curls up with a decorative clip at her crown and let them flow down her neck. She allowed other errant wisps of curls to frame her face. She took extra care with her make-up and when she zipped up the side of her new black dress with its mid-calf length and its soft scoop neckline she twirled in excitement.

When she heard the knock at her door her heart lurched. She took a steadying breath and splaying her hand across her stomach to steady her nerves. She checked her emotional fortification before swinging the door open with a broad smile. She squelched the feeling of disappointment to see Jake standing there.

"You look lovely, Kenann."

"Thank you. Are you going with Danny Mac and me?"

"He had something come up. He said he would meet us there."

She kept her smile firmly in place and offered her arm, "Shall we go?"

"You betcha."

"You look very handsome in that tux, Jake." And he did. His tall, broad chested frame filled out the suit to its best advantage.

"It was delivered this afternoon. I guess Mrs. Gage didn't want me to show up under dressed."

"Or she wanted to show you off in grand style."

A few minutes later they were winding up the curved drive to Mrs. Gage's spacious home. The first to arrive, they pulled into the parking area across the drive from the front steps.

Jake said, "Sit still and let me do this right."

He came around and opened the door extending his hand. Kenann laughed, trying to look languid and graceful as she swung her legs out and rose from the seat.

"Wow, get a load of this place!" It could only be described as Gothic. Lots of heavy gray stone. They rang the bell at the over-sized front door expecting to be greeted by a manservant. To their surprise the diminutive Mrs. Gage opened the door wide extending her arms in the same manner. She clasped both their hands and squeezed.

"I'm so glad you are here first." She was wearing her signature flowing silk and smelled of exotic places. Jake was consumed by her presence as she was in his.

"Where is Danny Mac?"

"He'll be along later." Jake responded absently.

"Lovely," her eyes rested on his.

Kenann drifted toward the sound of the band warming up leaving her hostess and escort in the foyer still holding hands. She could see through the large arched doorway into the ballroom that its ceiling reached easily to 20 feet in height. She looked up from the foyer to the second story. The grand staircase went wide and straight to join the stone balustrade walkway that framed the second level of the main hall. The light grew thinner, but she could see an identical balcony walkway on the third level as well. Were those gargoyles looking down at her through the shadows?

She sensed intrigue in this massive home. She vowed yet again to learn Mrs. Gage's story. Jake and Mrs. Gage continued their intimate conversation near the front door. Kenann wandered through the archway into the ballroom. The back wall consisted of a succession of French doors opening onto a terrace and stone balustrade. Potted plants and vines softened the Gothic ambiance. The food table was loaded with delicacies for every taste bud. Mrs. Gage obviously loved to entertain.

People of all ages, shapes and sizes began to arrive. No Danny Mac. She mingled and nibbled from her plate and was surprised to find herself being flirted with by some very attractive men. She was going to have to socialize without Judy more often. The dancing began to start in earnest, so she escaped onto the balcony. She hadn't seen Danny Mac enter the ballroom a few seconds earlier. Andy had followed Danny Mac from a discreet distance to the entrance to Mrs. Gage's estate. As Danny Mac walked up the main driveway Andy decided to explore the grounds.

Danny Mac caught a glimpse of Kenann leaving through the terrace doors and was stunned by her transformation. By the time he made it out to the balcony she had walked down the steps into the large garden that served as the backyard. She stopped at a small alcove to admire a statue. Danny Mac took the opportunity to admire her, without restraint, under the soft lighting. She was so sweet and yes, innocent. Despite that, he felt the knot of desire growing in his gut. That dress wasn't helping. He permitted himself the luxury of allowing his gaze to linger along the line of her neck and shoulders when he saw the figure step from the shadows. Everything happened in seconds.

The man lifted Kenann and turned to run. From her vantage point over her abductor's shoulder she saw Danny Mac leap one handed over the balustrade and land on the path at a dead run. In that instant, she filled her lungs and expelled an ear-splitting scream meant to shatter eardrums. The man faltered from the assault on his senses and Kenann's last image before being catapulted into the bushes by the impact, was Danny Mac in mid-air, his feet connecting with the other man's spine.

By the time Kenann gathered her wits to come to her feet, Danny Mac had the man pinned against a tree. He held the man's arms at an unnatural angle behind his back with one hand, the other appeared to be curled around the man's windpipe. Danny Mac spoke in a rapid tongue Kenann did not recognize. The man's eyes flickered. Angelo had said to be careful of this man. Andy appeared from the shadows dressed in jeans and T-shirt and pressed a gun behind the man's ear. Jake and Mrs. Gage hurried down the back steps. She never missed a beat at the scene before her.

"Would you like a private place to continue your discussion with this man?"

Danny Mac gave her a sidelong glance.

"I have seen and done many things, my dear. I am not so naive as you might think."

"What I really need is some crowd control."

"My best talent," and turned to the group gathering on the balcony. With consummate skill she had everyone back inside enjoying the party again in no time. Andy had the man bound with zip ties like a rodeo calf. He was lying on his stomach as the police arrived. When Andy pulled his ID from his pants pocket, the officers came to attention and made no comment about the weapon tucked into the back of his jeans. Danny Mac took off his tuxedo jacket and put it around Kenann who stood shivering quietly on the sidelines. Her dress had been torn on one side and her hair had been shaken loose from its clip.

"Jake, can I borrow your car?"

"Of course, son. What do you need me to do?"

"Stay with Andy and help these black and whites cage this guy. I'm taking Kenann someplace safe. Jake handed Danny Mac his keys and went to stand with Andy. Mrs. Gage returned and placed her palms on either side of Kenann's face and smiled a reassuring smile.

"You will be fine, dear. You go with Danny Mac now."

CHAPTER SEVEN

They drove in silence for several blocks. Danny Mac continually checked his rearview mirror for a tail.

"Where are we going?"

"I don't know. I'm thinking."

"What in the world just happened?"

"It's a long story."

"Well I suggest you start telling it." The anger in her voice surprised them both.

"I never wanted you to be a part of this."

"A part of *what*?"

"Someone is after me. It looks like they planned to grab you to get to me." He was pulling into a hotel parking lot. "I'll get you a room here till I can figure out what to do with you."

"*What to do with me?* Look Buster, take me back home. This is ridiculous!"

"I'll grant you that, but until I know more of what is going down, I want you out of the way. Please don't argue, okay? I think you'll agree that guy who grabbed you wasn't playing games."

"I want some answers and I want them soon."

"Agreed."

They walked into the lobby to book a room for Kenann. As soon as the words were out of his mouth and he saw the smirk on the desk clerk's face, he realized how it must look. His tuxedo jacket around Kenann's evening dress - no luggage. Kenann realized it at the same instance and flushed. As soon as they had the room card and were walking down the corridor, Kenann whispered sarcastically, "Well, that was awkward."

"Sorry for putting you in this position."

"It's a good thing one of your church members wasn't working behind that desk. How would you have explained yourself?"

"I guess they would need to have some faith in me."

Danny Mac held the door open for Kenann and locked it behind them. Kenann chided herself for suddenly feeling nervous about being alone in the hotel room with Danny Mac. She crossed the room and looked out the sliding glass door onto a small patio attached to the rear parking lot. Danny Mac was pacing and seemed to have forgotten her altogether.

Guess he's not too concerned about being in a hotel room with me. Kenann knew she was being petulant. She had resolved herself to the possibility that Danny Mac was attracted to Judy. She knew what she saw when she walked in on them. There had been enough electricity in the air to peel the wallpaper. And she couldn't blame Judy if she secretly desired Danny Mac. Just watching him move was exciting. He had such controlled strength. She had never given lust much thought, but she had a suspicion that the feelings churning in her at times bordered on just that. Her face flushed at the thought and she turned again to look out the glass. The only consolation is that she felt sure she had been successful in hiding these feelings and once again found great solace in retreating into that little world known only to her. She was not sure how long Danny Mac had stood transfixed in thought in the middle of the room. His mind was reviewing and analyzing all known data points. She doubted he would have heard her if she had spoken to him at that moment. She finally sat at the table by the sliding doors to wait him out.

Suddenly Danny Mac's head shot up. He growled, "Stupid, stupid."

"What?!" Kenann squealed as he grabbed her wrist and propelled her toward the door.

"My credit card! This room will be registered in my name. They'll have my information tagged. Come on." He jerked the door open and froze, pulling Kenann up tight behind him.

Standing in the doorway was a man with a Beretta aimed at Danny Mac's chest. The man waved them into the room with the barrel of the gun and shut the door behind them. Kenann looked around Danny Mac's shoulder. The man was as tall as Danny Mac but more heavily built. He was dark but not Middle Eastern. She guessed from her travels that he was Bulgarian or Romanian. For what seemed forever, both men simply stared at each other.

"Looking for scars?" Angelo sneered.

Danny Mac did not answer.

"Oh, believe me there were plenty. But I was pieced back together by the best money could buy. It was weeks before I was able to leave the hospital."

"What do you want?"

"Many things, many things. All in good time. Let me see your little girlfriend."

"She's not my girlfriend, Angelo." He tried to sound as convincing as possible. "She's just some dumb kid who had the bad luck to move in next door to me. She's nothing to me."

Kenann's head shot up as she searched Danny Mac's face for confirmation.

His eyes never left Angelo's face. Angelo noted the wounded look. Oh yes, there was something here he could use.

"Well, you won't mind if I have a go at her then." Instinctively Danny Mac drew Kenann closer.

"No, I think not. You like to gather the little wounded birds, eh my friend. This time she must be our, shall we say, security."

"Who is we?"

"You will know soon enough." Danny Mac had edged Kenann slowly to a chair as he spoke tugging her to sit down. He moved away from her listening for signs of reinforcements. Angelo seemed to be alone. Then Danny Mac began baiting Angelo to make a move on him.

"What's the matter Angelo? You still playing second fiddle? Somebody's flunky? Of course, you never were good enough to be top man."

"Shut up!"

"Why don't you try me, Angelo? Man to man once and for all. Best man wins. Or are you afraid you already know who the best man is?" The challenge was too much. Despite his strict orders not to touch Danny Mac - just bring him back - he threw his gun on the bed and lunged with a guttural roar. Danny Mac sidestepped slightly to deflect the impact of the larger man and used his forearm to deliver a forceful chop to Angelo's windpipe as he stumbled forward. In another swift move, Danny Mac wrenched Angelo's arm back and up slamming him onto the floor with his knee in the middle of Angelo's back. He used the small needle in his ring to administer the sedative. He jerked the lamp off the night stand using its electric cord to bind Angelo in the same fashion Andy used in the first attack.

Kenann had just reached the bed and retrieved the gun when two men stepped into the room through the terrace doors. Kenann gasped. Danny whirled just in time to see the gun butt that knocked him unconscious. The men did not see Kenann slip the pistol into the pocket of Danny Mac's tuxedo jacket. She kept her eyes warily on the two men but knelt beside Danny Mac and laid his head in her lap. The men spoke in Arabic.

"Angelo was a fool to challenge this man alone. He wanted to be a hero for Katerina. Look at him. Trussed up like a pig. Take him to the van. I will sedate this lion and deal with the girl."

Angelo was very lethargic but starting to gain consciousness. The second man released his bonds and dragged him to his feet. Angelo shook off the other man's hand and staggered out the terrace doors. The man who had spoken pulled out a needle and reached to plunge it into Danny Mac's neck. Kenann reacted instinctively and blocked the man's thrust. He knocked her back and successfully injected the already unconscious Danny Mac with a sedative to ensure his complete cooperation. Kenann quickly returned to Danny Mac's side but was hauled to her feet as the man threw Danny Mac across his shoulder. Carrying Danny Mac's dead weight as if it were nothing, he dragged Kenann by the forearm to the terrace door. He stopped long enough to check the parking lot. Kenann could see a van was parked directly in front of them with its side door open. The man had them loaded swiftly. They pulled away slowly and quietly. No one would remember hearing anything unusual that night. She had considered screaming but realized they would only drug her or knock her unconscious. She wanted to remain alert in hopes of seeing an opportunity to escape or at least witness something that might help Danny Mac later. The man dumped Danny Mac into a long box in the back of the van. He turned to Kenann speaking in rapid Arabic and gestured for her to get in. She hesitated a moment too long and found herself hoisted by an arm and leg over the box and dropped unceremoniously on top of Danny Mac. She looked up and the man gestured not to make a sound. The quick slashing movement across his throat was a universal gesture. She nodded her acceptance. A sense of panic welled up in her throat as an insert loaded with textile goods was settled on a ledge over them. As her eyes adjusted, she saw small points of light in the box around her giving her some reassurance of air to breathe. But her panic returned when she heard the sound of the insert being locked in place. She began to breathe through pursed lips to control the rising hysteria. A few minutes later she recognized the sounds of an airport as they were unloaded and placed on a moving conveyor rising steadily into a cold cargo hold.

She heard the engine accelerating and wondered if the increase in airport security would serve her today. What she couldn't know is that these men had filed a flight plan with all proper authorities as dealers in textiles. They had come to Memphis to invest in the cotton trade with Ellenburg International Textiles. Anyone who cared to check would learn of a very lucrative deal made the day before between simple businessmen. There would be no one to save Kenann this day.

CHAPTER EIGHT

She twisted in the space and was able to move Danny Mac's legs and torso enough to make room to stretch out beside him. She was relived to feel the soft padded surface under them. It seemed like an eternity but in actuality, it was less than 20 minutes before they were airborne. Her sense of despair at not being detained by airport security was lessened by the sounds and movement of Danny Mac coming awake. She softly spoke his name. He responded with a throaty murmur and reached out for her in the dark. He drew her close to him in an intimate embrace as his hands made slow sensuous movements up and down her torso murmuring her name.

Kenann was too stunned to speak when he began to caress her breast and then too aroused to protest. He began to nibble on the soft inner curve of her neck with great skill. Kenann managed a choked whisper in his ear, "Danny Mac. Do you know where you are?"

"No, but I know where I want to be." And pulling her into an even more intimate position began to caress and kneed her hips. Suddenly he stopped.

"Is that a gun in your pocket?'

Kenann still dazed by growing desire murmured, "I thought that was supposed to be my line?" Danny Mac laughed heartily. The extra blood flow lessened the narcotic haze somewhat and he began earnest attempts to orient himself. He remembered Mrs. Gage's party and how lovely Kenann had looked. Kenann? Oh, good Lord no.

"Kenann." He spoke her name sharply. She jumped and came to full alert.

"What?"

"What are we doing?'

His sharp tone turned the warm glow he had so skillfully created into shame and guilt. She responded with an equally slicing tone, "How in the world do I know? As far as I can tell, we are nailed into a pine box heading for parts unknown at jet speed."

The memory of the attack, seeing Angelo and the man who knocked him unconscious came flooding back. He wondered how far he had gone with Kenann before he came to himself.

"Did I hurt you? He moved away from her to reduce the intimacy of his arousal. The distance he created both physically and emotionally hurt her far worse than anything he had done in the minutes before. He seemed truly disgusted that he had allowed himself to touch her. 'Just some dumb kid. She's nothing to me' echoed in her mind.

"No." Her voice was flat. "You didn't hurt me."

Danny Mac's heart wrenched at the sound in her voice. He had betrayed her trust. What kind of man of God was he? He was completely disgusted with himself. Her voice broke the silence. "I think I deserve some answers."

"Yes, you do. What do you want to know?"

"Well, we've got nothing better to do. Why don't you just start at the beginning?"

He began slowly as if to himself. "It started in the Gulf. I was a part of a special ops unit. Andy and Angelo were there too."

Kenann broke in. "Is Angelo the goon in the hotel room?"

"Yes. It was our job to go in and do some things the larger units couldn't do."

"Assassinations?"

He hesitated briefly. "Among other things. Angelo and I could blend in."

"I can't see Andy blending in in the Middle East."

Danny Mac chuckled. "He usually handled operational communication behind the scenes." Danny suddenly rolled back to his side in the small space. "You've still got on my tux jacket, right?"

"Yeah."

He started to speak and then he realized there might be someone close by who could hear them, so he put his lips next to her ear. He could feel her stiffen in wariness. He forced himself to ignore this and whispered softly, "Inside the right breast pocket feel for a small listening device."

"Yeah, I feel something. What are you doing with it?"

"Andy gave it to me along with that sedative ring in case Angelo made his move on me. By the way, whose gun do you have?" He continued to whisper into her ear.

"It's that guy's - the one you call Angelo. He threw it on the bed when you goaded him into a fight. Why does he hate you so much?"

"He wasn't American military. We employed him for his knowledge of the area. He was anxious to make a name for himself in Intelligence circles and," he paused, "he saw me as his competition."

"So why is he here now? You're out of all that cloak and dagger stuff." She remembered Andy's gun and their suspicious behavior. "Aren't you?"

"Yes, I am. But Andy continues to work for the CIA and received information that Angelo was gunning for me. He asked me to help bring him down." Danny Mac considered and decided to level with her completely.

He sighed. "Angelo killed a young boy in cold blood just to spite me. It was a street kid I had sort of adopted. The kid wanted to please me, so he started bringing us information. Angelo accused him of selling us out and cut his throat before I could stop him."

"Oh, Danny, how awful. Why would he do that?"

"I don't know. I guess it was to get to me. He thought I was trying to make him look bad. On one of our operations Angelo gave us bad information and was about to get a bunch of us killed. I just knew something wasn't right and I told our commanding officer that I thought we should abort the mission that night. They called it off, but Angelo persuaded some of the men, boys really, to go off with him to prove me wrong. They were all killed except Angelo. He was discredited, and our commanders canned him. He disappeared for several weeks. Then I got a message to come for the kid."

"What happened?"

"After he killed Ramalla, I went berserk. I have thought all these years that I killed him. He's been working for someone, but I have no idea what their agenda is."

"So, what's with that transmitter in my pocket?"

"It's actually a GPS tracker and short-range listening device. Andy will know exactly where we are as long as we have it."

The airplane banked sharply throwing Kenann on top of Danny Mac. His arms encircled her in reflex. One hand was splayed across her shoulder blades and the other across her hips. She held herself up on her elbows and their eyes met. Neither moved. The moment was neither awkward or uncomfortable. Time seemed to stand still as they simply looked into each other's eyes. The plane banked again in the other direction. The force of their shifted weight knocked their crate off its shelving onto the floor. The impact was bone jarring and Danny Mac landed on top of Kenann.

"Jeez, MacKenzie. How much do you weigh? Get off me!"

He laughed as he rolled onto his side and then came alert. "We're landing."

CHAPTER NINE

Judy had stopped by Kenann's after her late shift to see how the evening had gone at Mrs. Gage's party. She used her key to let herself into the front foyer. She stopped. The apartment doors to both Kenann and Danny Mac's apartments were wide open, and she could hear a buzz of activity in both. Mrs. Gage was hurrying between the two when she saw Judy. The look on her usually serene countenance put Judy on alert.

"What's the matter?"

"Come in and sit down dear."

"Where is Kenann?"

"Come along dear and we'll start from the beginning."

"Is she alright?" she was beginning to shout. "Oh God, tell me. Is she alright?" She felt a fear she had never known. She had made herself numb for so many years that this rush of sheer terror turned her spine to water. She felt arms encircle her as she swayed.

"Please tell me where is Kenann?" she was pleading now and starting to go down.

Andy scooped her up and carried her to the couch in Kenann's living room. Judy was too overwhelmed to even consider fighting him. In a corner of his mind, Andy was aware of every curve of her body and the pleasant weight of her in his arms even as he remained fully focused on the job at hand. He sat her beside him encircling her shoulders with one arm and covering her clenched hand with his other hand.

"Judy, Kenann is in safe keeping with Danny but she is in a bit of a situation."

"What are you talking about?"

Andy looked up as Jake joined Mrs. Gage's side behind the couch. "Sit down folks. I feel you deserve some information. But keep in mind it is classified for national security. We're not playing games here, okay?"

Everyone nodded. Judy needed to reach out and hold on. She turned her palm into Andy's and linked their fingers. He squeezed her hand before he went on.

"Jake you know most of it already."

"Angelo?'

Andy nodded.

"I guessed as much."

Mrs. Gage spoke up. "Gentlemen, this is not a cigar club. Judy and I are full and equal partners."

Andy smiled. "Of course. When Danny, Jake and I were in Kuwait City we knew a man named Angelo De Morte."

"Angel of Death?" Judy's voice was regaining its old confidence.

"Not his real name, I'm sure. He was a hired gun we used in some of our Intelligence operations. He had grand illusions of becoming a super spy for the United States CIA. Most of the guys never took him too seriously. We underestimated his ambitions and his hatred for anyone who got in his way."

"What does this have to do with Kenann?"

"She is being used to ensure Danny's cooperation. Let's just say Angelo knew Danny's Achilles' heel and is using it to control him."

"Things are still very unclear Andrew." Mrs. Gage was now sitting on the ottoman with Jake in the chair behind her.

"Okay, let me try to bring you up to speed." His eyes met Jakes. "We thought Angelo died in Kuwait City. But he surfaced a few weeks ago in intelligence communiques and we knew he was coming to the United States. No matter what his objective, we knew Danny would be a target." Andy hurried on before he could be interrupted by more questions.

"Someone killed two of our operatives in Kuwait City who were closely tied to Danny."

Jake gripped the armrests. "Bhina and Saulie?"

"I'm sorry, Jake. I forgot you knew them too. They were tortured before they were killed. Danny had stayed in touch with them."

Jake added. "He just visited them last summer. They were like parents to him."

"It was apparently an expedient way to get to Danny Mac."

"How do you know it was this Angelo character?" Mrs. Gage asked.

"He left DNA evidence behind – one hair that didn't match anyone else. This information didn't register with the techs who were processing it but when Carter saw the ID on the hair, he contacted me and sent me to tell Danny."

"Who is Carter?" Judy still held Andy's hand even though her color and strength had returned. She did not allow herself to analyze it.

Andy's eyes again met Jakes. "He's our station chief."

"You're CIA." It was not a question.

Andy paused briefly before looking down into Judy's eyes. "Yes."

"Was Carter in Kuwait City?" She was all business now.

"Yes. We were a regular Marine unit ordered to work with Carter. After the war, Danny and I both went to work for him. Well, he wanted Danny. I just came along for the ride." He grinned at Jake.

"What happened that Danny Mac left the CIA?" Judy asked.

Andy looked to Jake who responded. "I think I can best answer that. After a few years, the work he did with CIA began to trouble Danny Mac. He felt tormented in his soul. I had retired and settled back here in Memphis. He was on leave and showed up on my doorstep one night. During that week of soul searching and introspection, he found the Lord and was able to find himself again. Carter blames me for 'brain washing' him but it was Danny Mac who hounded me with questions. He became desperate to know everything he could about Jesus. I had the privilege of baptizing him into Christ myself."

Andy continued. "Danny came back to headquarters to quit. Carter didn't take this lying down. Danny was his best man. He has spent the last 5 years trying to get him back and using me to do it. Actually, I think it had become a game for Carter."

"Is that why Danny Mac reacted the way he did when you showed up here?"

"Yeah, he thought I was here for another try at getting him back. But Carter really is trying to give him a break. Angelo is working for an organization we are anxious to crack. Carter knew if the National Security Council figured how crucial Danny was in bringing Angelo in, he'd be forced back into the game."

"Can they do that?" Judy was appalled.

Jake and Andy responded in unison. "Yes."

"Carter gave us one shot. Bring Angelo in and Danny stays out of it. Otherwise all bets are off." Andy said.

Judy asked. "So, what happened tonight?"

"One of Angelo's men grabbed Kenann at Mrs. Gage's party. Danny stopped him, but he knew then what their game plan was. Get Kenann and he would do whatever they asked. So, he took her to a hotel here in Memphis for safe keeping."

"How do you know that, son?" Jake asked.

"Global Positioning, sir. I put a device on Danny before he left for the party. It is a listening device at close range and a GPS for tracking. My people have been tracking them. I had to call Carter too." Just then his cell phone buzzed. He released Judy's hands to grab the phone but instinctively pulled her closer to him with his other arm. He took note that she didn't resist.

"Yes, sir." Andy's face took on a grim expression of intense concentration as he listened. He released Judy to stand.

"Yes, sir, no I understand, sir. I'll be ready when the call comes."

He broke the connection on his cell phone and stood staring down for several seconds. When he looked up, he turned first to Jake as much out of habit as a need for assurance from his former commanding officer. "They've got them, sir."

Jake stood up as the women gasped. Judy was the first to speak. "Where are they? They must know exactly where they are if they're tracking them like you said. Call in the Marines or whatever it is you people do and go get them."

"I have orders to sit tight until they arrive at their final destination and then I am to go and organize surveillance."

"Our government is going to use them as bait." Mrs. Gage stated in a very quiet, controlled voice.

"I have probably discussed more of this that I should, Mrs. Gage. We will do everything in our power to protect them. Danny is a trained professional. His experience in this situation will be vital to us."

"And what about Kenann? Is she expendable?" Judy's voice was flat.

"No, Judy. She is probably the safest one of all. She is their insurance that Danny will cooperate. She will be kept safe at all cost. If anything happens to her, they know they'll lose Danny. She'll be fine."

"You can't know that. Where are they going?"

"We don't know yet. Their plane is heading for Canada but the original flight plan listed Alexandria as their destination. I'm to wait here until the arrangements are made for me to follow him. I'm sorry for all of this Judy." He saw the coolness return to her eyes and felt deep regret at the loss of her earlier tenderness.

"If you'll excuse me, I need to brief my team in Washington." With that, he left to return to Danny Mac's apartment.

The three of them remained quiet for several seconds wrapped in their own stunned silence. Each was assimilating this turn of events in their own way. Jake understood the strategic advantage Danny Mac's capture could mean to our forces. Judy once again slammed the door shut on trust for anyone or anything but her own strength and wits. Mr. Gage had formulated her plan. She came to her feet in a fluid motion and took command of the room.

"The first thing we must do is ensure we have their exact location. Judy, dear, we may need you for this."

Judy looked up at Mrs. Gage through the haze of her own troubled thoughts. She squinted and blinked her eyes to clear her mental fog and the most she could offer was a weak, "Huh?"

But Jake knew exactly what she was about. He recognized a general forming a battle plan when he saw one.

"Now you wait one cotton pickin' minute, Missy."

She merely smiled at him in an infuriatingly patronizing manner.

"You need to stand down, Gabrielle."

Judy looked from one to the other. Gabrielle? The more agitated Jake seemed to grow the calmer Mrs. Gage became. Judy watched them in fascination.

"I'll hog tie you and put you in protective custody if I have to."

Judy saw a flash in Mrs. Gage's eyes, but she continued her patient silence. The two stood staring at each other from several feet apart. Jake loomed large as usual. His tall solid frame and strong chiseled features cast a striking image. Mrs. Gage, in contrast, was all soft curves and diminutive silk but she showed no signs of intimidation. On the contrary she appeared impregnable and valiant in her own right. A miniature Boudica. The warrior goddess of the Celts.

Judy smiled and thought, *You, go girl!*

When Mrs. Gage finally broke her silence, her deep voice held quiet command.

"Jake, you can either join us or be shut out completely. Your choice. I personally would value your experience and strength of character on our side."

He raised his voice. "This is ludicrous!"

Mrs. Gage turned to Judy. "Dear, would you care to join me upstairs?"

Judy stood. Jake reached out with his big hand. "Gabrielle, wait." She merely raised an eyebrow. He heaved a mighty sigh. "You realize you could get in the way and cause more harm than good."

"Well, we'll just have to make sure we don't do that, won't we, my sweet man." She was all smiles to him now as she knew she'd won the day. Jake certainly did look defeated. Mrs. Gage glided to him and standing on her tiptoes, placed her manicured hands on either side of his face looking at him for several seconds. The tension fell from him like scales and he grinned. The transformation was unsettling. Judy had a sense of being an intruder on a very intimate moment. Although neither seemed the least bit aware of her presence. Jake bent down to within a breath of Mrs. Gage's face. A silent communication passed between them. Mrs. Gage heard it loud and clear and smiled.

He added aloud in a soft but commanding voice, "I will protect you with my life but if you do anything to put yourself in harm's way," he paused, "I will kill you myself."

"Yes, dear."

Jake picked her up and embraced her. Mrs. Gage winked at Judy over his shoulder.

CHAPTER TEN

Kenann and Danny Mac felt their pine box lifted off the floor and carried. They remained quiet and waited to see where they were being taken. Danny Mac heard one of the men say in Arabic to hurry before the Lion wakes up. Danny Mac placed his forefinger across Kenann's lips to ensure she remained silent. They felt the change in temperature as they were carried off the small Lear jet onto the tarmac. They could hear men talking as they were placed on a flat surface and wheeled for several feet and hoisted onto another conveyor into yet another plane. Once aboard they heard the cargo doors close and seal. They continued their silence. The engines came to life after a few minutes. After becoming airborne they heard the movements of the lid being removed from their coffin like cell. Kenann was dragged from the box as ungraciously as she had been tossed in. The man spoke to Danny Mac in his native tongue and he was allowed to climb out under his own power. Kenann noticed the men took great pains to remain out of arm's reach of Danny Mac at all times. They motioned for them to proceed toward the front of the plane. The men followed behind them.

They continued forward until they entered the main compartment of the aircraft. The DC9 commercial craft had been converted into a private transport. Danny Mac turned and raised a quizzical eyebrow at their captors. They motioned for him and Kenann to sit on one of the long couches against the wall of the plane. When they sat, Danny Mac wrapped an arm around Kenann pulling her close to his side. She looked up at him in surprise. He leaned close to her ear and whispered. "They think we're lovers. Play along with me."

She muttered under her breath, "Thought I was just some dumb kid?"

He pinched her earlobe. Not in the mood to be playful, she ground the spike of her high heel into his instep. He turned her face to his with his free hand. He leaned in and biting her lower lip in what looked to be a loving gesture he glowered at her.

Danny Mac growled in a whisper. "You are safe as long as they think you are my lover. Got it?"

Angelo came through the opening from the cockpit. Kenann felt an imperceptible stiffening of Danny Mac's muscles - like a large cat watching its prey. Angelo went to the bar and poured a drink. She took the time to observe him further. He was powerfully built. She could tell he was trying to be smooth, but he was too rough edged to pull it off. He turned to them and spoke.

"I've been instructed to be a gracious host. Would you care for a drink?"

"No thank you."

"Could I have a Diet Coke?" Kenann looked at Danny Mac apologetically. "I'm thirsty." She whispered.

"It's okay." Danny Mac smiled at her.

Angelo reached beneath the bar and produced the drink from the small refrigerator.

"Would you like a glass?"

"No, thank you."

He crossed the body of the plane and handed her the drink sitting down in a chair to their right.

"You see, Danny Boy. I can be quite civilized. And you will soon see that I am a man of great power with the people with whom I work. This time you will answer to me."

"For whom do you work?"

"You will see. You understand what will happen if you refuse."

"I know the drill, Angelo. But you and your people also keep in mind, one hair on her head is harmed all bets are off."

Angelo narrowed his eyes. "Do you dare to threaten me?"

"Nope, just laying the ground rules, pal."

"You will do what we say. That is all."

"You were the ones who decided to use Kenann to make me cooperate. I'm just taking it to the next level."

Angelo stood up abruptly. "Go to sleep. We will not land for several hours and you will be taken directly to my people. You must be ready to receive your instructions." With that he left them alone.

Angelo knew he needed to find a gun somewhere fast. He chided himself for leaving it back in that hotel room and hoped Katarina did not discover this blunder.

Kenann asked, "Where do you think we are going?"

"The only thing I know is we are heading east." Danny Mac tapped his ear as he spoke and Kenann understood his caution about microphones. He leaned in closer and his whisper tickled her ear. "Make sure you hang onto my coat."

Kenann nodded.

"Let's get some sleep. We need to be sharp for whatever lies ahead."

"Have they got any blankets? I'm freezing." Danny Mac got up to check for something to cover Kenann. Low voices came from the next compartment. His blood ran cold at what he overheard.

*   *   *

Sunday morning dawned on four weary faces sitting at Danny Mac's dining room table. Andy, glad they had decided to forgive his part in Kenann and Danny's current situation, had gladly welcomed the trio back into his information circle. Judy was particularly glad to forgo any attempt on her part to extract information from Andy using her 'feminine wiles' as Mrs. Gage called it. Jake had argued against deceiving Andy, but Mrs. Gage had cleverly pointed out they were not lying to him. They were merely keeping their own counsel about a few things.

Judy was back to her remote self where Andy was concerned. He was grateful she conversed with him freely, but he missed their earlier intimacy. They had learned from Andy that Danny Mac and Kenann were flying across the Atlantic overnight. The government had transport on standby along with the tools of Andy's trade to leave within the hour from the naval base in Memphis. They could monitor the abductors location from the air and alter their course accordingly. Mrs. Gage subtly interrogated Andrew about the suspected destination. He remained convinced based on their current flight pattern that they would land in Alexandria, Egypt.

So be it, Mrs. Gage thought. *If I have to chase them across the Sahara, I'll not stand by and watch two innocent people be used by merciless tyrants.* she raged in her mind. *Never again.*

Andy gathered his electronic and personal belongings and the others helped him carry them to his rented car. He felt awkward - almost like a son leaving his family for the first time to go off to war. But that was ridiculous. Except for Jake these people were strangers to him. Yet, he felt like he had known them and been a part of their lives for years. He tried to turn up the volume on his Irish charm to conceal his feelings to no avail. He shook Jake's hand, he kissed Mrs. Gage's but when he turned to Judy, he froze. His glib remark died on his lips. Hers were the saddest eyes he'd ever seen. They appeared dead and at the very same time alive with yearning. He made himself take her hand, squeeze it and walk away. He had a job to do but if the fates willed it, he would come back and somehow erase that horrid sadness from her eyes.

*   *   *

Once again Mrs. Gage took command. "We must get busy. There's much to do."

Jake interrupted. "First, I must go to church services this morning and help fill in for Danny Mac. The other elders will have to be told something. They can be trusted with basics. It is hard to tell how long we will be away, and someone will need to carry on the work here. You both are free to join me for the early service."

Mrs. Gage looked at Judy. "I think it would be good, Judy. We need to focus our minds and hearts on our task ahead and what better way than in church."

"Oh, I can think of a few." She sighed then relented. "Oh, all right, but they'll have to put up with me in my scrubs. I'm not going home for a change of clothes."

"You'll see every kind of clothing imaginable. Nobody cares what you wear. Give them a chance, honey. They're good people."

Judy's eyes darted to Jake's face ready to rebuke him with a biting '*don't* call me honey' but the tenderness in his eyes stopped her and compelled her to return his smile. "All right, Jake. It's your show."

*   *   *

Jake met with the Elders to explain Danny Mac's absence. The elders knew all about Danny Mac's background and former occupation. Jake told them he had been called back into service temporarily (he omitted 'against his will'). It was decided that the associate minister would fill in during his absence. Jake also told them he would be away for an indefinite period as well. He offered no explanation and these men who respected and trusted him as a brother, asked for none. They wished him God speed, assured him of their prayers and told him if they could help him in any way he need only ask. He was once again overwhelmed by God's love manifested in His people, the church. He knew these Christian brothers would give their lives for him if called upon as he would for them. He took great confidence and courage in that.

Mrs. Gage and Judy sat near the front. (Mrs. Gage's choice not Judy's.) They were welcomed warmly by the people sitting around them. Jake came to sit with them. He put his big arm around Mrs. Gage and squeezed

Judy's shoulder in encouragement. Judy turned to him and smiled over Mrs. Gage's head. She felt more comfortable that she had anticipated. It had been many years since she darkened the door of a church building. She had been a regular growing up, as well as a leader among her youth group, back in Missouri. But circumstances the summer after her senior year in high school had forever altered her perceptions about men and God. Her mind drifted toward that and she visibly stiffened. Mrs. Gage reached out and took her hand. The cool, soft feel of that supporting hand seemed to diffuse Judy's tension until she was able to focus on the moment and join in the service that had begun.

Mrs. Gage sang with a surprisingly mellow alto voice. Judy was surprised to hear herself hitting the high notes so easily after being so long out of practice. Jake's deep base added a rich quality to the trio. The sweet music they made had people looking their way in admiration although some of the teenage boys had noticed Judy long before. Even weary from lack of sleep and dressed in hospital scrubs, she was beautiful woman. Her hair pulled into a ponytail framed a finely boned face. Her large blue eyes and well-formed lips could easily have graced the cover of Cosmopolitan or Vogue. She disdained her beauty and rejected any efforts to draw attention to it and was usually oblivious when others noticed her.

When it came time for the lesson, Jake stood and approached the platform. He still wore his tuxedo from the night before. The tie was gone and the collar open, but he made a handsome picture standing before them. He explained to the congregation that Danny Mac had been called away suddenly on business. Since it was such short notice, he would deliver the morning's lesson and then would turn the pulpit over to the associate pastor for future sermons.

Jake sighed deeply and looked out over the crowd with deep affection. He knew these people - their joys and struggles - their sins and their triumphs and he loved them. He wasn't sure how long it would be until he was with them again, so he left them with the words of John the Apostle of love quoting from 1st John.

"Dear friends, let us love one another, for love comes from God.

Everyone who loves has been born of God and knows God. Whoever does not love does not know God, because God is love. This is how God showed his love among us: He sent his one and only Son into the world that we might live through him. This is love: not that we loved God, but that he loved us and sent his Son as an atoning sacrifice for our sins. Dear friends, since God so loved us, we also ought to love one another. No one has ever seen God but if we love one another, God lives in us and his love is made complete in us."

"God is love. Whoever lives in love lives in God and God in him. In this way love is made complete among us so that we will have confidence on the day of judgment because in this world we are like him. There is no fear in love. But perfect love drives out fear, because fear has to do with punishment. The one who fears is not made perfect in love."

"We love because he loved us. If anyone says, 'I love God' yet hates his brother he is a liar. For anyone who does not love his brother, whom he has seen cannot love God whom he has not seen. And he has given us this command: Whoever loves God must also love his brother.'" Jake closed the Bible in front of him.

"These words of the Apostle John penned two thousand years ago still reverberate to us today. And God's love and salvation are as fresh now as then. I pray that everyone who hears my voice will ensure their peace with God by accepting his salvation through grace and have their sins washed away in the waters of baptism. Baptism that symbolizes the death, burial and resurrection of our Lord Jesus Christ. Church, I love you. Please come if we can help you in any way." The congregation stood to sing the song, inviting anyone who had a need to come to the front and let it be known. A young woman and an old man stepped into the aisle at different points in the hall and walked up to the front seat. Another elder joined Jake and they began speaking quietly with each of the people individually. After a few minutes the other elder stood and announced that the young lady whom he identified as Mary wished to be baptized into Christ. She stood and confessed Jesus as her Savior and was led away with some of the ladies to prepare for her baptism. Jake stood and related that the older gentleman, Chester, came asking for the prayers of the church and to be restored to their fellowship. Jake offered the prayer for the repentant man.

Following this, Mary entered the baptistery and was lowered into the water by the Associate minister. He seemed a little nervous with the task as he proclaimed to the audience "in the name of the Father, the Son and the Holy Spirit" before lowering her back to immerse her in the water. As she rose joyously from the water, he seemed to find his confidence as his voice burst out in a song of praise.

Jake felt Judy's eyes on him. He smiled at her warmly and uttered a silent prayer she would allow Jesus to heal whatever had broken her heart.

* * *

Danny Mac came back to Kenann carrying a blanket and pillow. She reached for them and stopped.

"What's wrong?"

"Nothing."

"Don't give me that. You look like you've seen a ghost. Sit down and tell Auntie Kenann all about it." She patted the seat beside her and grinned.

He looked at her a moment and matched her grin. "How can you be so chipper? Our situation is less than ideal."

"Oh, I've been in worse."

He arched a beautiful black brow.

"Oh okay, maybe I haven't. But Granny always taught me to play the hand I'm dealt. I'm just not sure I know the rules to this game."

"I used to know them but I'm a bit rusty. I'm not exactly the same man anymore."

"So, use what you've got, which is the best of both worlds. Didn't Jesus say to be as cunning as a serpent and as harmless as a dove?" She grew uncomfortable at the way he looked at her so intently.

"How did you get to be so wise?"

"Oh, I'm great at advising everyone else. It's me I have problems with."

"So, what's your problem?"

"You."

It was out before she realized she'd said it aloud. His eyes widened slightly and then she laughed if maybe a bit nervously.

"This is another fine mess you've gotten me into, Ollie." The tension of the moment passed. He pushed her forehead back with his palm in their now familiar gesture.

"You'd better get some sleep." He took her pillow and propped it against his leg. "Here, lie down and cover up."

"What about you?"

"I can sleep sitting up. No problem."

"Well if you're sure. I don't want to be a wimp but I kind of hate to be too far away from you."

"That's fine." She curled up under the blanket and laid her head on the pillow propped on his leg. He laid a hand on her shoulder and she covered his with hers. They both felt comforted.

He thought about Kenann's advice from God's word 'Be as cunning as a serpent and harmless as a dove'. It gave him renewed courage and he prayed, 'Lord, have you brought me here for a reason? Is there something you need me to do? I want to be in your will, Father. Do you want me to use what I've learned from my former life to accomplish that will? Show me. Lord. I need you desperately. Mixing these old ways and my new life in you is the hardest thing I've ever tried to do."

His mind returned to what he had overheard a few minutes ago. The men were taking their orders from Katerina. Hearing her name catapulted him back to a dark time in his life. He let his head fall back as memories and sensations flooded over him. If this plane was rushing him toward an encounter with Katerina Troika, he was in bigger trouble than he had thought.

CHAPTER ELEVEN

M rs. Gage lightly touched Jake's arm as the three of them walked across the street to Danny Mac and Kenann's house to continue planning.

"That was lovely, Jacob."

"Thank you, Gabrielle."

Judy had been touched by the simplicity and sincerity of his words, but she could not bring herself to voice it. Instead she said, "I'll fix a strong pot of coffee and throw together some lunch before we reconnoiter."

"Great, dear. I have some phone calls to make." They both looked at her quizzically.

"Travel arrangements," was all she said.

They both nodded. Judy used her key to let them into Kenann's apartment. Judy went to the kitchen and Jake followed her while Mrs. Gage began her calls.

"Can I help?"

"Yeah, sure. Check out the fridge and cupboards to see what our options are. Kenann's never been known for her cooking skills." She started out with a smile but then her face screwed up and the tears spilled over onto her cheeks. Jake's big hand rested lightly on her shoulder. His instincts told him she would feel too threatened if he tried to hold her.

"She'll be all right. Andy was telling you the truth. They won't let any harm come to Kenann."

"I know but what if she's scared?"

"Danny Mac can be a formidable force to reckon with if need be. And thanks to his new heart in Jesus he will take pains to comfort Kenann if she is frightened."

"You really love him, don't you?"

"Like a son. I was so proud he came to me when he needed someone. He was hurting from all the years of killing and deceit his job called him to do. When he showed up on my doorstep here in Memphis, I hardly recognized him."

Jake could see it again clearly. He had walked in without saying a word, sat down on the couch and leaned forward, arms on his knees, hands clasped, his handsome dark face staring at the floor. They sat in silence for a long while. Jake had given him all the time he needed. He finally broke the silence with, "I can't take it anymore." His voice was flat and lifeless. He poured out all the poison filling his heart. He talked until it turned dark outside. Purged and emotionally spent, he fell asleep on Jake's couch. Jake had covered him with an afghan his late wife had made still draped across the back of the couch. Jake sat in silent vigil with him while he slept, offering up prayers for his peace of mind. Most of all, he wanted him to come to know the Prince of Peace.

"Judy, Danny Mac's heart was healed."

She met his steady gaze and knew what he was saying to her. Mrs. Gage had come to stand beside Jake. Her loving expression mirrored Jake's. Judy sighed.

"It takes a lot of energy to keep certain things at bay." Mrs. Gage nodded. Judy went on. "Kenann deserves the best I have to offer her. And right now, it takes everything I have to hold it together."

She sat down at the table and looked up at them through eyes shimmering with tears.

"We know dear. Let us help you carry this burden. It will make it easier, I promise you."

Suddenly all her vows to keep her past locked tightly behind doors of steel seemed ludicrous. She wanted free of it and its power over her. She said simply, "Okay."

Jake and Mrs. Gage sat after Jake had filled coffee mugs for all of them. Judy looked at them and took a deep breath.

"My preacher asked me to go on a mission trip with him to Europe after I graduated from High School. There were two other women of the congregation going too so I readily agreed." She stopped for another deep inhalation of breath before plunging on.

"He raped me repeatedly throughout the summer." Mrs. Gage grabbed Jake's hand as if to steady herself. She knew Judy did not want to be touched as she relived that horrid time.

"The first time I was so shocked I couldn't function. I stayed in my room curled in a fetal position and threw up anything the women tried to get me to eat. I didn't know what to think or what to do. The women pressed him to get me to a doctor. On the way he basically blackmailed me into silence. My Dad was an elder and he threatened to ruin my family if I said anything. Now I can see how foolish I was not to blow the whistle on that jerk but at seventeen, I didn't know much of anything. He was such a slime ball. He said God had created his drives and knew he needed this from me in order to continue God's work. I tried everything I knew to stay away from him, but he managed to manipulate things to get me alone."

She remembered her parents concern when she came home sullen and hollow eyed. They considered it pre-college nerves and didn't press her to talk. When she left a week later for the university, she felt she was escaping the nightmare. She shut the door on that summer never to open it again. She quickly earned the reputation as the Iron Maiden. She had to keep such Herculean control over her emotions in order to keep that door shut that soon it became second nature. Kenann had recognized and accepted this need in Judy and forged a friendship in spite of it. One of the only real friends Judy had. And now it was time to repay Kenann for never asking anything of her except to simply be her friend. Remembering Kenann's unconditional acceptance of her, broke down the last vestige of her wall and at last her emotions flooded out. Her tears began to flow freely down her face. Jake got up and came to kneel at her side. She turned in her chair to face him and he took her hands in his.

"Sweetheart, what happened to you can't change the core of you. The part that is really you. God loves you. That's just who He is." He paused. "And I love you."

She felt swamped by the warmth pouring from him. She whispered in a choked voice, "I was a virgin," as sobs wracked her body.

Jake wrapped her in his big arms and she clung to him like a child. Mrs. Gage encircled them with her arms and laid her cheek on the top of Judy's head. When the sobbing quieted, Mrs. Gage slowly turned her and dried her tears with the cool silk of her blouse tail. Words poured from Judy in a stream.

"My parents couldn't understand why I quit going to church. Once they asked if I had turned communist." This produced a watery laugh. "Pretty soon I made excuses not to come home. Nursing school is demanding so I could hide behind that. Made top of my class with all that concentration. Then once I started working, I took all the overtime they would give me. It's worked until now. I know my attitude is not really healthy, but it was the only way I knew to survive. But now Kenann needs me. I've got to be strong for her."

She took a steadying breath and finished. "I'll need your help."

She clasped Mrs. Gage's hand and turned to capture one of Jake's.

"Sure thing, honey." Jake's smile made anything seem possible. Mrs. Gage spoke. "Judy, you are going to feel a little shaky for a while. Please talk to us. Don't close up again. We'll help you through whatever you're feeling, okay?"

"If you are sure I won't be a burden with everything else we have to worry about."

"This will be new territory for all of us, honey. We've just got to trust and depend on each other."

As if on cue, Jake and Mrs. Gage drew their hands together over Judy's, forming a pact. Judy smiled the smile of a happy child.

"Okay, Chief. Where do we start?" she looked at Mrs. Gage.

"We leave Tuesday morning. I've arranged private transport to Alexandria. This will give time for you to take a leave of absence and call your parents to let them know you are taking a long-deserved vacation. We need to tell Kenann's employers something first thing in the morning. Remember she had her first client tomorrow at 9:00. We'll think of something. Jacob, you and I will discuss weaponry."

Jake choked on the sip of coffee he had just put in his mouth. "Now Gabrielle..."

She cut him off. "We are all very tired now. Let us return to my home where there is ample space and provisions. After a long nap for all of us we can discuss things with clearer minds. Agreed?" They nodded obediently.

CHAPTER TWELVE

Danny Mac watched Angelo approach from under hooded eyes. Angelo stood for several seconds and finally pulled back his foot to deliver a brutal kick. In one swift, fluid movement, Danny Mac pulled back his outstretched legs and stood to the side of the couch out of reach. When Angelo's leg met no resistance, the momentum flipped him onto his back in the middle of the room.

His companions laughed raucously as they bent over him. One of them chided him,

"When will you learn, this Lion has sharp teeth." Angelo scrambled to his feet and went for Danny Mac, but the men restrained him.

They continued in Arabic to Danny Mac, "Tell your lady to put on the belt. We are landing."

Kenann had been awakened by the noise and sat up rubbing her eyes. Danny Mac was struck by her child like nature and yet again felt a pang of guilt for getting her involved. He gently turned her around and fastened her belt and then secured his own. She was fully awake now.

"Where are we?"

"I'm not sure." He posed this same question to the guards.

"You will discover soon enough I suppose. We are in Alexandria," they supplied. Danny Mac thanked him. The man nodded. Danny Mac decided to try again with Angelo.

"You know, Angelo, it looks like we will be working together again.

How about a truce?" His only reply was to make the motion of spitting on the floor.

So much for that thought Danny. Yet he kept hearing the admonition to love your enemies. If Angelo did not fit that description no one ever would.

'Lord, show me how this works. I know I don't have to like my enemies but show me how to love him.'

Their arrival was uneventful. They were passed through Customs with minimal inquiries. They obviously had papers for them. A nondescript van was waiting to receive them. The only luggage belonged to their captors and since they were on private transport, they did not have to wait with the other travelers to receive their bags. Danny Mac held Kenann's elbow as she stepped into the van. He felt her trembling slightly and slid in beside her pulling her over next to him with a friendly jostle.

"So, have you ever been to Egypt?" She knew what he was trying to do, and she appreciated it.

"Actually, I have. I was 12. I think I imagined myself a reincarnated princess. I had a dream about it and for years I liked to tell myself that dream was a vision."

"Maybe it was."

"Don't make fun of me."

"I'm not. You've been around the world enough to know there are many things that cannot be explained away."

"Well, how do you reconcile that to your fundamental religion?"

"It's not *my* religion, Kenann."

"You know what I mean."

"God is an awesome God. There are mysteries in the spiritual realm we will never understand until heaven and maybe not even then. I don't usually rule anything out completely."

"Keep talking like that and they're gonna kick you out of your little preacher club."

He raised his hand that had been lying comfortably across her shoulder and pulled her hair. Their captors remained silent, so they took the opportunity to look at the city. Danny Mac pointed out the Quaitbay Fort built on the site of the famous Pharos Lighthouse which had been one of the Seven Wonders of the World. He told her about the ancient library that was destroyed by fire in the 5th century that was believed to house literature on Troy and even Atlantis.

They pulled up in front of the Metropole Hotel. Kenann still wore Danny Mac's tuxedo jacket over her evening dress. Her hair was lying in loose curls across her shoulders. Danny Mac's dark skin against his white shirt made him look attractively native. As they made their way through the lobby, other guest wondered at their identity. They obviously had enjoyed a long night of revelry and they must be important to be surrounded by bodyguards. They came off the elevator and were ushered into a suite. Danny Mac and Kenann stood in the middle of the room waiting expectantly.

They did not have to wait long. The door opened and a woman in black robe and veil entered. Her movements were seductive despite the traditional attire. She moved within a few feet of Danny Mac before she stopped. She slowly and deliberately began removing the veils and slipping the robe off one shoulder, she then allowed it to pool at her feet. The woman exuded style in her white blouse with gray silk trousers. She was stunning. Long, sleek black hair. Almond eyes and flawless olive skin.

Danny Mac lightly squeezed Kenann's hand that he had continued to hold. She wondered if it was to reassure her or simply a reaction to this woman's impact.

"Hello, Danny Boy." Her voice was deep and mellow. No real accent that Kenann could detect. These two obviously knew each other. And from the look in her eyes they had known each other *very* well.

"Hello, Katerina." His voice was flat and without emotion.

"I've missed you." She moved slowly and sensuously toward Danny Mac. She stopped so close Kenann cocked her head and lifted an eyebrow. You couldn't slide a piece of paper between them. Danny Mac continued to hold Kenann's hand as he made direct and steady eye contact with Katerina.

Completely ignoring Kenann, Katerina ran her hands over Danny Mac's chest and encircled his neck. She was only slightly shorter than Danny and had no trouble leaning forward and covering his lips with her own. Despite his lack of response, she made the kiss very convincing. When she released him, she looked down her nose to Kenann's much shorter position and sneered, "Who is this child, Danny Boy?"

Before Kenann had a moment to consider her precarious situation she smiled brilliantly up at Danny Mac and said, "Honey, you were right. She really is pathetic."

A blur of movement and Kenann's forearm blocked the vicious slap aimed at her face. Danny Mac had executed his own lightening quick block and found his hand covering Kenann's. The look of easy affection that passed between them sealed Katerina's rage into granite.

"Enough! Take them away," she barked to the men standing nearby. Danny Mac and Kenann turned to go with the men who had accompanied them from America. Katerina called to Danny Mac and spoke to him in Arabic.

"Keep a muzzle on her lest I lose my patience."

He answered her in Arabic, his voice low and menacing.

"This arrangement is of your own making, Katerina. She stays healthy and happy or it is over. You will do well to remember that."

"Do you threaten me?"

"I speak the truth." He turned and taking Kenann's elbow, guided her into the hallway. Katerina slammed the door behind them. They proceeded in silence down the corridor, flanked front and back by the men until they stopped at another room. They were ushered inside and left alone. Kenann heard the sound of a traditional key locking them inside. Daniel went to the window that looked out onto a plaza. He surveyed the iron bars over the windows designed to keep people out but was just as efficient in keeping them in.

When he turned back into the room, he found Kenann standing very still watching him. He stepped toward her.

"Are you okay?"

"I think so. What now?"

"We wait."

She nodded and swayed on her feet. He lifted her into his arms as her legs gave out beneath her. She uttered an expletive.

"Sorry, Danny. I hate a swooning woman."

"You're entitled, Kenann. I'd say you've been a trooper. Hey, by the way. Where did you learn to block a blow like that?" He sat in a chair still holding her across his lap. She was limp with exhaustion. She laid her cheek against his chest and murmured, "Oh, my Dad's assistant had his black belt. He became my private Sensei as we traveled around the world."

Danny Mac smiled. He sensed her breathing evening out as she drifted off to sleep. When he was sure she was sleeping soundly he gathered her close and rocked her gently. He wasn't sure if it was for her or for himself.

* * *

Refreshed from four hours sleep at Mrs. Gage's mansion, the trio gathered once more around a small table in the breakfast nook off the kitchen.

"What's our game plan, Mrs. Gage? I don't mind telling you, I'm feeling out of my league here."

Despite her concern for their impending adventure, Judy felt freer and more alive than she could ever remember.

"Well, we will approach much of it as it comes. But there are some things we can know and work on now. We know they've gone to Alexandria. Since people on both sides would recognize us if we show up and wander through the city, we shall have to assume disguises."

Judy and Jake exchanged glances.

"I'm afraid I shall have to exploit your beauty, my dear. I know in light of your recent revelations this may be difficult for you."

"I meant what I said about doing whatever I could to get Kenann back. Now that I've let the demons out, so to speak, I feel," she hesitated, "I don't know, less vulnerable I guess."

"Wonderful dear. Because your beauty will be a valuable tool, but I wouldn't want to hurt you in any way."

"Hey bring it on. I feel like taking on the whole world thanks to you two." She looked at them and beamed.

"I am so glad. We'll get you a wig, so you won't have to dye that lovely hair."

"What about me?" Jake asked.

"You my handsome man will be a dashing American tourist. And I'm afraid hair dye *is* in your future. Men simply cannot pull off the look of a wig."

"And you?' Judy asked.

"Me? I think I'll don lots of those mysterious veils and robes. There is absolutely no reason we can't have fun while we fight terrorists and save the day."

Judy and Jake joined Mrs. Gage in a hearty laugh.

*   *   *

When no one returned to the room, Danny Mac pulled back the covers of the large bed and laid Kenann down pulling the covers over her. It was then he remembered the gun and GPS in Kenann's jacket pocket. He reached for them but then realized their movements might be on video monitor. He got under the covers next to Kenann and gently pulled her to him without waking her. He was successful in retrieving both items and slipping them under his pillow surreptitiously. He could only hope and pray that Andy was on his way and could listen in as soon as he was in range. He lay back and finally succumbed to the bone numbing weariness. He was asleep in less than a minute.

He woke with a start when he heard the door being opened. He instinctively reached out for Kenann. She was awake and watching him. Angelo stood glaring at them from the foot of the bed. Danny Mac sat up against the headboard and pulled Kenann close to him. He was sending a clear message that 'this woman is under my protection'.

"She wants to see you."

"Let's go Kenann."

"No. She said to leave her here."

"Not an option. She will not leave my side."

"Danny Boy, you can come easy or you can come hard. It makes no difference to me."

"Angelo, I'm not trying to play hard ball. Kenann is my responsibility. She is in this mess because of me and I am not leaving her. Now I'm sure whatever Katerina has in mind for me doesn't include me having knots all over my head. At least not yet."

Angelo considered this for a moment. "Then you can deal with Katerina. I'm tired of her tongue taking the hide off my bone."

"That is one thing we can certainly agree on." Kenann observed a hint of a smile play at the corners of Angelo's mouth and mentally filed it away. Danny Mac noticed it too and drew hope from it.

Danny Mac continued, "Well, let's get this over with." Taking Kenann's hand, he pulled her with him out of the bed.

As they made their way back down the hallway, Kenann lowered her voice to a growl, "I am not your responsibility. I can take care of myself."

'You know what, I believe you can. But I'm still going to look out for you so deal with it."

Before she could reply they had arrived at Katerina's suite of rooms. She was lounging on the couch when she called for them to enter. She had changed into an oriental number designed to entice. No question what she had in mind when she had summoned Danny. The fury on her face at being thwarted was also clearly evident. She came off the couch with a flourish.

"I gave explicit orders, Angelo. Are you such a fool you cannot do even this without failing?"

"You cannot blame Angelo, Katerina. Like the good soldier he is, he weighed the options and chose wisely." Angelo's only reaction was a slight lifting of one eyebrow.

"And what were these options, Danny Boy?' Her soft voice belied her anger.

"Either I came with Kenann or I didn't come."

"You are pushing me, Danny. I will not tolerate this for long."

"And as I explained to Angelo, I plan to cooperate with you fully as long as I am assured of Kenann's safety. Wasn't that your reasoning for bringing her into this?"

She glared at him in response. He was using her own strategy against her. He had her in a box and she knew it. Danny Mac went on.

"I will not give you any resistance except where Kenann is concerned. If I don't feel comfortable about her, I will dig in and fight. Now, can we get down to business?"

"I give the orders here, Danny Boy." An awkward silence ensued until she whirled and led the way into the dining area of the suite. Large windows overlooked the city. Kenann felt a thrill despite herself at being back in Egypt. Danny Mac pulled a chair out for her and sat down close to her. It was obvious he was not letting her get two feet away from him. Danny Mac could feel the tightrope he was walking. If he played it too hard or too soft, he could lose the delicate balance and Kenann would pay the price. He remembered all too keenly what cruelty Katerina could dish out if he so much as blinked. He waited for her to speak.

"We have been very busy since we last saw you, Danny Boy." He acknowledged this with an imperceptible nod of his head.

"Angelo had the foresight to join forces with us. Unlike you, he realized there are no good guys or bad guys. Only smart ones. You Americans make so much of groups like Al Qaida, the Taliban and ISIS. We have discovered an organization so powerful it defies description."

Katerina's face glowed. "All of civilization is being controlled by the people of whom I speak. You see terrorists in turbans and robes, when your real enemies walk among you daily in suits carrying laptops and mothers who drive children to soccer practice."

"Katerina, spare me the social lecture and tell me what you want me to do." Danny hoped to keep her off balance and somehow maintain an edge. He could tell he had broken her stride, but not for long.

"Oh, you think you have the upper hand, don't you Danny Boy? We traveled half way around the world to bring you to us. That makes you valuable. In that you are right but think ahead lover. You are mine now. No going back. And no escape now for your little girlfriend either. If you remain useful to me, she lives. And when you stop being useful, I will take great pleasure destroying both of you slowly and painfully."

"Yeah, Katerina I get it."

Her eyes narrowed to slits. She could not shake him or make him show an ounce of fear. But isn't that why she had sent for him? She had always desired his steely courage and sharp mind. So be it. But he would not always be so bold. She would make sure of it.

"We have discussed enough for tonight."

"But we're just getting started."

"Enough!" She could feel her control slipping.

"Maybe you're right Katerina, you seem a little tense. Perhaps a little rest will do us all some good. Could I prevail upon you for some clothing and toiletries for myself and Kenann?"

"See to it." She gestured to Angelo and then waved them all away in sharp strident movements.

When they were back in the hallway Angelo scoffed, "You have more guts than brains, Danny Boy."

"What do you mean?"

"Don't try that innocent act with me. You were deliberately antagonizing her. That is very dangerous."

"Are you worried about me, Angelo?"

He barked a laugh. "This is not about you. She is like a viper. When she is riled, she strikes at whomever stands closest. For years I have dreamed of your undoing. I will relish watching Katerina sink her fangs into you."

He switched to Arabic and his voice purred, "And when she has had her fill of you, I will take my fill of your little lion cub."

Danny replied in Arabic. "If you have any decency, you will not dishonor her in any way."

Angelo faltered a moment and seemed embarrassed but quickly

shook it off laughing nervously. "Don't you know, Danny Boy? There really is no honor among thieves."

They had reached the room and Angelo ushered them in. "I'll send a woman to get your sizes. Tell her anything you need."

"How will we pay for them?"

"Oh, it's all on Katerina. She has big plans for you Danny Boy. And don't bother trying to bribe the lady. She works for us." He backed out locking the door with a key. Danny and Kenann both stood staring at the door, deep in their own thoughts. Kenann was the first to move. Putting the length of the room between them she turned and asked, "How do you know Katerina?"

She saw his back muscles tense ever so slightly beneath his white shirt. He turned and looked at Kenann debating how much to tell her and decided.

"She and I worked together as an assassins' team."

"And?"

"We were lovers."

"She hopes to renew your acquaintance, you know."

"That's too bad."

"Tempted?"

"Did I look tempted?'

Kenann suddenly burst out laughing and flopped on the bed.

"No and I have to say that warmed the cockles of my heart - whatever cockles are."

Danny felt the grin spread across his face. "Why so chipper?"

"Oh, get real?" She effected a perfect impersonation of Katerina's throaty voice, "Hello Danny Boy. I've missed you."

Kenann giggled. "She expected you to form a puddle at her feet. Way to go, man. You shut her down big time - like a big block of ice."

"Thank you, I think."

He sat down next to her on the bed and leaning next to her ear and whispered, "I haven't had time to search the room, but we have to assume we are being listened to and probably videotaped. She started to bolt off the bed looking up at the ceiling. Danny caught her in his arms and kissed her before she could get up. He meant to merely distract her but once he started, he took it deeper despite himself.

He felt her go limp against him as she responded to him. When he finally broke contact he laid his forehead on hers.

She mumbled, "If that was supposed to calm me down, it failed."

"What did it do?" Danny Mac asked quietly, pulling back to look her in the eye. She looked back for several seconds and then shook her head as if to break the spell she had been about to go under.

Kenann affected her best southern drawl. "Why Danny Mac, I do believe you are trying to flirt with me."

Before he could respond, the key in the lock turned and a tall raw-boned black woman entered, sporting the hotel concierge name plate and notebook in hand. She was followed by a man pushing a cart covered in white cloth. She quickly and efficiently took their sizes and a list of their personal needs. She left without any indication this process was out of the ordinary. They heard the now familiar click of the door being locked from the outside.

They both dashed to the cart and were pleased to find smoked salmon, roast beef, cheeses and something Kenann couldn't identify but dove into, nonetheless.

When they were sated, Kenann asked Danny Mac, "What time is it anyway?" He checked his watch.

"Well, it's 9 o'clock Memphis time but to tell you the truth I don't know if that's pm or am. I am about to drop so I say we go to bed until we are summoned again."

They turned as if on cue to look at the one king size bed dominating the room. Kenann sighed, "I suppose we better establish some boundaries."

Danny moved to her quickly and pulled her into his arms lowering his voice against her ear. "Don't give our platonic relationship away, Kenann. They think we're lovers."

"Is that why you keep kissing me?' she whispered.

"Partly." He gave her a wicked grin that had served him well with women all his life. Kenann felt her heart flip. He really was flirting with her. Why? Was he relieving stress, using her as a diversion? She knew their relationship had grown into a loving friendship, but this new behavior was throwing her a curve she wasn't sure how to handle. When all else failed her, she reverted to humor.

"At last. I was born to be an actress."

Danny Mac felt irritation rise. Did she have to manufacture sexual attraction for him? He pulled back and gripped her shoulders tighter than he realized.

"Yes, darling by all means let's do that."

He turned and called over his shoulder. "I'm taking a shower." He jerked one of the hotel robes off the hanger and stalked into the bathroom.

Kenann looked after him. She stopped herself from speaking out loud but questioned herself silently, *What's his problem?*

When he returned wrapped in the soft white robe towel drying his hair, he seemed calmer.

Kenann took her robe from its hanger and adopted a light tone, "Next."

"Watch the water. It gets pretty hot."

"Thanks." She hesitated, wanting desperately to return them to their easy footing but didn't understand what had changed, so she just went in and shut the door. When she came out the overhead light was off, replaced by the lamp on her side of the bed. Danny was already asleep. She sat down and watched the rise and fall of his even breathing. She was puzzled by his sudden change in mood. But she decided to cut him a break. He was under a lot of pressure and even though he seemed cool and confidant she figured he was entitled to be a little testy at times. She turned the light out and crawled under the covers. Since Danny was hugging the edge of his side of the bed, she followed suit and was soon fast asleep. When her breathing evened out Danny turned on his back and stared at the ceiling.

CHAPTER THIRTEEN

When Judy had called her parents, they knew instantly she was different. She sounded like their little girl again. They had learned not to press her, so they didn't ask what had happened to prompt this call and a return to her easy affection. She told them she was going on a trip.

"Who will you be going with honey?" Her mom wanted to know.

"Oh, it's one of those group things."

"That's good dear. They are much safer. Where will you be going?"

"The Mediterranean."

"I'm so glad, sweetheart. You work so hard. Will you call us when you return?"

"Sure, Mom." She paused. "I love you."

"Oh baby, I love you too."

"Is Dad there?'

"Yes, would you like to talk to him?'

"Yeah." She could tell her mother covered the phone and called urgently to her Dad who was probably kicked back in his recliner watching Wheel of Fortune.

"Hello, cupcake."

Judy felt a lump constricting her voice. "Hi Daddy."

"Is anything wrong?"

"No, Daddy. I've been doing a lot of thinking. Thank you for always being there. I know I haven't always been the easiest person to deal with."

"We've worried about you."

"I know. And we'll talk about it soon, but I wanted you to know I'm getting some things sorted out. I'm going on a trip. Mom will fill you in. When I get back, I'll come home and we'll talk okay."

"We'll be here, cupcake." After they said their good-byes and hung up, Judy sat there for a few minutes. She felt energized. She was reclaiming her life. A smile spread across her face.

Mrs. Gage looked up from her desk when Judy came in. "How did it go?"

"Great."

Mrs. Gage beamed. "Is your work agreeable to your sudden departure?"

"They were ecstatic. They've been trying to get me to take a vacation for eons. And I spoke with the Director of Kenann's counseling agency. I think you were right about telling him the truth. He deals with confidential information as his livelihood, so he can keep a secret even one as unbelievable as this. He knows me from my work next door, so I had credibility. He agreed to cover for her with other staff and assured me her job would be secure when she returns."

"Good. Everything is proceeding smoothly. We will leave in the morning."

"What do I need to pack?"

"Bring your own personal items. You will be traveling as yourself. I did not have time to get an altered Passport."

"Mrs. Gage! Who do you know that alters Passports?"

"There's a lovely little man in Jackson, Mississippi who does excellent work."

Judy shook her head in amazement. Mrs. Gage continued, "Once we are settled in Alexandria, I will outfit you with your new persona."

"You're the boss. After I get my things, I think I'll go to Kenann's. When we get her, I think it will be comforting for her to have some familiar things."

"How considerate and insightful of you dear."

Judy smiled shyly. "What are you going to do?"

"Oh, there are plenty of last-minute details to tend to. You run along, dear. We'll all spend the night here if that is agreeable?"

"Sure." Judy let herself out through the kitchen and walked the few blocks back to Kenann's to pick up her car. She had her key in the lock when she noticed movement out of the corner of her eye. She turned and was stunned to see Granny James rise from one of the wicker chairs on Kenann's porch.

"Granny! What are you doing here?"

"Kenann was supposed to call me yesterday. I waited until this morning and when she did not answer her phone, I knew something was wrong. I took the earliest flight I could get out of Charleston and used her address to get a taxi from the airport."

"How long have you been sitting out here?"

"Oh, about an hour. I figured the preacher who Kenann said lived next door would be home eventually."

"Oh, Granny."

"Judy, tell me what's happened."

"It's complicated."

"Is Kenann alright?"

"She's not hurt but she's been taken."

"Taken! What do you mean taken?"

"Kidnapped, I guess. That's where it gets complicated."

"Can we go inside? This heat has about drained me."

"Of course." Judy used her key to let them into the main entry hall and on into Kenann's apartment. She got Mrs. James a glass of tea from Kenann's refrigerator.

"What happened, Judy?"

"Well, Kenann went to Mrs. Gage's party Saturday night. While she was there, she was grabbed by a man in the garden but Danny Mac, the preacher, he rescued her but later on both of them were taken."

"Judy, this is unthinkable. Who would want to kidnap them?"

"Some group that knew Danny Mac from his military days. They took Kenann, I think, to make Danny Mac cooperate."

"Do you know where they have taken them?"

"We think its Alexandria, Egypt."

"What?"

"I know it all seems pretty bizarre, but Mrs. Gage has taken charge and organized a rescue party. We are going after them."

"Take me to Mrs. Gage."

"Okay." Judy drew the word out with a sinking feeling.

"I'm going with you."

"Now, Granny."

"Don't you now Granny me. If you think I'm going to sit by and let someone else go after my baby you've got another thing coming."

"Okay, okay. Just let me get some things from Kenann's room." She packed a small bag and helped Granny carry her own small suitcase out to her car. She ran by her place for a few things and then drove them the short distance back to Mrs. Gage's mansion.

"Oh my," was the only thing Granny said when they pulled up in front. Judy had planned to take Granny's elbow going up the wide front steps, but she skipped up them while Judy tried to catch up. Granny rang the doorbell before Judy could tell her to go on in.

Mrs. Gage opened the door with a smile of greeting already on her strong face. She waited until Judy broke the silence.

"Mrs. Gage, this is Kenann's grandmother - Mrs. James."

"Oh, come in. Come in, you poor dear. You must be worried sick."

"I'm going with you." Mrs. James spoke without preamble.

"Of course, you are."

Judy's head snapped around to stare at Mrs. Gage. "She is?"

"Of course. There would be no way to prevent her short of ... what is the phrase?"

"Hog tying." Mrs. James supplied.

Mrs. Gage laughed heartily. "Precisely."

Despite her anxiety over Kenann, Mrs. James found herself grinning too.

Look out Egypt, here we come. Judy thought.

*   *   *

Both Kenann and Danny Mac slept soundly for several hours. Danny Mac was the first to awaken. He felt under his pillow for the gun and the GPS device. He relocated them between the mattress and box springs trying to shield their view by his body in case of video monitoring. He felt better having them secured. He wasn't sure the listening device would pick up laying under the mattress, but he would try to find a better location later. He rose quietly and went to the bathroom. When he came out, he noticed several boxes and bags lying on the credenza near the door. He turned when he heard the key unlocking the door. Angelo walked in.

"You have changed more than I imagined." Danny Mac raised an eyebrow in response.

Angelo continued. "You sleep next to a beautiful woman and do not touch her. Where is that man I knew?" This confirmed Danny Mac's suspicion that the room was on video monitor.

Danny Mac weighed his options and decided he needed to be completely honest and let God protect them in His way. Originally, he thought if they knew he and Kenann were not lovers it would jeopardize the balance that was keeping Kenann safe. It felt good to put himself completely back in God's hands. He had forgotten how draining it was to try to juggle everything on his own.

"Kenann and I are not lovers, Angelo. We are friends. And even if we were in love, we would do our best to wait until marriage to make love." Once again, he felt the great gulf between the man he used to be and the man he had become. Angelo looked at him incredulously.

"Does this religion of yours take away what is between your legs?"

"No, but it asks me to control it. Not let it control me"

"This religion makes you weak," he paused, "Not a man."

94

"On the contrary, Angelo. I like to think it makes me stronger."

"You are crazy. Enough of this! She wants to see you again. I will be back in an hour. Be dressed and ready to go out when I return." He turned and held the door open for a young woman pushing a food cart. She took the other cart without a glance at Danny and left as quietly as she came. Angelo locked the door behind them.

Danny turned and found Kenann lying on her side watching him. "You decided to tell him about us?"

"Yeah, the more I thought about it, I realized I was trying to protect us by my own power."

"And now?"

"I gave it back over to God where it belongs."

"Does that mean you're not going to kiss me anymore?" She grinned, dissolving the knot he had forgotten lying in his stomach. He answered her with the same lighthearted manner.

"No, it means I'm going to make your life miserable with unwanted advances. Come on. Let's eat. He'll be back soon."

Kenann, pondering what Danny would do when he found out his advances weren't unwanted, got out of bed and began fixing herself a plate. Danny said around a mouthful of egg and biscuit, "I get the bathroom first. Women take longer."

"Chauvinist."

"Realist." He laughed and became absorbed in opening some jelly.

She was glad the hours of rest had restored them to an equilibrium. She had grown to depend on Danny Mac's friendship as a stabilizing force in the short time they had known each other. She always felt like she was 'coming home' anytime she was with him. It was that 'kick off your shoes and put your feet up' kind of comfort that she had never felt with anyone else. It scared her to realize how much she needed him. The therapist in her saw this as unhealthy dependence. The woman in her knew she was powerless against it. And because she needed him in her life at all cost, she wasn't willing to risk losing him by a failed romance. Sexual attraction may come or go but she knew, with care, Danny Mac would be a friend for life. So, she would be his friend and feel secure that this part of him would be hers, forever.

He emerged from the bathroom later in sharply pressed khaki pants and black polo shirt. His black hair falling becomingly across his forehead made him look all the more like a native to this country.

"Looking good, MacKenzie. Now it's my turn. Let's hope Miss Efficiency got my hip size right. Nobody likes a wedgy."

Danny Mac laughed and started to perform the now familiar nudge to her forehead. She dodged expertly out of his way.

"Hah! I think I'll start practicing my karate moves on you, old man to keep in shape."

"Anytime you think you can handle it you jump right in, James."

"Ooh, that sounds an awful lot like a challenge."

"No, it's more like a warning." They both were smiling as she went into dress. Her outfit turned out to be tailored perfectly for her shape. The black pants and hounds tooth jacket complemented her well. Even the bra fit which amazed Kenann who could never find one that did.

"That's it. I'm taking this woman away from Dragon lady. She must become my personal shopper."

She did a runway modeling turn for Danny. She stopped and turned sober.

"This is getting weird, Danny Mac. I'm actually enjoying myself. How sick is that?'

"I'm sure it's all part of the plan to keep us cooperative and in line." He looked up to the ceiling fixture. "Isn't that right, Katerina?"

"Oops, I forgot." Kenann giggled. "Guess that crack about Dragon Lady wasn't so good, huh?"

"It was perfect." Danny Mac placed his hands on either side of Kenann's face. "And so are you. You've been very brave and bold through this whole thing. I'm constantly amazed by you." He leaned in and whispered, "And because I know this will irritate her as much as being called Dragon Lady," he leaned in further and slowly captured her lips with his. He took his time changing the angle of the kiss to deepen it. Kenann couldn't help responding and brought her arms up to encircle Danny's neck. When he finally released her, he pulled back just enough to look her in the eye. She met his gaze squarely.

He whispered more to himself than to her, "What's happening with us?"

Kenann realized he was as scared of their intimacy as she was. A tiny spark of hope erupted into a flame. From somewhere deep within her she answered, "Inshallah, as they say in these parts."

Danny Mac grinned. "Yes, as God wills."

That's how Angelo found them - locked in a close embrace and looking at each other.

"Friends, my ass," he muttered.

*   *   *

Katerina was all business this time, but she completely ignored Kenann as if she was not standing directly beside Danny Mac. He made note of this and put his arm around Kenann pulling her close. She laughed softly. She couldn't help it, she really enjoyed baiting Katerina. She was also comforted by the warmth of being tucked under Danny Mac's protective arm.

Katerina drew in a deep breath exhaling slowly as she looked at them. It was costing her not to scratch the smile off that little minx face. All in good time. All in good time.

"Your work begins tonight." Kenann felt Danny Mac's muscles contract slightly. "Sit down while I brief you."

They sat around the small round table in the suites dining area.

"There is to be a dinner party tonight - a very important event for the organization. We will go so I may introduce you into the inner circle of the society I mentioned earlier. It has taken me several years to get this far. I have earned their trust and now with you at my side, I will begin the process of taking control."

"And how do you plan to do that?"

"You will assassinate the current leader."

"I'm not killing anyone, Katerina." Before either of them could react, Katerina had grabbed Kenann by the hair and jerked her away from Danny's side, pulling her to her feet. Danny jumped up, knocking the chair over but stopped cold. Katerina had a dagger poised at Kenann's rapidly pulsing jugular.

"Does this remind you of anything?" The color blanched in Danny's face. "You see, even then Angelo was doing my bidding. That kid was ready to blow my cover and the whole operation. I couldn't take the chance that he had told you anything, so I wanted you to think he could not be trusted. I never dreamed you cared enough for that kid to almost kill Angelo over him."

Danny Mac hadn't moved. Katerina wound her hand tighter around Kenann's hair and pulled her head back farther, exposing more of her neck.

"You choose, Danny Boy. Her life or the life of a man you've never met."

"Let her go," Danny's voice sounded hoarse.

Katerina laughed and shoved Kenann, who landed in a heap on the floor. Danny Mac knelt, put his arm around her and helped her to her feet.

"Katerina, you brought me half way around the world to kill someone you could have killed yourself at any time?"

"No, Lover. I plan to have an iron clad alibi when the deed is done to remove all suspicion from me."

"Then have one of your goons eliminate him while you're busy being seen somewhere else."

"But you see, I need your mind as well as your skill. This man has an elaborate system of protection that surrounds him. I have been unable to find his Achilles heel. That's why I sent for you. This must be flawlessly planned, executed and completely untraceable to me. So tonight, you will begin the process of studying Monseigneur Montefort. You will give me the plan and you will kill him, or I will kill her."

Danny Mac instinctively stepped in front of Kenann before she could speak.

"Alright, Katerina. You hold all the cards. We will be ready tonight."

"No. You go with me. But to show you I am a good sport, she can go with Angelo. As it so happens, he is in need of a date." Kenann cut her eyes over to where Angelo stood as still as a statue. He met her gaze and gave her an unholy smile. She felt her stomach roll. For the first time since this whole thing started, she was truly afraid.

They returned to their now familiar room and sat together on the side of the bed. Danny Mac reached over and took Kenann's hand.

"It will be alright. God will be with us."

"Danny Mac, I don't have the same kind of trust in all that stuff that you do. The only thing I know about God and going to church is from the little bit I have been around Granny James."

"Kenann, trust in God is very simple really. You can look at all the evidence and there is plenty of it to be convincing, but when it's all said and done, it really is a 'leap of faith.'"

"But that is so scary."

"Yeah, it is the first time or so, but it doesn't take long to see that he really is taking care of you. Then it is gloriously reassuring and liberating."

"Okay, how do I take this leap of faith?"

"Well, I don't mean to sound like a preacher, but have you accepted Jesus as your Savior?"

"Well, I know about the whole dying on the cross thing for the 'sins of the world' but I'm not sure I understand what you're talking about with accepting him as my Savior."

"Believing he died for the sins of the world is a beginning. Believing he died for you gets a little more personal. And when you truly believe that and all that goes with it, it will produce a response. Call it gratitude, devotion, maybe even relief to be freed from the burden that sin weighs on us, but when that change happens people want to get as close to Jesus as they can."

"Well, how do you do that?"

"Do you want book, chapter and verse?"

"I will eventually. That's one thing Granny James did drum into my head. 'Speak where the Bible speaks.'"

"Good for Granny James. I will show you the scriptures but basically once a person truly believes that Jesus is the Son of God then they will automatically repent or be sorry that they are so imperfect compared to him. They feel pretty unworthy of this wonderful gift they have been offered. But the good news is that once a person has been baptized, they take on the symbolic death, burial and resurrection of Christ. Their sins are forgiven, and the holy blood Jesus shed on the cross continues to cleanse us of our sins every day. You've seen the bumper sticker 'Christians aren't perfect, they're just forgiven'? It's true."

Kenann listened as Danny Mac continued. "At baptism you become 'in Christ'. It's a mysterious thing, but the Holy Spirit comes to dwell in the new Christian to help them. It is a wonderful life, Kenann."

"It sounds pretty good."

"I'm always here if you want to talk about it. And if you decide you want to become a Christian, I'll be the first one in the water."

"Thanks, Danny Mac. You have been very sweet to me."

Danny fought the urge to take her into his arms. This was a crucial point in Kenann's life and he didn't want to cloud the issue with his own growing desire for her. They sat there for several moments deep in their own thoughts. Kenann turned to Danny.

"Will you pray for me about tonight, that God will keep me safe while I am with Angelo and he won't, you know, do anything to me?"

Danny felt his stomach tighten. The thought of Angelo laying a hand on Kenann filled him with rage. He offered his own silent prayer for strength and took her hand again. "Sure."

They bowed their heads out of years of habit.

"Father, you know all things. You know how frightened we are and how weak. Please be with us in a mighty way. Send angels to surround Kenann in protection and allow them to make their presence known so she will be comforted. And be with me, Lord. Give me wisdom in how to handle what lies before me and the strength and courage to do your will in all things. Thank you for Jesus and it is by the power of His name that I pray. Amen."

Kenann turned into Danny Mac's arms and clung to him. "I especially liked the part about the angels. If I remember right, they have been known to kick butt."

Danny Mac chuckled.

"Yes." He stroked her hair.

"The biggest and baddest warrior angels will be with you tonight, baby."

CHAPTER FOURTEEN

G ranny had a current passport in case she needed to return home to Waterford for her family. She made a habit of keeping it in her purse, so she would always know where it was along with her driver's license and social security card. This proved to be advantageous in their efforts to leave as scheduled. Mrs. Gage had called for a limousine service to pick them up and take them to the airport that morning. They were processed through and boarded a private transport aircraft. The trunks and cases had also been picked up by a cargo carrier and loaded onto the plane without a hitch. Judy asked Mrs. Gage what was in the large containers.

"I have accumulated many things over the years that would be useful in the task ahead of us. Things to use in disguises and some equipment we might find useful."

"Why would you have the occasion to collect that kind of stuff?"

"Well, my dear," she smiled and dropped her head. When she looked up, she offered, "I have many interests. Some of which have placed me in unusual circumstances. Now shall we get settled, I imagine the captain will be calling for takeoff very soon."

Judy knew an evasion of a topic better than anyone. And this lady had some secrets. She hoped that one day Mrs. Gage would grow to trust her enough to share them with her. They joined Jake and Granny James in the seating area. The captain came back and checked personally with Mrs. Gage to see if all was ready. He had obviously flown for Mrs. Gage before, judging by his deferential manner. They buckled their seat belts and their journey began.

*   *   *

Judy had just finished serving refreshments to the others from the fully stocked galley kitchen when a man dressed in coveralls came in and whispered something to Mrs. Gage. The imperturbable Mrs. Gage stood up and shrieked, "What! Where?"

At that moment, a young dark-skinned child stepped into the seating area from the back of the plane. Judy recognized him as Blade, the boy who had been coming daily to Kenann and Danny Mac's duplex apartments.

"Blade, come here." Mrs. Gage sounded deadly serious. Everyone held their breath. Blade walked slowly across the room and stood in front of her with his head bowed as far as a head can be bowed.

"Can you explain why you are on this plane illegally?"

His head was up, and he pleaded, "I'll pay you back for the ticket. I promise. I have my paper route and I'll pay back every cent, honest."

"How did you manage to stow away without being caught?"

"I overheard y'all talking about how you were gonna go get Danny Mac and Kenann back. So, I got up real early this morning and came in through your side door in your kitchen and crawled into a big green trunk and covered up with the stuff."

Mrs. Gage sat down as if all the air had gone out of her.

"Blade, what if no one had found you? The men could have piled several heavy trunks on top of yours and you would have been trapped. The temperature gets so cold at high altitudes. Oh child," she grabbed him and enveloped him in silk and perfume.

He sniffed. "I didn't mean to make you mad, Mrs. Gage. I just wanted to help Danny Mac and Kenann."

"I know sweetheart, but we have to call your mom and get you on the first direct flight back to Memphis."

"Oh please, let me stay with you. I couldn't do nothing to save my Dad when he got sick. Since he died, Danny Mac has tried to, you know, keep an eye on me and I just gotta help him. Please."

His face was so earnest. Jake cleared his throat.

"Gabrielle, a little boy with dark skin will be able to blend in places we could never go."

"Jake, he could never pull it off without knowing some of the language."

Blade interrupted. "I could pretend I couldn't hear or talk!"

There was complete silence as the simplicity and ingeniousness of this tactic sank in. Everyone began to laugh. Blade looked from face to face to try to determine if he had won his case.

Mrs. Gage said, "Oh alright but at the first sign of trouble your little skinny behind is on the first plane home. Is that understood?"

His fist clenched, and he pumped back his elbow, "Yes!"

Mrs. Gage raised an eyebrow.

He added, "Ma'am."

*   *   *

Leticia Daniels was relieved beyond words to know that her son was safe. They had taken a vote and decided not to tell her all the details of their impromptu trip. She scolded Blade about pulling such a fool hearty stunt but was pleased that they were willing to let him tag along on their holiday. They rung off with promises to keep in contact and assured they would have him home before school started. Mrs. Gage went into closed quarters and began working on the problem of getting Blade into the country without a Passport or papers of any kind. No one asked her any questions. When she came out, she nodded to Jake and it was understood that the obstacles had been overcome. Judy pondered the seemingly endless network available to Mrs. Gage to arrange things. She was turning out to be an international woman of mystery.

CHAPTER FIFTEEN

D anny pretended to drop a cuff link on the floor by the bed. He steadied himself by the mattress and was able to retrieve the GPS receiver and conceal it in his breast pocket. He decided it was time to check in with Andy who he hoped to God was listening.

He went to the door of the bathroom and talked loud enough for Kenann to hear through the door.

"Let's go over everything so we'll be on the same page."

She called back, "Now?"

"Yeah, I'll be leaving soon."

"Okay. I'm all ears."

He hit the highlights he thought Andy would need the most. "So far we know that Katerina brought me here to the Metropole to kill someone as yet unknown who is head over some secret organization that no one has ever heard of. She wants to be above suspicion, so she can step into the leadership of this said organization. He will be at this party tonight and I am to begin my observations in order to devise this assassination plan."

Just then the door opened, and he lost his voice. Her white diaphanous gown flowed around her like a Greek goddess. She did not have any pins or ornamentation for her hair, so she allowed it to curl naturally which only enhanced the aura of ancient and bygone days. Danny Mac stood motionless.

"What?" Kenann looked pained. "Do I look stupid?"

Danny Mac swallowed. A woman who had no clue of her beauty could be a dangerous thing.

"No, Kenann. You look lovely."

She beamed like a child. "Really? Cool! Do you think my angels will approve? I do sense them, you know."

"I know."

"You look yummy Danny Mac. Let me let you in on a well-known secret." Danny shook his head in confusion in that logic.

"There is not a woman alive from 9 to 90 that can resist a man in a tux."

"Including you?" Danny asked quietly.

Kenann got that flutter in her stomach again. What was she supposed to do? How much could she reveal of her heart and not be destroyed. She looked into his eyes as he waited patiently for her response and she couldn't bring herself to be flippant.

She answered softly. "Including me."

He took a step toward her. The hunger in his eyes caused her to catch her breath. The door opened, and they froze. One of the Arabic guards entered and spoke to Danny.

"The Boss said you are to come with me. The little lion is to wait here for Angelo."

Danny took both of her hands in his.

"I'm going to have to leave you now. I will be nearby at all times. And you won't be alone."

Kenann understood that Danny Mac was talking about celestial protection and could feel that strength surrounding her. She smiled bravely and meant it.

"I'll be okay, Danny Mac. Thank you for well, you know."

He released her hands and brought his up to cup her face.

"We'll get through this, Kenann, and then we have some talking to do, okay?"

"Okay." She whispered. He gave her a brief hard kiss and left.

She stood motionless for several moments and then her thoughts began to race.

Okay, God. I know we aren't really on speaking terms, but Danny Mac makes it seem so easy. Could you, like, show me what I am supposed to do. I mean about all of this and maybe even about You. I do feel the presence of strength and I do not believe that's a coincidence. So, I guess I'm asking You to help me, okay? Well, that's it for now. I, um, guess I'll talk to you later.

She sat on the bed and waited to be summoned. She didn't have to wait long. Angelo unlocked the door and came in. He had a scowl on his face and motioned for her to come with him. She was relieved to see his cocky attitude gone and wondered what had taken it away. She could not know that Katerina had given him strict orders to leave her alone. If they had any hope of controlling Danny Mac, she had to be off limits for the time being. It grated that Danny Boy was getting treated like a King and he was ordered around like a lowly servant.

Kenann followed Angelo down the hallway to the elevator. They got in together and he had yet to speak. She certainly had nothing to say to him, so they continued down to the lobby in silence. They turned down a wide corridor toward a large archway. Kenann could see chandeliers and white tuxedoed waiters milling among the 'beautiful people'. She paused at the top of the stairs leading to the ballroom and scanned the crown anxiously looking for Danny Mac.

They saw each other at the same time and smiled. She took little notice of Katerina and the other distinguished man standing with them. He was almost as tall as Danny Mac with silver at the temples of his dark hair. He was staring up at her with rapt attention. He moved forward and stopped.

Katerina observed this with keen attention. Angelo took Kenann's elbow at a signal from Katerina and led her down the steps. The other man followed her every movement and as she reached the ballroom floor, he came to her.

"Pardon my boldness, Mademoiselle. I must confess your loveliness left me speechless. May I ask your name?"

At that moment Danny Mac was at their side and offered smoothly, "Monsieur Montefort, allow me to introduce my sister, Kenann."

Danny Mac was pleased to see Kenann never missed a beat but extended her hand, which Mr. Montefort grasped, and promptly brought to his lips in a gracious kiss. She smiled demurely which Danny Mac knew was a very sincere response to this genteel behavior.

"Kenann, what an unusual name."

"It was a combination of my," she looked at Danny and corrected, "Our parents' names."

"Is this gentleman escorting you?"

She looked at Angelo and nodded.

"May I be so bold as to steal her from you this evening?"

Before Angelo could respond, Katerina interjected. "Of course, Pierre. You are our guest of honor. You only have to request your desires."

Pierre Montefort beamed and extended his arm to Kenann who gracefully came to his side. She smiled up at him and was drawn into his obvious warmth and enamoration of her.

Katerina continued, "Shall we find our table and relax a bit before the dancing begins?"

"Yes, that would be perfect." Pierre beamed down at Kenann.

Angelo drifted away, no longer needed. Kenann had no idea what was happening in this sudden turn of events, but she knew she was enjoying herself much more than she ever anticipated. This would give her the added benefit of being near Danny Mac since this man was obviously the man Katerina had targeted. She faltered as the implication of that realization hit her.

Mr. Montefort took her other elbow. "Are you alright?"

She said the first thing that came to her mind. "I'm a little hungry. I was so excited about tonight I just realized I haven't eaten much today."

He quickened their pace to the table and clucked over her like a mother hen until she was seated and one of the servants was dispatched to bring their food. Katerina sat across from them and made no indication of her earlier hostility toward her. But she was taking advantage of the situation with Danny Mac by stroking his arm and leaning into him at every opportunity. Now it was Kenann's turn to want to claw her eyes out. Danny Mac must have sensed something and winked at her when they made eye contact.

"Mr. McKenzie, what brings you and your delightful sister to Alexandria?"

"I had some business here and Kenann tagged along."

"Most fortunate for me that she did. How long will you be here?"

"I'm not sure. Kenann is recently graduated with her master's and hasn't begun looking for a job so I suppose she can stay with me as long as she wants."

"And what do you say, young lady?"

"Danny Mac is a pesky big brother but as long as he is footing the bill, I will stay until he runs me off."

Mr. Montefort laughed heartily and patted her hand on the table. Just then the waiters brought their food and they were busy with this endeavor. Once they had eaten and the dishes had been cleared away the band began to play. Mr. Montefort scooted back his chair and held out his hand to Kenann.

"Would you do me the honor?"

Involuntarily Kenann looked at Danny Mac who nodded. Mr. Montefort grinned at Danny Mac.

"I can see you are a very protective brother. I assure you my intentions are honorable."

Without thinking Danny spoke from his gut. "They'd better be." And then softened his words with a smile.

Once they had entered the dance floor, Katerina spoke. "Well, this is certainly an interesting development."

"See if you can get Montefort to dance with you and find out what is prompting his attentions to Kenann."

"Jealous?"

"Should I be?"

"Well, Pierre is a very skillful lover and usually gets what he wants."

"Not this time."

"Don't you think that will be her decision?"

Danny Mac knew she was enjoying bating him, so he did not respond. "We need to find a way to spend time with Montefort without making ourselves obvious."

"Well it appears we have it. You keep playing the protective brother and insist on tagging along. If I know Pierre, his questions about your plans were prompted by plans of his own for your *little sister*."

At that time, they returned from the dance floor and they heard Kenann say, "You make dancing with you very easy Pierre. Thank you."

"The pleasure was all mine, Mon Ami."

"Well, how about letting your big brother drag you around the dance floor next?"

She sighed heavily. "Oh, I suppose if I have to," and laughed. "Will you excuse us."

"Of course, my dear. Katerina and I will catch up a bit."

Danny Mac and Kenann stepped onto the dance floor and turned to each other. The electricity between them was palpable. Danny Mac felt it sizzle and knew if they were not very careful Mr. Montefort would discover their deception or have serious concerns about family dynamics in America.

Whether it was the tension of the day or excitement of the moment, but Kenann shivered when Danny Mac splayed his left hand across her lower back drawing her to him.

"Cold?"

"Oh no." Kenann sounded breathless even to herself.

Danny Mac grinned wickedly. "Good."

"Why?"

"I was starting to think you may be developing a thing for *Pierre*," he could not keep the sarcasm out of his voice.

It was Kenann's turn to grin. "Good."

"You are doing great, kid. I can't believe I'm proud of you for falling so easily into covert operations but I'm beginning to think you are a natural. I wish I had had you with me in Europe a few years ago."

"What would you have done with me if you had?"

"Oh, let's not even go there. I'm trying desperately to be good. If you put that mental picture in my mind, I may dance you out of here and not look back."

Kenann was suddenly breathless. If she thought she had experienced passion before, she was mistaken. This was the most overwhelming feeling she had ever experienced, and it bordered on terrifying.

"Oh Danny Mac." She felt tears well up.

"Hey, hey. It's okay. Why the tears?"

"Oh, I don't know. I'm feeling so many things and I don't know what to do about them."

Danny Mac drew her closer into his arms. "Listen. We'll take everything very slow. One day at a time. Okay? Are you feeling pressure from me?"

She looked up into his face. "No. My fears are all about *my* feelings. Don't pay any attention to me."

The song ended, and he hugged her fiercely but briefly in what he hoped passed for a brotherly squeeze.

They came back to the table and both were feeling edgy trying to reconcile what was happening between them. Katerina was all smiles and joviality. Kenann thought Katerina was pretty good at this 'covert thing' too considering her raw resentment toward her not a few hours before.

"Pierre and I have been all abuzz with plans for tomorrow. He will only be in town a few days and he wants to spend them with us. Danny, I told him how protective you are about Kenann, so we have decided to make a foursome out of tomorrow. I told him I could clear my calendar and I assured him you should be able to as well. What do you say?"

Danny Mac made a pretense at hesitating and after a few moments said, "Let me make some phone calls and see what I can do. Mom and Dad would be furious with me if I let Kenann out of my sight for very long. They practically made me take a blood oath before we left."

"Oh, I'm sure Kenann knows all about blood oaths." Pierre gave her a knowing look.

Kenann looked at him quizzically. He took her hand and said, "Don't worry Mon Ami. All will be clear soon. Shall we dance?"

Kenann found herself once again looking to Danny Mac for approval. Danny Mac smiled at her reassuringly and she got up and took Pierre's proffered hand. When they were out of earshot Danny Mac turned on Katerina.

"What does he mean about blood oaths?"

"Calm down, lover boy. He's talking centuries ago. Since you haven't heard the whole story about our little cabal, it will seem strange to you, but Pierre is convinced that your stupid little friend is the reincarnation of Inanna. That's the reason for his sudden and complete fascination with her."

"Who or what is Inanna?"

"She was a goddess worshiped in ancient Sumeria – a forerunner of Isis. The reason you have never heard about her is part of the extreme secrecy of the people with whom we are dealing."

"You have got to be kidding. What kind of whacked jobs are you dealing with, Katerina?"

"Don't underestimate them, Danny Boy. This organization has been in existence for millennia."

"What do you mean like some ancient cult?"

"I'd really rather not get into it right here. Let's reconnoiter in my room later tonight and I can fill you in."

"No, let's not."

"What's the matter, Danny Boy, afraid?"

"No, I don't trust you."

"Are you sure it's not yourself you don't trust? How long has it been since you've had a real woman?"

He looked over at Kenann and Pierre on the dance floor.

"I'm beginning to think I never have."

He didn't notice the shock followed by complete venom that coursed through Katerina as she followed his gaze to Kenann.

CHAPTER SIXTEEN

hey arrived at the International Airport in Alexandria and disembarked with remarkable speed considering their growing number
and the amount of things Mrs. Gage had to get through customs. She
scurried them off to a private villa on the outskirts of the city near a large
market and within easy access to bus transportation. She made everyone
comfortable in private rooms except Jake who graciously accepted Blade
as his ward for the duration. She gave them an hour to refresh themselves
then asked that they return to the main floor parlor.

Upon their gathering in the spacious seating area of couches and
overstuffed chairs Mrs. Gage once again took center stage.

"As some of you may have guessed, I have had some practice in what
we are about to accomplish. So, let me assure you I am in charge. For your
own safety, you must do *exactly* as I say. No exceptions. Understood?"
Everyone nodded.

"Good, now onto our strategy. In just a few minutes we will begin
assuming our respective disguises and going over each person's agenda
and assigned task. We know that Andrew O'Hanlon is in the city too,
along with whatever entourage he has brought with him. We do not want
to come to his attention as he will do his best to then thwart our efforts in
some misguided attempt to protect us from harm. To the man, or should
I say boy, we have all counted the cost to the best of our abilities and are

willing to accept the risk. Now let's begin the business of getting our dear friends back."

"Blade, your very quick-witted suggestion to pose as a deaf, mute boy was inspired. You will be assuming the guise of a street child. Your biggest task will be to become as invisible as possible. Blend in and observe and listen. I will provide you with a dirty scrap of paper with the statement of your infirmities written in Arabic. You are to make guttural sounds if anyone approaches you and asks anything. Point to your mouth and ears and shake your head no. If you cannot make yourself understood, pull out this paper and show it to them. If anyone tries to write anything to you, shake your head no as if to say you cannot read or write as well. Understood?"

Blade sat mesmerized at the thought of the adventure before him and nodded. Mrs. Gage continued, "We will get you some dirty clothes and make you look the part."

"Granny James, I have not decided what role we need for you. Bear with me for a few minutes while I sort out the others. All right?"

"All right." She sat very straight with her hands folded in her lap.

"Jacob, I will be dying your hair dark and putting you in Armani. You will be a very wealthy business man vacationing here and looking for a little action. I am looking for a caricature of this type. Do you understand what I am saying?"

"I think so, Gabrielle."

Judy smiled. Jacob already had all the action he could handle right here whether he knew it or not. Mrs. Gage turned to her.

"My dear, with Andrew in this city we will have to do an exceptional job at concealing your identity. I imagine he will have radar out where you are concerned."

"I imagine he has radar out for anything in a skirt."

"Maybe on a superficial level, dear. I could dress you down into a character like I am going for with Jacob but, as I mentioned before, my plan will be to use your beauty as a diversion. Since you are already a blond, I have a black wig for you and we will do a little magic with the make-up. Once I show you how to walk to disguise your identity, I think we will be almost ready."

"But what to do with you, my sweet lady," she tapped her pen against her teeth as she studied Granny James. She came over and reaching out her hand had Granny stand up and step out a pace or two. She circled her and pondered. Finally, she decided.

"A change of plans. But I will reveal all that in good time. Jacob, let me get you headed off to dye your hair. Angelina will help you." Jake looked dubious, but he was accustomed to following orders, so he followed the quiet house servant out without a word.

"Mrs. James, you and Judy follow me. Blade, I will have someone come back for you with your clothes. Now they won't smell very good, but you'll be a brave little fellow, won't you?"

"Hey, I like dirt."

"That's my boy. Will you be alright here for a few minutes?"

"Yep. I mean yes ma'am," and was rewarded with a loving smile from Mrs. Gage.

The ladies trooped after Mrs. Gage like the soldiers they were quickly becoming. She quickly worked her magic on Judy, who now looked like a fashionable woman of haute couture. She received a quick lesson on a runway walk and affecting the bored look of a woman who is used to being watched. Judy then excused herself to check on Blade. Mrs. Gage turned to Granny.

"We have had little time to chat privately much less get to know each other, have we?"

"Well, my baby is out there somewhere, and I'm just glad you have a plan to get her back."

"As I pondered a disguise for you it was hard because I have not had time to learn your personality or your ways. But as I studied you for a few moments, downstairs, I decided to change scenarios a bit and make you into a rich entrepreneur's wife."

Granny James' only reaction was a raised eyebrow.

Mrs. Gage continued, "I realized I was being swayed by your moniker of Granny and not looking at you properly. How old are you if I may ask?"

"That's no problem. I'm 68."

"You can pass for a much younger woman you know."

"Well, until now there hasn't been much call too."

"What I would like to do is pair you up as Jacob's wife."

"Why, land sakes, I've probably got more than 10 years on him."

"It makes no matter. Either people will assume by your looks you are younger, or they will assume he prefers older women. Jacob is a brave and wonderful man, but I need a good intuitive woman with him to complement his strength while I am busy in other arenas. You are, what do they call it in your country, fey, aren't you?"

Granny James didn't bother to deny or confirm it as she knew Mrs. Gage already had the answer. Mrs. Gage went on.

"That will be very helpful in a country where you are not familiar with the language or the customs. If you can sense danger, you will be one step ahead. So, let me begin our transformation of you."

"Is this going to hurt?" Granny James laughed.

They were reassembled into the parlor by the afternoon. Jake was looking a bit uncomfortable in a silk, grey Armani suit. Blade sat next to him smelling of things no one wanted to identify. Judy was stunning in her straight chin length black hair with bangs, short skirt and long boots. But the real transformation was Granny James. Her hair had been wound into a complex chignon and she wore a soft suit in a stunning silver blue. Her make-up was flawless, and her high heels were the exact shade of the suit. Mrs. Gage observed them for a few minutes while they all looked at her for their next set of orders.

"I simply cannot continue to call you Granny James, my dear. What is your first name?"

"Moira."

"Well, Moira, may I say you look absolutely stunning. Well, onto our change of plans. Jacob you will now become the entrepreneur husband of this fine women. We will get you two set up in the Metropole Hotel for observation purposes. Jacob, you will be known as an insatiable gambler, which will allow you to roam the main floor at all hours of the day or night. Moira, you will accompany him occasionally as the need arises, but you will also spend time in the bar. Can you hold your liquor?"

"I'm Irish." Everyone laughed and the break in tension was a welcome relief.

"You will also be doing a lot of listening. Judy, you will be positioned at the Cecil Hotel. Hit the club scene and anywhere else a young attractive model would care to go. Blade, once I don my black traditional robes you and I will hit the streets ourselves. We will meet back here for our briefings on a regular basis. I will provide you with these details as we go. Any questions?"

Judy raised her hand, "Should I ignore Moira and Jake if we end up in the same place for some reason?"

"That's an excellent question. And the best answer I can give is to use your instinct at the time. And once one of you commits to a certain scenario, the others can follow along as needed. You three are very bright and I trust your instincts in this matter. Any other questions?"

No one replied.

"All right then, I have identification papers for each of you with sufficient currency for a few days. Should you run into Danny Mac and Kenann or Andrew O'Hanlon try to remain calm and if possible do not give your identity away. Should they recognize you and appear to be on the verge of quizzing you, don't let the situation become awkward and thereby raise unwanted suspicions. If this happens, take the upper hand by approaching them and asking what they are doing here etcetera, etcetera."

She took one last opportunity to scan their faces. She lifted her teacup in a toast.

"Here's to bringing our friends home!"

CHAPTER SEVENTEEN

B y two am the party had wound down sufficiently for Danny Mac to suggest he and Kenann call it a night. Katerina started to protest because she had yet to coax Danny into her bed but was cut short by Pierre. He established their point of departure for tomorrow's activities for the foursome. When Kenann came to her feet, Pierre was there. He took both of her hands and turning them to expose the vulnerable flesh of her wrists, took his time kissing each in turn.

Danny cleared his throat. Pierre smiled and released her hands. "Till tomorrow then, Mon Ami."

"Goodnight everyone." Danny Mac quickly led Kenann toward the stairs to exit the ballroom. At which point they were met by two of Katerina's men.

"Why are they under guard, Katerina?"

"Not guard, Pierre, protection. My friend Danny is very important in certain circles and if any harm came to him under my care I would pay dearly."

"How intriguing. So, he is not merely a simple businessman?"

"No."

"And his sister?"

"She, I'm afraid, is exactly what she seems."

"Lovely. I knew the moment I saw her that the prophecy had come true in my lifetime."

"Pierre, don't you think that is a bit melodramatic?"

Pierre Montefort's usually pleasant face turned hard as flint, with a very dangerous glint in his eye. He spoke very softly. "Do you challenge me, Katerina?

She felt a cold prickle of fear at what this man was capable of doing to another human being.

"No, of course not, I would never presume to do that."

"Good. We understand each other then. I shall have her for myself. Her virginal manner is not an affectation. My seed and mine alone shall grow in her to bring about the new order as promised."

Katerina's men let Danny Mac and Kenann into their room. In almost the manner of a man servant, one of the men asked if they required anything before morning. Danny Mac graciously said they would be fine and actually wished them good night. The two men were halfway down the hall to their post when the absurdity of the situation hit them. They laughed to themselves at how quickly The Lion had gained control of them. Katerina had better watch herself very closely.

There were several awkward minutes of silence between them. Kenann moved about the room picking up personal articles and trying to look busy.

Finally, she asked. "Who is that guy anyway?"

"Apparently, he is the head of this cult or ancient order that Katerina wants to control."

"Why is he paying so much attention to me?"

Danny Mac looked at her directly without blinking.

"He thinks you are the reincarnation of the goddess Inanna."

"You're joking, right?"

"Afraid not."

"Well how in the world did he come up with a hair brained idea like that?"

"When you walked into the room his *spirit spoke to him*. This guy is very dangerous, and I want you to steer clear of him."

His tone rankled her.

"Well, how in the name of Pete am I going to be able to do that?"

"Don't let him touch you."

"I repeat for the slow to learn - how do you expect me to stop him?"

"I don't know. Kick him between the legs."

"Does that really work?"

"Trust me it will slow him down."

"Won't you be with me all the time, *big brother*?"

"If I have anything to say in it, I will, but I have a feeling he will maneuver both of us to get what he wants."

"Which is?'

"You."

"How did I suddenly go from Katerina's insurance to make sure you were a good boy to becoming center stage in this mess?"

"You're just lucky I guess."

"Yeah, a real rabbit's foot."

"Are you tired of dancing?"

She gave him a quizzical look. "Why?"

He walked over standing very close and leaned in to whisper very softly in her ear, "Because I wanted to have the last dance."

And he didn't want to have a video audience when he did it. At the last minute he remembered the listening device in his pocket. He took her hand and led her near the door. She stood looking up at him unsure what he was doing. He very deliberately reached over and turned off the switch plunging them into total darkness. He took the GPS receiver out of his pocket and put it into the side of his shoe to negate its reception. Having created as much privacy as he could under these difficult circumstances, he drew her close to him.

He took her hands in much the same way as Pierre had done. And when she felt his warm lips caressing her wrists, it was almost too much.

"Danny Mac, what are you doing?" She was breathless.

"I'm erasing any memory." And boy was he. He trailed his lips up the inside of her arm and then draped it around his neck. She felt limp with sensuous pleasure. He took her other hand and placing his hand at the small of her back drew her to him in an intimate embrace he had been denied on the dance floor.

They stood there very still for a few seconds. Danny Mac's mind was warring with his heart. He knew he was playing with fire but, God help him, he needed her in ways he couldn't even articulate. Slowly he began to move with her. He guided her in the dance with his hand on her back and the pressure of his hips against hers. He felt like he might explode but he couldn't stop now. Slowly, sensuously they moved back and forth together. Instinctively Kenann pressed herself to him with her own pulsing need. He whirled her around and pushed her up against the wall and plundered her mouth.

Kenann made soft whimpering sounds against his mouth as she clutched frantically at his arms and sleeves. All she could think was *please don't stop*.

He groaned deeply within himself and pulled her away from the wall. Picking her up, he carried her to the bed laying her down gently. He wanted desperately to lay on top of her and continue his plunder but made himself lay beside her and stroke her hair and face. She tried to turn and press herself to him again. He could tell this was not from experience but sheer instinct. She was being driven by needs as old as man and he was being unfair to her. He should not be initiating her into these feelings if he could not give her ultimate satisfaction. He was ashamed at how selfish his behavior had been, so he worked as hard to bring her back down as he had in thrusting her into hot desire.

As he whispered calming sounds and stroked her shoulders, he could feel her heartbeat returning to normal and her breathing ease. He was reminded of his days tending horses when he worked a ranch in Oklahoma. He soothed them when a wolf was in the area. Only this time he had been the predator and he felt no pride in knowing how close he had come to stepping out of reason into that realm of pure animal instinct.

Kenann finally lay quiet beside him. She suddenly wanted to cry. Something inside her felt unfinished and raw and she didn't know how to make that feeling go away. This was all new territory for her - *virgin territory* - she though ruefully. Danny Mac is probably thinking, 'What a dolt.'

Danny Mac suddenly felt awkward not knowing what to say. He sat up and turned on the bedside light running his hand through his hair. His break in contact left her feeling cold. Finally, he pulled her up to sit beside him. He turned toward her with his bent leg creating a barrier to further intimacy and spoke from his heart.

"Kenann, I'm sorry."

"Don't be. I understand."

"What do you understand?"

"That I'm not ... I don't know... what you want in that way."

"Do I act like a man who doesn't want you?"

"Well, why did you stop and turn away from me?"

"Kenann, sweetheart, you were within seconds of having your gown ripped off and your body driven into that mattress?"

Kenann turned and looked down where the aforementioned activity was to have occurred. She turned back and grinned like a mischievous child.

"Really?"

He started to laugh. He felt he had been saved by the grace of God from something he would have felt shame over for the rest of his life. When he made love to Kenann, and that hope was his lifeline at this point, it would be right, and it would be beautiful. But he refused to dwell on that thought any longer lest he lose his head again. He squeezed her hands and stood up. He tugged on her to stand but she sat looking up at him with her eyes brimming with tears.

"Danny Mac, I love you."

He dropped to his knees in front of her overwhelmed by emotion. She leaned forward and cradling his head against her breast began to stroke him like a frightened child. Somehow, she knew that was what he needed. He had known love throughout his life. The people at the church-run orphanage had loved him in their own way. His men and comrades in arms shared a love forged from facing their battles as brothers. But this was warm, and this was exclusive. This was home sitting by the fire kind of love, pouring out your very being to someone without having to say a word. This was snowball fights on the front lawn and warming each other in the shower later. This was grocery shopping and laundry, and this was kids. He suddenly looked up into her eyes.

She was smiling, and he sent up an offering of praise for the God of the universe who had better things to do than bring him his hearts desires and yet here it was looking at him.

He whispered, "I love you too, Kenann."

Kenann framed his face in her hands and kissed him tenderly. "I think I get it now. You are trying to save it - us - for later, huh?"

"Yeah."

"That is the sweetest thing I've ever heard."

"Oh yeah, I'm a real prince of a guy."

"Hey, I'd be really miffed at you if you didn't want to rip my clothes off. And when you stop wanting to do that, I'm going to inject you with something. Are we clear?"

"Crystal."

They looked at each other and burst out laughing. Danny Mac wrapped his arms around her and held on for dear life.

CHAPTER EIGHTEEN

anny Mac and Kenann clung to their respective sides after getting in bed. They dared not touch. They lay wide awake and talked of simple things, but as with anyone who is newly in love, even those simple things felt very important. The next morning Kenann was having a wonderful and warm dream when she heard Danny Mac's voice whispering in her ear.

"You're killing me here."

She opened her eyes and found him looking down at her. She was cuddled up against his side and had thrown her leg over him in her sleep. She yelped and scooted away from him. She laughed.

"Sorry."

He grinned back at her.

"No harm. No foul. But you snore."

"I do not."

"You do."

"Well, how delicate of you to point that out."

"Hey, if I'm going to spend the rest of my life with you, it's good to know these things."

She came to her knees in the bed and faced him. "The rest of your life?"

"Well, yeah."

"What are you saying?"

"What do you think I'm saying?"

"Well, I know what you're saying but I want to hear you say it."

"This is starting to scare me because I understood that." He got up and held out his hand. He helped her out of bed and then paused.

"Come on," and led her into the bathroom. "If they have this room under surveillance, they're sicker than I thought."

He closed the door behind them, dropped the lid on the commode and taking Kenann's shoulders, sat her down on top of the lid. He got down on one knee in front of her.

"This is the best I can do under the circumstances, but Kenann will you be my love and my life until death do us part?"

Tears immediately swamped Kenann's eyes. "I cannot believe you love me."

"Believe it. So, will you or not?"

"I am. I will." There was a moment when they both looked at each other and absorbed the enormity of what had just happened. They were pledged to be married. It was so fast and under crazy circumstances, but it was right. And they knew it. Kenann stood and pulled Danny Mac up with her. He wrapped her in his arms. She wriggled her arms free, so she could encircle his neck and standing on tip toe with her fingers entwined in his hair, she pulled him in for a kiss. She thought she was prepared for the jolt of electricity and desire. But it was nothing compared to the reality. She was beginning to understand why God said the two shall become one flesh. If she could have taken him into herself, into her very core, she would have gladly done it. His strength didn't scare her. She reveled in the force of his hands as they pressed her to him and deepened the kiss even further. She could feel the effort it required for him to reign in his desire, and to gentle his love making until he brought his hands up to frame her face.

"Without knowing it, Katerina has created a new torture for me." Danny Mac sighed.

"Oh yeah?"

"Yeah. You're mine but not mine. It may be a blessing we are on video camera out there, or else my good intentions might get swamped by other more pressing intentions."

"Well, there's always the bathroom." She laughed.

"Don't tempt me," and reached to open the door.

*   *   *

Judy turned more than a few heads when her long legs stepped out of the limo in front of the Cecil Hotel. She kept repeating her secret mantra, 'this is for Kenann, this is for Kenann' as she walked into the lobby of the Hotel and secured a room. She then made her way there to catch her breath and devise her own personal recon strategy. They had all been given the same general task. Mingle, listen, remember anything and everything, whether significant or not, and report back to command central in order to plan their next move. Judy had been provided with several beautiful outfits and laid out a dress for that night.

Jake and Moira also arrived at their respective hotel without incident. Moira was glad to see the two large beds in the bedroom of the suite. Sharing Jake's bed would have been a bit awkward even at her age. Mrs. Gage and Blade were trying to learn what was being said on the streets- anything out of the ordinary going on in Alexandria which may have precipitated Danny Mac being brought to this place in particular. Mrs. Gage could not speak Arabic well enough to be convincing as a native, but she was passable on a receptive level. She made sure she stayed primarily in areas of the city around men because she knew they would never approach or speak to her dressed in her traditional robes, but if she ventured into the company of other Arabic women, she was sure to be spoken to and discovered. Blade was instructed to stay within visual sight of Mrs. Gage. Their first location was near the American Embassy. They were hoping to get a glimpse of Andy and follow him to his command post if possible. All were in place and now began the tedious task of waiting and watching.

Judy started out by going to the bar in the hotel. She was still trying to find her way with her character and had practiced an accent in front of the mirror. She finally came on the one she felt would be convincing as Eastern European and hoped Mrs. Gage's genuine accent had rubbed off on her. She chose Prague if anyone asked her where she was from and hoped she didn't run into some expert on the area who wanted to chat about familiar sights. One thing at a time.

She chose a corner booth in order to have the best view of the bar's entrance and the lobby beyond and sat down to wait. She felt silly because she did not know what she was waiting for. Mrs. Gage had warned them how tedious this could become, and to not get discouraged. She concentrated on memorizing every face in the room and their language or accents as best she could guess. She lost track of time sitting there but felt it had been sufficient to one setting. She got up, paid her bill and walked out onto the street. She stuck her finger in her mouth and held it out to see which way the wind was blowing and followed that course. It beat flipping a coin. She ended up at a relatively quiet spot on a corner halfway between the Cecil and the Metropole, where Jack and Moira were staying. She went in and sat down at the only available place at the bar and ordered a glass of Chardonnay. She turned to scan the room and looked into the face of Andy O'Hanlon.

She froze while he stared at her and was about to speak when he beat her to it.

"Pardon me for staring, Mademoiselle, but your eyes remind me of someone I met recently, and it startled me."

Judy took a deep breath and steadied herself. *Show time,* she thought.

"It is no problem. This woman, she is a friend?"

"How did you know it was a woman?"

Judy waved her hand. "Is it not always a woman?"

"Yeah ain't that the truth." and he grinned at her.

Judy felt like a rat to use the situation for selfish purposes, but there you have it.

"This girl. Do you like her?"

"Oh yeah, I can't get her out of my mind."

Judy felt herself grinning back at him.

"Pretty pathetic, huh?"

"Actually, it is very sweet." and meant it. "Why are you not together?"

"I had to leave town in a hurry and she was pretty steamed at me when I left."

"What do you do?"

"I'm in communications." He did not elaborate, and she did not pursue. She was more interested in hearing how he felt about her.

"Will you go back to her and try to work this out?"

"I have no idea where this job will take me or for how long. That's the other problem. She's settled in one location and I'm always on the road."

"People find a way to make that work all the time. If you truly have strong feelings for this woman, you should not let her get away without a fight."

"Do you really think so?"

"Of course. People say all the time that life is too short, but it is true. We do not know what lies before any of us and we should not waste time by being timid. We should grab life." Judy realized how passionately she truly felt these words. She had wasted her last minute of life feeling afraid or unworthy.

"You know, I think you are right. I'm going to call her and see if we can start building something while I'm on this," he hesitated briefly, "job. All she can do is take my heart out, slice it up into little pieces and toss it aside, right?"

"Right." and smiled with him.

"Hey, thank you. Seriously, thanks very much. You have been a good listener. Can I buy you a drink?"

"Why not. I can continue to help you with your lady friend could I not?"

Judy had a brain storm. "May I make a suggestion?"

"Shoot."

"Excuse me?" Judy pretended to be ignorant of the meaning.

Andy laughed. "Go ahead and tell me your idea."

"Do not call her or try to reach her by phone." She won't be there anyway, she thought. "Instead, send her an email. No woman can resist a love letter, even an electronic one."

"You may have something there. That way I can't go on and on and make a love-sick idiot of myself. I can polish it all I want before I hit send."

"Precisely."

"I just realized I don't have her email."

"I'm sure someone in communications would find this - a minor detail."

"Oh, right. Man, it's like my mind goes right out the window when I think of her. You are very kind to help me this way."

"Let us just say it makes me feel as good as it does you."

*   *   *

Jake and Moira were in the process of checking out the Casino and Bars downstairs, when Moira spotted Kenann. She would have run to her if Jake had not put a gentle but restraining hand on her arm. Moira concentrated on breathing while Jake observed and mentally recorded what he saw. She was with Danny Mac but not with him. It appeared they had paired off to make two couples. The gentleman with Kenann was tall with black silvered tipped hair at the temples. He had a lithe athletic body for a man who was at least 50 and was giving Kenann his undivided attention. Danny Mac was watching him with intense scrutiny. Jake had seen that look on Danny Mac before. The boy was poised to attack at a second's provocation. So, obviously no matter how amiable the foursome looked, this man was a threat to them on some level.

He noticed the lady standing by Danny Mac with her back turned to them. He was not immune to her curves and undisguised sexuality. It was not until she turned that he stopped breathing. That explained a lot of things. No matter how discreet his men were, he always knew when they had taken a lover. Danny Mac never mentioned his affair with Katerina, but Jake had known. They had worked well together in a way only people who have been extremely intimate could. He wondered what she had been into since waving good-bye to them at the airport in Kuwait City.

Jake said, "Wait here, Moira, I'm going to check in with Gabrielle. Don't let Kenann see you in case she reacts before she thinks." Moira nodded and continued to watch her baby smiling and acting as if she was on holiday instead of a victim of kidnapping. Something strange indeed was happening here.

*　　　*　　　*

Before their drinks were finished, Andy's cell phone rang. He excused himself and turned away to answer it. Judy heard him say, "When? Where are they headed? Well, get on it and keep me posted. You've got the GPS, use it! If you lose them, you will be cleaning latrines by nightfall, am I understood?" Andy was visibly making an effort to control his agitation. Judy knew it had to do with Danny Mac and Kenann but had to feign casual interest.

"Problems?"

"Huh? Oh yeah. I'm at risk of losing a couple of my clients. I've gotta go, but thanks for everything, really. Hey, my name is Andy. What's yours?"

"Inge. Good luck with your lady friend and with your runaway clients." Andy paid for both of their tabs and smiling down at her a final time, left the bar. She waited until he had cleared the door before bolting off the barstool. She slowed her pace when she stepped out onto the street and looking both ways spotted Andy half running up the street. He jogged up the steps to the same hotel where she was staying.

CHAPTER NINETEEN

"We've had a profitable day. Let's review what we know so far?" They were congregated back at the villa in the main parlor. Mrs. Gage had a flip chart to record their information.

"We know that they are staying in the Metropole Hotel and Andy is set up at the Cecil. We obviously made wise choices in our locations. Andy is using the GPS device he had put on Danny Mac back in Memphis, so it has obviously not been discovered. Andy is probably at the Cecil because, as Jake discovered, our nemesis is known to him. And he to her. We know that for some reason both Danny Mac and Kenann are playing the role of willing visitors or guests and probably for the benefit of the gentleman with Kenann. We need to find out who and what he is. Jacob informs us that this Katerina Troika worked with them in Kuwait and we can only assume she and Angelo are in league together. For how long and to what extent, we do not know. We also know that according to their appearance and lack of accoutrement, the four of them were out for a holiday and not changing locations. We will maintain our original set up with the exception that Blade and I will be monitoring the Metropole in order to follow if Danny Mac and Kenann leave again. Between us - a little boy and an old woman- we should be able to get in about anywhere. Judy you are to stick to Andy as closely as possible. My commendations, by the way, on how you handled the situation earlier today."

Mrs. Gage winked at Judy. She had set Judy up at her office computer, so she could monitor her emails. Andy had wasted no time in tracking down her address. The letter he had written had been fraught with nerves, which made it all the more endearing to her. Her reply was as encouraging as she dared be without giving herself away. Judy smiled back at Mrs. Gage, obviously pleased with her discretion.

"Gabrielle," Jake interjected, "Can we try to make contact with the kids?'

"Yes, I have considered this, and I need everyone's feedback. What do you think?"

Moira spoke first. "It might give them great encouragement to know we are near."

Jake responded, "Or it may distract Danny Mac because then he will feel responsible to keep everyone safe."

"But Darling, don't you think he will leave that to your capable hands once he knows you are with us."

Jake smiled proudly down on Mrs. Gage. "Yes, I suppose that is right." He was warm inside at hearing her call him darling.

Judy spoke up, "Why don't we keep with what you told us at the beginning Mrs. G?" Mrs. Gage smiled at her new moniker. "We can all be responsible to use our judgment at the time. Let's not force the issue but when the time is right, and we need to declare ourselves, we can. Agreed?"

All were in agreement. Blade was considered an equal member of the team with full voting privileges and gave his assent as well.

"Let's all have a spot of dinner and then we can return to our respective posts."

"Gabrielle, I'll not have you and Blade sitting out on the streets at night."

"Oh, you dear man, I have no intention of doing that. We will observe from the comfort of a luxuriously appointed car and pursue in same, until such time we are required to follow on foot. Is that better?"

"Yes." He looked a little sheepish for trying to strong arm her. They all relaxed and enjoyed easy banter at dinner. A sense of relief had descended on them after making visual contact with Danny Mac and Kenann.

Mrs. Gage coordinated their return to their respective hotels and they settled in for the night. Except Jake, who positioned himself in the Casino, in an effort to catch another glimpse of Danny Mac or Kenann if possible. He felt his body tense when they walked through the lobby. They continued to look the part of four friendly tourists coming in from an afternoon of sight-seeing, but Jake observed that Kenann looked strained. Danny Mac obviously noticed it too because his gaze never left her as they walked through the lobby.

The gentleman with them was the only person who appeared none the worse for the day's activities. Even Katerina looked tense. Danny Mac appeared to take charge before anyone else could initiate their agenda. Jake overheard him.

"Thanks for our great tour, Pierre, and the offer of a nightcap but I think we'll head up to our room."

"Do you wish to take a break from your big brother's watchful eye, Mon Ami?" The man asked Kenann.

"Not tonight. Actually, I am very tired. We had a busy day and I'm still not used to the heat here. But thank you."

"We must all meet in the morning then and bring your swimming clothes. I know a private beach we can use for the day. Shall we say 9 o'clock?"

Katerina jumped in before Danny Mac had a chance to refuse. "That sounds lovely, doesn't it darling?" and turned to Danny Mac.

"All the more reason to turn in. We'll meet you here in the lobby at 9 then. Good night," and taking Kenann's arm, led her toward the elevator. Katerina hurriedly said her good byes to Pierre and jumped in the elevator before the door closed.

"What are you two up to?"

"Katerina we are tired, and we have had quite enough of playing the happy tourists for one day."

"You will play whatever role I want you to play. And you will come to my suite, so we can discuss our strategy."

Danny Mac knew he could bully his way out of her demands but did not have the energy for the battle. He turned to Kenann.

"Will you be alright for a while?"

"Sure. I'll probably be asleep when you come in."

"If anything happens, scream bloody murder. I can be there in a matter of seconds."

She smiled at him reassuringly. "I'll be fine."

Katerina sent her a smug smile as she locked her in the room to take Danny Mac back to her suite. She had plans for him and wasted no time in trying to seduce him. But no matter how subtle or blatant her behavior, she elicited no response from Danny.

He outlined his plan as he saw it in its early stages and remained completely focused on that, despite her wandering hands. These he calmly removed from his person at each overture from her. His plan was very simple, and he relayed it to her in a matter of fact manner. Since they were constantly followed as they toured the city and surrounding sites, Danny Mac planned to stage a car bombing on a rural road. The bomb would be strategically placed to take out the driver since he was in Pierre's employ. By the time his bodyguards made it from the second car, Pierre would be killed swiftly. His death would appear to be the result of the bomb blast. The rest of them would be equipped with articles to fake their own injuries thus sealing everyone's alibi. Of course, Danny Mac had no real intention of finalizing these plans, but he needed something in order to pacify Katerina and buy all of them some time.

Katerina stopped her assault long enough to ask how he planned to bomb their car without killing all of them. He explained that the bomb would be more 'smoke and mirrors' than real explosives and the driver could be quickly dispatched if it did not take him out. He could detonate it by remote control when they were stopped to avoid danger to them. Pierre would meet his end due to blunt force trauma strategically executed for a swift demise. Danny Mac had already worked out most of the details in his mind but indicated otherwise in order to make his escape for the night.

Katerina made one last attempt to reach him by dropping the straps on her already revealing top. Danny Mac responded by going to the door like a dog begging to be let out.

He tossed over his shoulder, "Set me up with your explosive guy."

Katerina hit a buzzer by the couch with enough force to break it. The door opened, and a man received curt instructions to take Danny Mac back to his room. At one time Katerina's very skillful efforts would have been a sore temptation indeed. No longer. She was a pathetic substitute for what he felt for Kenann.

Now that was a problem. His desire was growing stronger by the day and his restraint growing weaker. He offered up a silent prayer for God to give him renewed commitment to purity until he and Kenann could make their union official.

She had left on the light at his side of the bed. The absurdity of the situation hit Danny Mac. They were becoming like an old married couple before they could experience the honeymoon. He tried to be quiet as he finished up in the bathroom and slipped under the covers. He longed to pull her to him and hold her as they slept but he knew it wouldn't end there. He turned out the light and tried to relax enough to drop off to sleep. He slowly became aware that Kenann wasn't asleep but was actually lying on her side of the bed crying silently. He sat up and turned back on the light.

"Kenann, what's the matter."

"Nothing," and sniffled loudly.

"Now don't give me that. Why are you crying?"

"Girls are allowed to cry whenever they want. Didn't anyone ever teach you that?"

"I didn't say you weren't allowed to cry. I'm asking you *why* you are crying. Now turn over here and talk to me."

She slowly turned onto her back and then her side to face him. Her eyes were swollen, and she obviously had been at it awhile.

"There are you satisfied?"

"Are you mad at me about something?"

"No." She sounded petulant even to herself.

"Are you sure?"

"Why were you gone so long?"

So that was it, he thought. He wasn't sure of the best way to reassure her. Against his better judgment he pulled her to him and cradled her in his arms.

"Kenann, Katerina made her move, but I am not interested."

"How could you not be interested in her. She is gorgeous."

"That's a matter of opinion."

"Oh, get real. You'd have to be a blind Monk not to be attracted to her."

"Or very much in love with someone else," he pointed out.

Good answer, she thought. She looked up at him under her lashes.

"So, nothing happened?"

"Scout's honor."

"Were you ever a boy scout?"

"Well, no."

"Then you can't use their honor. Try again." She was starting to smile.

"How about if I promise on the blood of my Native American ancestors?"

"Are they going to come and do some sort of spirit dance if I say yes?"

"Possibly."

"Then I accept."

"Now, there is a tradition when one accepts an oath on the blood of my ancestors."

"Does it involve kissing?"

"No, it involves," he paused for dramatic effect, "Tickling!" He flipped her onto her stomach and proceeded to attack her rib cage. She screamed and laughed until she couldn't catch her breath. He finally had mercy and let her roll over and sit up.

"That wasn't fair," she laughed between catching her breath.

"Get used to it sweetheart. I don't fight fair."

Kenann got a wicked gleam in her eye he didn't like. She turned and moved toward him on all fours. He began inching away unsure what she had in mind.

"Good, cause, neither do I."

She kept coming toward him slowly until he was out of the bed and on his feet. He didn't trust that slow smile on her face. She slowly stepped off the bed and continued advancing as he made a corresponding retreat.

"What are you doing, Kenann?"

"Not playing fair."

"Well, cut it out."

"Chicken."

"Kenann." He tried to sound stern, but the word caught in the dryness of his throat.

"Yes?" She had him up against the wall by this time. She didn't touch him but came within a hair's breath between them and stood looking up at him. He could feel the heat from her body and knew his breathing was speeding up along with his heart rate.

One part of him prayed she wouldn't touch him, and another part was silently begging her to. She slowly splayed her fingers on his heaving chest. He stood motionless waiting for her next move. She looked at her hands on his firm chest and then moved them slowly down over his stomach. Danny Mac flattened his palms against the wall and held his breath. She grasped the bottom of the grey t-shirt he was wearing and slowly brought it up. His limbs became weak and she easily pushed his arms up, so she could pull it over his head. She dropped it to the floor beside them and running her hands over his chest and torso whispered, "You are so beautiful."

He brought his hands down and gripped his hair. Dropping his head back against the wall he closed his eyes. Kenann brought her hands up to encircle his neck and saw the anguish on his face.

"Oh Danny, what am I doing?" She moved away from him abruptly.

He continued to maintain his rigid posture with his eyes closed. He didn't respond.

She stepped back further and whispered, "I'm sorry."

This brought his head up and he looked at her. "Kenann. I love you. You know that, but we can't do this."

"I'm sorry." It was the only thing she knew to say. She was so embarrassed. She turned away from him and went to the barred window looking out into the night sky over the city. She sensed more than heard him come to stand behind her. He didn't speak for several moments.

"Kenann, this is an extraordinary situation for both of us. It's not normal in any stretch of the imagination. We'll get through it. Let's just be patient."

In her confused state a painful thought came to her. What if they were experiencing some bizarre form of Stockholm Syndrome and he realized he did not love her once they were out of this mess. The thought left her even more embarrassed by her brazen behavior. How could he really know how he felt? He was under too much strain to be thinking clearly about such an emotional issue. She needed to get a major grip on herself before she made a complete fool of herself. She drew in a deep breath and let it out slowly to steel her resolve. She turned and smiled.

"You're right. I'm sorry I got so carried away. Let's get some sleep now. We'll probably have another long day tomorrow."

She moved past Danny Mac and got into her side of the bed. The shutters over her heart had closed with an almost audible sound. He wanted to say something but didn't know what, so he let the silence hang between them. He got into his side of the bed and turned off the light. It was a long time before either of them slept.

CHAPTER TWENTY

A ngelo sat glued to the video monitor. He knew the others were laughing at him behind his back. They thought he was hoping to catch some skin action with the little lion, but how could he tell them he was actually watching Danny Boy. There was something different about him. He had lost that hungry look he had carried all those years ago. He occasionally saw a flash of the danger in him that he remembered, but there was definitely a change in him. He observed the heat between him and the girl, but yet they did nothing. This was also not like Danny Boy. He had been well liked among the ladies even after he and Katerina had become lovers. He had fed that hunger with lots of women and none of them complained. He says his God has made him different now. Could it be true? He heard the things he had told the little lion about having faith and God listening to their prayers. He pondered these things and continued to watch and wonder.

*   *   *

Kenann was the first up the next morning and into the bathroom. As she showered and dressed for the day, she steeled her resolve from the night before. She had gotten completely out of control but was thankful she had come to her senses before she made a fool of herself. She was in control now and planned to stay that way. Who was to say how Danny Mac would really feel once this was all over? She took a good hard look at the situation and realized there was no way someone like Danny Mac could be in love with her. He was a red-blooded male and just thought he was in love when actually he felt sorry for her. She couldn't be upset at him. He was an honorable man and apparently had not been with a woman for a very long time. Of course, he would get the two confused. She would deal with it when this was all over.

She hoped that day would be soon. This Pierre guy was starting to give her the creeps. Reincarnation or not, he had designs on her that were by no means holy. She wasn't the most experienced gal around, but she knew enough to know this guy was on the make and she was the prey. She planned to take Danny Mac's advice and pop him in the family jewels if it came to that. Her plan was to keep dancing around this guy and not give him any chances. Might as well get going. She put on her best smile and came out of the bathroom.

Danny Mac was not sure how she would feel this morning but took his cue from her and smiled back. Something was off. Her eye contact was short and to the point. She's pulling back, he thought. He decided that might not be a bad idea under the present circumstances but even as the thought congealed in his mind, he was missing the genuine warmth of her smile. He offered a silent prayer for God to lead them in their growing relationship and a special one for Kenann that she would know in her heart how much he loved her, even though he had to hold himself back for the sake of purity.

They both went through the clothing provided for them and found bathing suits as Pierre had requested. Kenann held up a tiny scrap of material and muttered. "They've got to be kidding. I've worn band aids bigger than this."

Danny Mac laughed until he opened the package containing his speedo. He groaned. It was Kenann's turn to laugh. "When in Rome, as they say."

Danny Mac's face sobered suddenly, "Kenann are you sure you can keep playing this charade?"

"Well, do I have much choice?"

"I could find a way out of it somehow."

"No. I'm fine so far. This guy seems all frill and polish on the surface, but I get the feeling he's a real stinker underneath. Oh, believe me, I'll be screaming bloody murder if I feel the need. I still haven't figured out what his game is with me except maybe a roll in the sheets."

"Which we will not be accommodating."

"No worries. So, how soon do we ice this guy?" Her look of wicked merriment was incongruent with her statement.

"As you so delicately put it, it will occur as soon as I have all the details ironed out in my head and not until. You are as bad as Katerina."

"You wound me unfairly."

They smiled at each other in an unspoken truce. Things were off between them but there was enough genuine warmth and affection to let it ride until a better time to deal with it. The sound of the key turning the lock in their door suddenly filled Kenann with a sense of dread. It must have shown on her face because Danny Mac took her hand.

"What's wrong, baby?"

Kenann felt a warmth fill her at his endearment but couldn't shake the feeling of panic. She had been rolling with the punches throughout this whole ordeal, but her courage was quickly abandoning her. She knew Danny Mac well enough to know he would endanger himself to protect her. Pierre was too dangerous to have Danny Mac challenging him as this point. She forced a smile and shook her head.

"I'm fine. I'm just worrying about that bikini." Danny smiled back but didn't buy it for a minute. He planned to keep her within arm's reach all day.

They were escorted to Katerina's room where they waited for her to emerge and accompany them to the lobby. Once again, she took great delight in linking her arm through Danny Mac's and pressing herself to him. She whispered to him that their demolition man was flying in that afternoon. He stared straight ahead with a look of complete disinterest until the elevator doors opened onto the lobby. His face was transformed by a smile (albeit forced) and he assumed the attitude of a man looking forward to a day in the sun.

Pierre was talking rapidly to a man near the door. He ushered him away when he saw them approach. He too adopted a benign expression that belied his intent. These men would engage in a battle of wills and Kenann's life would hang in the balance.

Chapter Twenty One

Kenann glanced over as she came down the steps of the hotel and was drawn to a little boy playing in the rubble near the curb. And something in the hand movement of the Egyptian woman approaching the boy made her pause. As they were being driven out of town, Kenann tried to adopt her own casual attitude. She laughed and said to no one in particular, "I must have had too much sun. I keep thinking I see people from home."

Pierre laughed too and pledged to erect a cabana on their beach to protect her from the offending rays.

Kenann smiled and then a thought struck her. She looked to Danny Mac and could see he had had the same thought. *Oh, they wouldn't. How could they?* But the more she tried to rationalize the idea away, she knew it was useless. They were here. Somehow, someway they had found them, and they were *here*! She forced herself to look away from Danny Mac and focus her attention on what Pierre was telling her. Katerina was watching Danny with a wary eye. Within minutes, they arrived at a small villa overlooking the Mediterranean Sea. The colors were beyond description. The blue of the sky competed with the turquoise of the water for brilliance. The white plaster facade of the villa with its red tile roof was a stunning contrast. When they stepped from the car, the breeze caressed them and Kenann stood transfixed by the loveliness. She was completely unaware of the picture she made poised and gazing out over the parapet. Katerina was the last to emerge from the car and when she saw the two men watching Kenann, she hurried to break the spell.

"Let's go in, shall we?"

Pierre ushered them into the foyer. It alone was magnificent with its terra cotta flooring and mosaic walls. Kenann was anxious to see the rest of the - dare she call it a house. She was not disappointed. They were treated to a tasty brunch in a room straight out of lifestyles of the rich and famous and shown to dressing rooms to don their bathing suits.

Kenann didn't know about Danny Mac, but she was more than thankful for her cover up. Unless they put a gun to her head that thing wasn't coming off. When everyone was ready, they met back in the foyer and Pierre escorted them onto a terrace overlooking the Mediterranean. It was breathtaking and, not for the first time, Kenann couldn't believe her good fortune to be seeing these sights again. She would soon be changing her mind. They made their way to the beach by a series of terraces built into the hillside. It was not a taxing decent and shouldn't prove to be a bad climb back to the villa. Danny Mac's eyes took in everything. He found himself on high alert. He noticed the conspicuous absence of Pierre's ever-present staff of bodyguards. That was odd. His gaze scanned up and down the beach. There was not a soul in sight. The hair on the back of his neck began to prickle. True to his word Pierre had seen that a small cabana was erected on the sand several feet back from the water. Pierre stripped off his outer garment and dashed to the water with shouts of encouragement for them to follow. If the situation had been different Danny Mac would have laughed. Kenann looked absolutely sick. She heaved a sigh of resignation and began unbuttoning her wrap. Katerina had no qualms about taking her clothes off. *She had probably done it many times*, Kenann thought peevishly. Danny Mac was not overly body conscious but seeing Kenann's discomfort made him feel uncomfortable for her. For once Katerina's attempts at distraction were welcome. She took his hand and drew him toward the water. He walked with Katerina allowing Kenann to finish disrobing and follow behind them. Kenann was extremely grateful. She had no qualms about going about in a bathing suit, but this was a couple of strings and a few scraps of cloth for goodness sake. Now all she could think was to get into the water as fast as she could. It felt deliciously cool to her heated body. Pierre approached her through the bobbing surf with a look not unlike a shark on the hunt. Kenann turned her eyes to Danny Mac. He saw the fear she was trying to hide. Danny Mac had just kicked off to swim to her side when he felt the piercing pain in his side. His last coherent thought was a prayer for Kenann.

*   *   *

Kenann saw Danny Mac convulse in the water and go under. She screamed his name and began running through the water to him. Her first thought was a shark, but in her panic, she was still able to process that there was no blood. She reached him in time to pull his head out of the water. Katerina helped her pull him onto the beach. He had a pulse, but he wasn't breathing. Kenann opened his airway to begin rescue breaths but the manipulation of his head and neck forced water from his lungs and he began coughing. She turned him on his side and was relieved to see his breathing even out. She was suddenly surrounded by people. It was disorienting. Pierre was standing back issuing orders to his bodyguards who had literally come out of nowhere. Danny Mac was picked up by these men and they began carrying him up the terraced steps. Kenann whirled around. Katarina looked away. Kenann went to Pierre.

"What happened?"

"It appears he was stung by something in the sea. I have instructed my men to call the physician as soon as they get to the villa."

Kenann ran to where her wrapper lay over a chair in the cabana and grabbing it up, ran to the stairs while putting her arms through her cover up. As soon as she was out of earshot Katerina looked at Pierre. She knew he had pulled his own scam on them and she felt powerless to combat him. She waited for him to show his hand.

"Katerina, you may return to the city."

"But I should not leave Danny and Kenann. I am responsible for them."

"Your only responsibility now is to handle any inquiries that come in about them. If any of their family try to reach them, you are to assure them that they have gone on a little side holiday and allay any concerns. Do you understand?"

"But, Pierre..."

"I said, do you understand?" His tone invoked no questions.

"Yes."

"Good. Now shall we go up to the villa?"

"Yes, Pierre." Katerina's mind whirled. What did he have in mind? Without Danny, her plans would dissolve. She might be able to follow through on his idea, but she had lost her confidence. If she were honest, that is why she brought Danny here in the first place. She never felt as alive and capable as when he was in her life. And even though she had not been able to entice him back into her bed, she still felt the old fire of their partnership. She knew that together they could pull off the coup she had so desperately wanted. Now she felt lost. When they arrived at the balcony of the villa, they found Kenann screaming and pounding the chest of a man twice her size and strength. She was demanding to see Danny Mac. The man had folded his arms and simply shook his head. Every time she moved to go around him, he blocked her way. The only way into the house was behind him as the balcony had no other exit but the path back to the beach.

Pierre stopped and, holding up his hand, signaled Katerina to do the same. He wanted to watch this spitfire in action. Kenann feinted one direction and dashed in the other. The man was momentarily caught off guard but was able to grab the back of her shirt with his beefy hand. What happened next surprised even Kenann, who was running on pure adrenaline. She whirled around and grabbing the man's outstretched arm for leverage, scissored her legs into the air and landed a powerful blow to the man's face. Blood spurted onto Kenann from the man's nose as he loosened his grip. She used the opportunity to fly into the villa without a backward glance. She was halfway up the stairs screaming for Danny Mac when Pierre called from the main hallway. She looked over her shoulder but kept up her ascent to the next level. She would find him if she had to knock down every door in this place.

"Ma Petit if you will wait, I will take you to him."

This finally got her attention and she paused. "Then you'd better get to it."

Pierre came up the stairs with a smile on his face. "You were magnificent."

"Cut the crap, Pierre, and let me see Danny Mac."

For a second, Pierre felt rage boil up. No one dared speak to him with such insolence. Not since he ran with a band of street urchins in Paris. And even then, he had gained control by cutting out the tongue of anyone who crossed him. He then remembered who she was and felt a great calm overtake him. He was on the verge of fulfilling his destiny to become the most powerful man in the world.

He smiled, "Of course, my dear, right this way."

Danny Mac looked dead when they entered the room. She ran to him and fell on her knees beside the bed. She laid her head on his chest and felt the steady beat of his heart. She was weak with relief. She had no doubt Pierre's men had drugged him, but it appeared he was in no immediate danger. She turned to look over her shoulder.

"I won't leave him."

"But of course, you will have to. He needs tended by the physician."

"I don't care. I will stay right here until he can be moved back to the hotel."

"There is no need for you to return to the hotel. I can meet all your needs much better here."

Yeah, I'll just bet, thought Kenann. "Where is the doctor?"

"He will be here shortly."

"I'll wait."

"As you wish." He stepped out and closed the door. She waited to hear the usual click of the door locking behind him and was relieved when the sound did not come. She laid her head back onto Danny Mac's chest and thought, *Now, what do I do?*

Chapter Twenty Two

"Something is up. They all went to a villa along the coast. Katerina left a few moments ago but without Danny Mac and Kenann. Another vehicle has arrived. I couldn't tell who was in the car. It doesn't feel right Jake, I'm worried." Mrs. Gage was calling from her car.

"You stay put and watch the villa. Moira and I will watch the lobby and see if Katerina returns. Maybe we can learn something here. I'll call Judy to keep her ears and eyes open with Andy. Did you see a tail from Andy's men?"

"Yes, they're here too."

"Good. Have they spotted you?"

"I don't think so. We have stayed in the car so far and we are fairly secluded. They are trying to blend in as tourists walking along the coastline cliffs, but they are keeping a close eye on things."

"That makes me feel better knowing they are there, to be quite honest. Do you think we should contact Andy?"

"No, not yet. They know as much, if not more, than we do. We have nothing to offer them at this point. And perhaps by working independently we can still be of service later."

"Alright, Gabrielle. Give me directions to this villa in case we need to get to you fast."

When he was satisfied that he knew how to reach her if needed, they disconnected, and he filled Moira in on the current situation as he dialed

148

Judy. Judy took it all in and decided. She went down to the desk and used every feminine wile she could muster, and finally got Andy's room number out of the desk clerk. She took a deep breath and headed for the elevator. Her nerve failed her as soon as she got out on his floor. She stood wringing her hands by a table with a huge arrangement of flowers, when he came out into the hallway putting on his suit jacket at a run. He saw her just as she was ready to turn and hide her face.

"Inge, what are you doing here?"

"Someone told me the spa was on this floor. but I could not find it."

"Follow me. I'm in a bit of a hurry now but I can at least show you the floor on our way down."

She followed him onto the elevator. "Have you had time to compose your letter to your friend?"

"Yeah, it sounded lame, but her answer was encouraging. Here's the floor for the spa."

"I've changed my mind. I think I'll go shopping instead. Do you want to share a taxi?"

Andy seemed to consider this and decided it couldn't hurt anything. "I have my own car. I can drop you in the shopping district on my way out of town."

His car had been brought around and he got behind the wheel. They chatted about mundane things as he made his way through traffic, but both of their minds were racing. Andy let her out in the center of the block. She thanked him and waved him away. When she was sure he was concentrating on the road ahead she hurriedly hailed a taxi and pointed to his car. Thankfully the driver spoke English and she was able to tell him to follow the dark blue sedan and provided the license number. She followed him out of town along the coastal highway. When he finally pulled into a wide place used as a scenic overlook, she asked the taxi driver to continue on until they were out of sight of his car. She used the cell phone Mrs. G had provided and called her.

"Where are you, dear?"

"I followed Andy by taxi. I am around the curve past the overlook on the right side of the road."

"I know the place. Pay the driver and we will be there to pick you up." In just a few minutes, Judy was sitting in the air-conditioned limo with Mrs. G and Blade.

"Did you learn anything from Andy?"

"Not a thing. He came out of his room like a bat out of hell but cooled it when he saw me. He was definitely distracted but he never gives anything away."

"Well, we shall send our little street urchin on a mission? What do you say, Blade?"

"Cool."

"Make your way down near the men by kicking stones or a can if you can find one. Be discrete, dear. Don't let them know you are listening to them. Try to remember everything you hear. When you think you have heard all you can, head back to the car. Understood?"

"Yep," and he opened the door and began looking for something to kick. Once he located a dented can in the alley, he made his way over to the short wall overlooking the coast and began to play. He made his way to the men standing at the overlook and appeared to ignore them completely as he played all around them. As he received the report from his men, Andy watched the little boy playing in the dirt.

CHAPTER TWENTY THREE

Jake and Moira waited in the bar by the lobby for what seemed like an eternity when Katerina blew in the door. She was barking orders into her cell phone.

Jake grabbed Moira's hand. "Come on. Let's go." and they followed her up to the elevator. Jake waited for her to push a number and then smiled and said, "Our floor."

Jake had no way of knowing that Katerina controlled the entire floor of that hotel. She eyed him warily. Moira laughed shrilly hoping to throw off Katerina's train of thought about where she might have seen this man.

"Oh, darling. That is not our floor," and punched the number below it. She chattered on shrilly about the wonderful little shop she had found while he spent his whole day at the Casino. She didn't understand why he had to waste his time like that. There was a wonderful city out there just waiting to be explored but no, he had to throw good money away. Katerina was more than relieved when they exited.

Once the door closed Moira quieted.

Jake exhaled. "Thank you, Moira. I was so anxious to follow her I didn't think about the possibility she might recognize me. Do you think she did?"

"No. But I think she was well on her way. She seemed very agitated. I wish we knew what happened out there at the villa."

"This is the hard part - the waiting and watching. I'll go back to the lobby and keep out of Katerina's sight."

"And I'll do a little snooping around of my own."

"Moira be very careful. Katerina is one of the most dangerous women I have ever encountered."

Moira smiled reassuringly at Jake and thought, *She should never have messed with my granddaughter.*

*   *   *

Kenann's head lay on Danny's chest. The sound of his heart beat was comforting to her. She had remained in that position for a long while when a plan struck her with such force she jumped up. Before she could consider consequences or chicken out, she went out to the hallway and looking down to the main floor from the balcony, she called Pierre's name. She cleared her throat and adopting her most imperious tone, called again. He appeared through the doorway and looked up at her. He did not speak but merely waited. She thought, *There's no going back now.*

"I request your presence."

He started up the long stairway. She stood in the doorway to their rooms. She felt her knees shaking and willed them to stop. She stiffened her spine and reminded herself what was at stake and felt suffused with resolve. When Pierre rounded the corner column at the head of the stairs, he was awestruck by the woman he saw. The shy naive young woman was being replaced by a Valkyrie- a goddess of war with fire in her eyes. Once again, he waited for her to speak first. She wasted no time.

"You are very aware of my identity, so I will not insult you by pretending any longer. I knew the first time I saw you that you recognized me as Inanna."

Pierre gasped. Even though he knew the legend, it was unbelievable to be standing here as she revealed herself to him. He took a step toward her but stopped cold when she raised her palm. She wanted to maintain her edge of authority.

"You have made a grave mistake in harming Daniel." Pierre started to protest but she cut him off.

"Do not pretend otherwise. It was not a creature in the sea who poisoned him. But you can redeem yourself if he recovers."

"Oh, he will, he will. He is only now sedated. He is in no danger. I swear to you."

"This is fortunate for you. The oracle purposely omitted Daniel's role for reasons you will soon see."

Pierre felt a surge of rage at the thought that Daniel would rival him for power with Inanna. She could see his reaction and the last thing she wanted to create was a power struggle between Danny Mac and Pierre, so she went on.

"Daniel will be the high priest in our international kingdom but the man to stand beside me is yet to be revealed." She saw him come alert.

"It is imperative that Daniel and I remain together at all times until my consort is determined. Is that clear?"

"Of course, Your..." he faltered

"Your Highness will suffice for now until my full identity is revealed. My full title is too cumbersome." Kenann bit the inside of her jaw to stem nervous laughter.

"Yes, Your Highness."

"I will have no further instructions until Daniel is awake and I know he is well."

And with that, she turned back into the room to continue her vigil beside the sleeping man. As she sat down and took his hand, she offered a silent prayer that she had done the right thing.

CHAPTER TWENTY FOUR

Moira had reverted to the familiar wardrobe of Granny James she had brought with her to the hotel. She donned a flower print dress with a small cardigan sweater and flat comfortable shoes. Her hair was once again woven into a large single braid down her back. No makeup adorned her face. She went to several floors before she found an unattended housekeeping cart. She hurriedly obtained anything that had the hotel logo on it and was pleased to find a staff apron draped over the bar on the cart. She scurried off with her treasures before the maid came back to claim her cart. She pushed the button for Katerina's floor and said a prayer for protection and guidance as she attempted to help her baby girl.

She kept her head down and eyes averted as she came off the elevator. There was no one in the hall so she stopped at every door and listened. All was quiet except for an occasional television set, when at the very end room, she heard Katerina screaming orders to unseen minions. There was no other voice but hers. Suddenly the door burst open and a large man in a dark suit almost bowled her over. "You'd better get in there and clean that mess up." He barked in Arabic.

Moira looked past the man and saw broken pottery and wet flowers strewn across the carpet. When he shoved her and spoke again, she knew what he wanted her to do. Moira busied herself with the task and tried to glean anything useful from the tirade coming from Katerina. At first the only words she understood were the names of Kenann, Danny and someone named Pierre. She took a count of the men in the room. There were three men who were obviously of Middle Eastern origin standing off by themselves. A lone man was on the receiving end of Katerina's tirade. She guessed this to be Angelo whom Jake had told her about. He was visibly upset by what Katerina was telling him. Moira had stalled longer than she dared in cleaning up the broken chards and flowers, but she hadn't learned anything of value. As if on cue or by divine intervention, Angelo switched to English and Katerina followed in kind.

"What are you saying, Katerina?"

"What I'm saying, you imbecile, is that everything is falling apart. Pierre is shutting me out. He wanted his little goddess to himself and he had to get Danny out of the way to do that. I don't know what he has in mind. He practically ordered me out of the villa. The Night of the Lion is in three days. If I'm not standing beside him during the ceremony, I have no chance of being chosen his successor when he dies. Not to mention that when Danny comes to and realizes I am not there he will find some way to make his escape."

"Let me go to the villa and handle it."

"You? What do you think you can do that I cannot?" Katerina fell into the corner of the couch with a flourish. Moira had faded into the bathroom and was making a pretense of cleaning it. No one was paying her any attention.

"I'm no threat to Pierre. I will take their clothing and personal items to the villa and remain. It is my guess he will forget I am there unless his guards make an issue of my presence."

"All right, see what you can accomplish. Something has to change quickly, or years of effort will be for nothing. Why he thinks that stupid little twit is the reincarnation of an ancient goddess is sheer madness. Hopefully when he realizes he's mistaken, he will use *her* for the human sacrifice."

"What human sacrifice?" Angelo seemed shaken by this news.

"The one offered every five hundred years to preserve the strength of the order. Don't look so horrified. It's no different than the assassinations we've both done over the years, you dolt. They will just find a nice young innocent off the streets and it will all be over in a matter of a few hours. The child will be doped up with hashish and feel nothing. Now get the things from Danny Boy's room and get out there."

Angelo had made it to the door when Katerina called to him. He turned, and she said, "If Danny Boy or his little girlfriend make an escape, kill them both."

*   *   *

Blade ran back up the hill to the alley where Judy and Mrs. Gage were waiting. He was excited that he had some news to share. They welcomed him into the coolness of the limousine and he began to relate what he had learned.

"Danny Mac is asleep for some reason. Kenann is pretending to be a princess and Danny Mac is her High Priest."

Judy and Mrs. Gage looked at each other.

"Andy said Kenann has bought them some time, whatever that meant."

Things were escalating. Mrs. Gage picked up her cell phone and called Jake. He answered on the first ring.

"Is Moira with you?"

"She is just coming off the elevator."

"We will pick you up in front of the hotel in 20 minutes."

*   *   *

They had convened in the conversation pit in the library. Mrs. Gage stood in front of the fireplace.

"I have special commendation for Blade and Moira. Good work. Let's review what they learned. Danny Mac and Kenann are temporarily out of Katerina's control. They are playing some sort of game of their own and at this point do not seem to be in any *worse* danger. This human sacrifice is troublesome. I am not sure what this Night of the Lion might be, but

156

we need to have a decisive plan by then. Are there any suggestions for our next move?"

The noise level rose as they bantered about their individual ideas. Mrs. Gage mused at how quickly they had become like a family. No, she challenged. We *are* family. She had lost everyone she had loved to the tyrants who destroyed her family and had felt that loss every day since. These lovely people were filling that emptiness she had believed to be beyond healing. She adored them. Not in that surface emotion she affected most days just to get by. No, she well and truly loved them. She felt Moira's eyes rest on her.

"What is it, Gabrielle?"

"I'm just taking a moment to count my richest blessings."

Moira gave her a knowing smile. She too had known loneliness and the pain of loss. She joined with Mrs. Gage in surveying the active room. Despite her fear for Kenann, she was having the time of her life and jumped back into the middle of the fray.

"We have got to find a way to get near enough to those kids to help them if things get rough."

"Any ideas on how to do that?" This came from Judy.

Everyone had an idea and the noise level rose again. They could not be assured any of their offered actions would not make things worse, so they retired for the night in indecision. They could only hope that further observation would lend them an opportunity to connect with the captives. Blade had remained uncharacteristically quiet during the vociferous exchange.

Chapter Twenty Five

Kenann jerked her head up. She had been in a half dreaming state with her head still resting on Danny Mac's chest when she felt him stir. He opened his eyes and looked at her for what seemed a long time. She waited for him to speak. She began to fear his drug induced sleep had produced some amnesia when he croaked, "Are you an angel?"

But then he grinned at her with that smile that had formerly won him many a female conquest. She smacked him on the arm.

"It's not funny. You had me worried sick."

"My apologies."

"Are you okay? Can you move?'

"Well, let's see." He raised himself up on one arm and tried to swing his legs into a sitting position. He pitched forward and falling into Kenann's arms, they both fell back onto the floor. He used that devastating smile on her again. He grabbed her by the arms and flipped her over so that she was lying on top of him.

"Danny Mac will you quit fooling around. Are you feeling alright?"

"How do I feel to you?"

"I think that drug Pierre used on you has made you simple."

But she couldn't resist taking her time sliding off him to stand. She took satisfaction in hearing the soft moan that escaped him. She stood up and extending her hand, helped him to stand as well. He grabbed the robe lying across the foot of the bed. It matched the one Kenann had donned from the closet. He made a thorough check of the room. By this time Kenann recognized a sweep for bugging devices and left him to it. He gave her a thumbs up, so she proceeded to explain her recent course of action.

"Your behavior is most unbecoming for the high priest of Princess Inanna.

"Excuse me?"

"I've been busy while you lay around snoozing."

"Apparently."

"I decided to go on the defensive. I presented myself to Pierre as the reincarnated Goddess and then issued a few edicts. He bowed and scraped and if I can keep this up it could be very useful to our situation."

"So, what did you tell him about me?"

"You are my high priest." She smiled

Danny Mac looked down to the general area of his speedo and said, "Did you hear that? Isn't she the greatest?"

Kenann wrinkled her nose. "Man, I always heard guys were obsessed with their," she paused and waved her hand toward his midsection. "But I didn't know they actually talked to it."

Danny Mac threw back his head and laughed exuberantly. He then reached into his speedo and produced the small listening device. Holding it up, he continued to grin.

Kenann rolled her eyes.

*   *   *

Pierre knocked on their door deferentially. Kenann bade him entrance. He assured her that Daniel would have no lasting effects from his sedation and apologized profusely about his actions. Had he known Daniel's identity, he would never have taken such a course of action. He asked them to join him for a meal. Kenann said they would prefer to dine in their rooms at present, but she would send for him later to discuss their future. She dismissed him perfunctorily and he bowed as he went out the door.

Kenann turned her regal gaze to Danny Mac, who laughed.

"You're good, girl. You are *good*."

Angelo entered the villa by way of the service door and found a couple of the bodyguards entertaining themselves with a game of poker. They reached for their weapons when they heard the door open but relaxed when they recognized him. He showed them his parcels and they waved him on through to the main part of the house. Before he left them, they asked if he knew what game Pierre and Katerina were playing. His response was vulgar and sarcastic and was met with bawdy laughter. He followed their directions to the rooms where Danny and Kenann were being housed. He walked in unannounced hoping to catch them off guard but found them sitting together talking quietly. They simply looked up when he entered.

Cool as usual, Angelo thought. He tossed the parcels onto the bed, closed the door and leaned back against it, folding his arms across his chest.

"You are in a precarious position, I fear."

"How so?" Danny Mac queried.

"Pierre has shut Katerina out. He wants the little lion to himself and he has plans for her in 3 days. She has to present a convincing portrayal of this ancient goddess and there is some vital information I need to give you."

"Why are you helping us?"

"I've been ordered to help you. Don't take it personally. And in case you harbor any doubts, I'll kill you both if you try to escape from this villa. Are we clear?'

"Pretty clear." Danny Mac smiled.

"Angelo," Kenann asked softly, "What do I need to know?"

Angelo willed himself to maintain his firm countenance even though he felt himself soften when he turned to her.

"There is a ceremony called the Night of the Lion. It occurs every

500 years in this society and involves a human sacrifice. Katerina was convinced she was to stand beside Pierre on the dais and be recognized as his successor, but things are off balance now. The situation is extremely volatile. And if it erupts it will have deadly consequences."

"I know firsthand that Pierre's nuts, Angelo, but what makes you think he's so dangerous?" Kenann asked.

"You still do not understand, do you? This organization that Katerina has been able to infiltrate, is more powerful than you can imagine. You have heard of the Knights Templar? This goes back 4000 years before that. It began in Sumeria in the cradle of civilization. If its own legend can be believed, it was instrumental in the rise and fall of Babylon, the Greeks, the Romans - even Hitler's Third Reich. Many world events are controlled by them and their web of influence at this very moment. That is what makes them so powerful. They work behind the scenes. Their agenda is their own. They are a network of office workers, housekeeping staff, generals and world leaders and their loyalty is to no one or nothing but the Society. It has been passed down through the millennia. Each generation is given the charge to control history and amass more power toward some unknown end."

Angelo stopped and shook his head.

"It doesn't matter. What matters is that you pull this off. There are scrolls. They will instruct you in the ceremony. See if you can get Pierre to show them to you."

"Kenann may have tipped the balance of power in our favor. She 'revealed' herself to Pierre as Inanna while I was knocked out. He is so awestruck. He practically quivers around her." Angelo turned back to her with a look of increased respect.

"She also has established me as her high priest which gives me an edge as well."

Angelo threw back his head and laughed. He spoke in Arabic, "Danny Boy, I swear, if you do not claim this woman I shall."

Danny did not want to break the tenuous thread of congeniality, so he answered jovially in Arabic, "I think I have finally met my match in this little one, Angelo."

"Indeed, indeed."

"Hey boys, English please."

Angelo smiled at her. "You have done well. Katerina will not thank you, but she will be pleased. Get the scrolls and wait to hear from us." He made to leave and turned back to them.

"Do not try to escape." But this time it held the air of a plea.

*   *   *

Angelo left the villa, walked down the steps to the coastline and threw stones in the lapping waves of the Mediterranean. He was reminded of his childhood along the Black Sea. Those were carefree days for the most part. He knew now that they were also hard times, but he didn't know it then. He parents had shielded him and tried to give him a good life. He sat down on a rock outcropping and looked out over the horizon. Ships in the distance were coming and going. He contemplated the path he had taken and for the first time, felt the dark emptiness in the center of his soul.

*   *   *

Katerina paced her apartment trying to figure a way to turn the things around. It was all that stupid girl's fault. No matter how this turned out, she was going down. Katerina was going to relish killing her with her own hands. Danny Boy would come around eventually. She would wear down his passing fancy with religion and return him to their own brand of worship, the kind that involved lust and every kind of carnal pleasure. She had been intoxicated by his powerful passion and at one time had resented the hold he exerted over her. She had spent years trying to forget him but now she had him back.

She had seen and experienced that dark side of him and she longed to drink from that cup again.

*   *   *

The next morning found everyone at their posts. Jake and Moira were ensconced in the hotel lobby with an eye out for Katerina. Mrs. Gage, Judy and Blade were once again watching the seaside villa behind the tinted windows of the limousine. Judy and Mrs. Gage were arguing their own views as to how to get into the villa when Blade bolted from the car. Before either woman could react, he was dashing down the hill toward the villa. Judy suddenly realized what he intended and clambered out after him. Despite her disguise of spike heels and short skirt, she ran at full speed calling out to Blade to stop.

Andy's attention was drawn to this activity as he sat in the back of a utility van parked along the street. Wasn't that the kid playing in the street yesterday? She was calling him Blade. Blade? Wait a minute! He looked closely at the woman running down the sidewalk beside the van.

"Oh, there is NO way!"

With lightning speed, he jerked open the side door on the van, snatched Judy around the waist and pulled her in on top of him in a tangle of arms and legs. One of Andy's men reached over them and pulled the door closed behind them.

Judy fought with fierce determination and was satisfied to hear a deep grunt of pain when her elbow connected with her assailant's midsection. When Andy could speak again, he grabbed her forearms from behind, "Judy, quit fighting me!"

She went still as a stone. Before he could speak again, the black barrel of a Glock appeared behind the left ear of the van driver and a voice drawled very slowly.

"Release my friend and you won't find your brains on the windscreen."

"Mrs. Gage?" Judy was incredulous.

"Yes, dear. If you are unencumbered, open the door and come stand behind me."

"But Mrs. Gage, its Andy."

"Oh my, I was afraid of that. Well, I guess the jig is up, as they say. If I put away my gun can we discuss our situation rationally?"

"Crime-in-Italy, as opposed to a shootout? Just get in the van and tell me what in the name of common sense is going on!"

Judy scrambled off Andy's lap, hurriedly tugging her skirt down over her hips. Mrs. Gage climbed in and sat beside Judy on the bench seat along the wall of the van. She squeezed Judy's hand and looked across at Andy who returned her gaze with a forbidding frown. The other man sat at a communication center along the back of the van. The driver continued to keep a vigilant observation of the villa in front of them. He seemed nonplussed by just having a gun pressed into his skull. The man at the communication controls tugged off the head set and handed it to Andy.

"You'd better listen to this, Boss."

Danny Mac heard several raised voices coming from the foyer below. He walked out onto the balcony and looked down to see Pierre's men surrounding a small boy in ragged clothing. He gripped the railing to steady himself when the child looked up and met his gaze.

The men were discussing their good fortune at having the lamb walk right up to the door and present itself. One man passed a note to another who threw back his head in laughter.

"A deaf and dumb lamb in the bargain!"

Danny Mac barked the order in Arabic, "Bring the boy to me."

The men looked up and sneered. They began calling insults when Pierre appeared and silencing them with an oath, telling them to do as Danny said. The men exchanged looks and shoved Blade toward the stairs. The boy turned back and grabbed the grimy note out of the man's hand and ran up the stairs. Danny showed no emotion but austerely pointed toward the room where Kenann stood waiting. She too maintained a stoic countenance as Danny Mac led the boy solemnly inside and she closed the door.

Kenann dropped to her knees in front of Blade.

"Are you alright?"

He nodded and looked wide eyed at Danny Mac who realized the boy thought he was angry. Danny Mac smiled and pulled Blade into a fierce hug.

"How in the world did you get all the way here, kid? No. Never mind. Mrs. Gage, right?"

"Yep, she is totally awesome."

"Apparently." Danny Mac's eyes met Kenann's over the boy's head.

"How did you talk them into letting you come along on this harebrained scheme in the first place?"

Blade told them the whole story.

"Mrs. Gage was really steamed and then she hugged me a lot. Jake told her I could help since I have dark skin. She called my mom and squared it with her. I don't have to be back home until school starts."

Danny Mac squeezed the boy's shoulder involuntarily. He hoped to God that he was alive when school started.

*   *   *

"Jake is here too?" Andy practically screamed it.

"Now Andy, there is no need to become upset."

"Upset? You haven't seen upset. I am going to bundle up your little band of misguided mental misfits and ship you back to Memphis where you belong."

"You cannot do that."

Andy merely arched an eyebrow.

"All right, maybe you can. But be reasonable. We could be of assistance. Blade is already on the inside."

"Yeah and scheduled to be the next human sacrifice. Great job, Mrs. Gage."

"But you must admit we have been able to learn a great deal in a short period of time without the benefit of electronics."

"No, you have other methods," he said sending a pointed glance at Judy who dropped her eyes.

Mrs. Gage hurried to draw the attention back to herself. "Moira was able to infiltrate Katerina's apartments yesterday and learn a great deal."

"Who in the world is Moira?"

Mrs. Gage felt a trifle chagrined when she offered, "Kenann's grandmother."

Andy dropped his forehead into his hands. "Carter is going to eat my liver."

CHAPTER TWENTY SIX

They sat staring at each other around the conversation pit in Mrs. Gage's drawing room. Andy's two deputies, Johnson and Whitaker, stood like Presidential secret service by the door – ramrod straight, hands clasped in front of their bodies. This might be the ladies place, but no one was going anywhere 'til the Boss said so.

Andy was taking secret delight in seeing Jake look so sheepish. He had hung his head when he arrived at their hastily convened meeting at Mrs. Gage's villa.

"I'm sorry son. She's a strong woman. She would have come with or without me. I figured if I tagged along, I could at least keep an eye on her."

Andy looked at Jake's dyed hair and raised an eyebrow. Jake burst out laughing.

"Like I said, son, she is a force to be reckoned with."

"I'm beginning to understand that."

Before they convened, Mrs. Gage had taken Jake aside and asked him to speak to Andy and explain without divulging any confidences that Judy played her deception as a request from them. She was concerned at Judy's behavior since Andy had discovered them. She reminded him how fragile Judy was since she had revealed her trauma to them only hours before they came on this misadventure. He had agreed readily and felt now was as good a time as any.

"Son, I need to explain something to you before we join the others. Judy is, well, delicate."

"Yeah, right."

"Son, you listen up and listen up good."

Andy's spine snapped to attention involuntarily. Force of habit.

Jake continued, "You don't know all there is to know here, so watch your attitude. Judy has carried some things on her heart that a person shouldn't have to carry, so you treat her gently and with kind care or you will have me to deal with. Do I make myself clear?"

"Yes, Sir."

Andy turned and walked to the fireplace. He willed himself to ignore his feelings where Judy was concerned. He promised himself plenty of time to explore all of that when this was over. He turned and was suddenly swamped with affection for the expectant faces looking up at him. These brave souls, who had struck out to help their friends, filled him with a longing to be counted as one of them. He mentally shook this off and got down to business.

"Blade is in good hands for the time being. Danny and Kenann have him with them. Kenann has begun playing the part of Princess Inanna with Danny as her High Priest. But this you have already learned by your own counter intelligence."

He tipped his head to Mrs. Gage in salute. She acknowledged the accolade with a slight nod of her head in return. He was also declaring defeat. For better or for worse these folks were in.

"I regret I didn't fit Danny with a two-way receiver in Memphis, but hind sight is 20/20. Our task now is to get one to them now, so we can coordinate our efforts. This organization needs stopped and we have an opportunity to take it down at its head. Now, I know your main concern is Danny and Kenann, but I have to be very clear on this. That is not my only objective here."

No one offered any comment, so he continued. "We are going to have a package delivered to them purporting to be from their family since their original guise was as brother and sister. At this point Pierre does not seem to suspect anything and Katerina certainly is not going to tip her hand at this point."

"That is an excellent plan, Andrew. May I make one small addition?"

"I'm listening."

"Suppose I play the role of Daniel and Kenann's mother and show up to surprise them here in Alexandria. You have already said Katerina would not risk exposing their duplicity."

"Now, Gabrielle, I don't like this." Jake bristled.

Andy considered her plan. "Sir, she may have a point. We will have an opportunity to eyeball them up close and we can then be assured the transmitter will be delivered without the risk of a package being searched. I accept your offer, Mrs. Gage."

Jake spoke again, "I will *not* sit around twiddling my thumbs, son."

"I have every intention of utilizing your talents, Sir. We need to continue keeping a close eye on Katerina. That will be your and Mrs. James' job. I want to know her every move. Got that?" They nodded.

Judy looked up and waited for her instructions. He said, "You'll be with me."

CHAPTER TWENTY SEVEN

When Pierre approached Danny Mac and Kenann to see if they needed anything, they indicated the articles Angelo had delivered would suffice for the present, but the boy required clothing and other articles. He must be treated well until the appointed hour and hoped this would explain their interest in Blade. Pierre assured them these needs would be attended to. Danny Mac and Kenann had discussed this next course of action at length and had decided a direct approach was best.

Kenann spoke, "Pierre, we will need to review the scrolls."

Pierre's raised eyebrow was his only indication of surprise.

She continued, "Daniel and I will sit down with you at your earliest convenience to discuss the Night of the Lion. We need to finalize the ceremony, don't you think?"

"Yes, of course. I'll gather them and call for you. Will that be acceptable?"

"Yes and thank you for your kind attention." Pierre glowed under her compliment and bowed his way out the door. They dressed casually in the clothes Katerina had provided for them and waited. They did not have to wait long. Pierre came for them and led them to a library in the back of the villa. It was all dark wood and leather and on a long conference table lay scrolls encased under glass.

"How old are these, Pierre?" She saw him look at her quizzically and added, "Just because I am reincarnated does not make me omniscient,

Pierre. That is why I have been revealed only to you. You are to guide me with any information I do not have."

"Of course, Your Highness. These are 1000 years old. This will be the third Night of the Lion they have seen."

She didn't dare hope they were written in colloquial English. What was she going to do now that she couldn't read any of it? She approached the table slowly. Danny Mac stepped forward and looking down said, "Your Highness, allow me to assist you."

She looked at him and nodded. He went around the table looking carefully at each panel. She realized she was holding her breath and released it slowly. Pierre watched him expectantly.

Danny Mac looked at Kenann and said, "I would like time to examine the scrolls if you will permit me?"

"Of course, Daniel. Pierre and I will be on the veranda enjoying the sunshine. Would you care for some refreshment?"

Pierre was slightly annoyed by the way they seemed to have taken over but accepted this as a natural progression of the prophesy. He led Kenann from the room. She stole a glance over her shoulder and Danny Mac winked at her. She smiled back and left the room.

Kenann decided to make use of her time with Pierre to quiz him about the ceremony. He was eager to impress her with his knowledge. She waived away his obsequious attempts to ingratiate himself and asked him to give her facts and details. She bade him leave nothing out. He complied.

When he had finished, she sat in stunned silence. She quickly regained her composure and complimented him and his predecessors on the accuracy they had been able to maintain to the original ceremony. Pierre beamed. He could not believe his true good fortune to be here at this moment with this woman, fulfilling a destiny determined centuries ago. Kenann felt herself losing steam. There was too much to assimilate. She indicated she would go to Daniel in the library. Pierre made to accompany her, but she raised her hand in refusal. He was stopped dead by the motion. She thought she could get used to this goddess thing.

Danny Mac was pouring over the documents when she entered the room. He looked up and shook his head slightly when she started to speak. She understood he was cautioning her against listening devices in this room. They were not necessarily for them. Pierre probably listened in on private conversations of unaware business associates in this cozy atmosphere. Kenann went to stand beside Danny Mac. She looked down at the play of lines across the papyrus and hoped Danny was not bluffing about being able to decipher them.

He spoke, "I'll be finished here soon."

Kenann nodded and watched in fascination as Danny Mac perused the document closely. He moved back and forth between the panels comparing something known only to him. Finally, he straightened and reached for her hand.

"Let's go, Your Highness." She thought she detected a slight note of laughter in his voice. She gave him her hand and he placed it on his arm. They left the library and proceeded to their suite of rooms.

CHAPTER TWENTY EIGHT

K enann whirled around as soon as the door to their rooms was shut. "You could read those scrolls?"

"Most of it. Hey, Buddy, how ya doing?" Blade came out of the adjoining bedroom eating a pear. He gave a nonchalant wave as if he were at home on a Sunday afternoon instead of the fast track to an execution. Danny was struck cold remembering another little boy who had trusted him with his life. Kenann saw the shift in his demeanor and touched his arm. She knew Danny Mac was worrying about Blade and wanted to comfort him somehow. He looked down at Kenann and attempted a reassuring smile.

"Should we set some sort of strategy?" She decided work would be his best diversion.

"Yes. Come over to the table. I need to sketch out some things on paper." They all went over to the small writing table near the window overlooking the street. Danny Mac took some paper out of the desk drawer and drew a rough drawing of a large room with pillars.

"The scrolls were written in the Coptic language. It was one of the languages we used for codes."

"Lucky for us." Kenann secretly thanked God for this providential help.

"Yeah, it mentions a great deal about the aim of the Society and why it was formed in the beginning. For the sake of time I will just put down the blueprint described about the ceremonial temple. Before we can plan any strategy, we need to know how the stage is set. Apparently, it has changed very little from Sumerian times. There will be a raised platform at the front of the hall here," Danny Mac drew on the paper.

"It will hold the leadership of the Society. Directly in front of this dais is the sacrificial altar." Danny Mac and Kenann involuntarily looked at Blade.

His only response was "Cool."

Blade felt no fear. He knew Danny Mac would take care of him.

Danny Mac continued, "On both sides running the length of the hall is seating for the members of the Society. Literally translated, they are called Instruments of Power. Before the ceremony there is a modern-day board meeting as people from around the world give their reports. I imagine there are similar meetings held at intervals, but this is a special one for obvious reasons. This Society was established on superstition and mind control techniques and this ceremony will be no exception."

Kenann broke in. "How do we stop this thing before it gets out of hand?"

Danny Mac knew what she meant - before Blade's life was in danger. "We need a diversion. A big one. I'm still working on that."

Just then came a knock at the door. Kenann stood as Danny Mac turned the papers over. She bade entrance. Pierre came in and went through his ritual of apologizing, bowing and scraping. He finally got to the point.

"Your Highness, we will be leaving in the morning for the ceremonial site. I know you will want to make the necessary preparations. The other members of the Society will not arrive for another two days." What he didn't mention was his plans to ensure she would name him as her consort. His leadership in the Society did not guarantee him that privilege but he hadn't come this far to lose out now. He would have her and she would carry his seed before the next new moon.

*   *   *

Andy's cell phone rang. He answered it and listened intently for a few seconds.

"Stay on it." He turned to the group. "Mrs. Gage, its show time."

Pierre appears to be taking Danny Mac, Kenann and Blade to another location in the morning. We can still track them via the GPS, but we need that two-way in place before they get away from us."

Jake spoke up. "What do you need the rest of us to do?"

"Unless you have a way to get into Katerina's apartments?"

Moira coughed, "Actually…"

*   *   *

Judy had not seen such synchronized chaos since her ER rotations in nursing school. Mrs. James was fitted with a uniform for the hotel housekeeping staff and a two-way transmitter in her ear so when the men talked to her in Arabic, the man at the com center would translate. Mrs. Gage needed little in the way of preparations. Judy imagined she could pull off any scheme like a pro.

Mrs. James was hustled back to the Metropole Hotel and was on her way up to Katerina's rooms within the hour. She knocked on the door and called Housekeeping in Arabic. She repeated this several times. Being Irish, she was a natural mimic and could get her tongue around the difficult sounds with relative ease. When no one answered, she used the pass key Andy had been able to procure on short notice. She entered cautiously at first but when it was clear no one was in the suite, she put one of the listening devices in the bowl of artificial fruit decorating the sideboard table in a central location of the room. Then she began looking for somewhere in Katerina's personal belongings to plant another device. This proved to be more difficult. Like a lot of women, she had a pair of shoes for every outfit with matching accessories. There was no way to determine what Katerina would wear at any given moment. It was then she saw it. A small pistol in a leg holster. The way things seem to be heating up, she figured this was one accessory Katerina was sure to put on.

She hurriedly planted the device the way Andy had shown her. Taking one last look around, she headed for the door when it swung open and Katerina stormed in. She had been out on the beach trying to calm herself. She could not assuage the boiling rage she felt toward Kenann for destroying all her hard-won plans.

She barked to Mrs. James in Arabic, "Get out."

Mrs. James repeated the words she heard in her ear, "I am finished," in Arabic.

"I don't care if you are finished or not. I said get out."

She bowed and left the room as instructed by Katerina and the voice in her ear.

She passed the men who were coming in behind Katerina and heard one of them whisper something softly to the other. The voice in her ear spoke to someone sitting nearby.

"That was very interesting." Mrs. James would love to have known what the man had just said. There had been enough venom in his tone to make the hair stand up on the back of her neck.

*   *   *

Mrs. Gage got out of the cab and looked around like an awestruck tourist. She tripped lightly up to the villa's entrance. Knocking, she opened the large front door and called, "Yoohoo, anybody home?"

She was met by a very large man in a suit. He blocked her from entering further.

"My but you're a big one, aren't you?" She used her best Memphis drawl and swatted him on the arm. He didn't move.

"May I help you?" His voice rumbled in his chest.

"Why you sure can, darlin'. My younguns are here and I want to see them."

"Excuse me?"

"Danny and Kenann. I came all this way to surprise them and then I find out they've gone off from their hotel. It was just the luckiest thing that the hotel clerk told me who they left with or I'd have never found them. Now if you would be so kind to go and fetch them for me."

The man took her to a room off the large foyer. He found Pierre and explained the situation. Pierre went hurriedly to the parlor but before he entered, he took a deep breath and assumed his most charming attitude.

"This is indeed a pleasure. When did you arrive and how were you so fortunate to find us?

"Like I told that other fellow, one of the hotel clerks said he saw you all leave together and since my kids hadn't come back to the hotel I asked around. It took me a while, but I finally found out where you live when you're in town. Can I see them? They are gonna be so surprised," drawing out the last word shrilly.

"By all means, madam. You wait here."

He went to their suite of rooms and ushered Danny and Kenann down to the parlor without any explanation. He was testing the veracity of this ladies' claims. When they came in, Mrs. Gage jumped up and cried, "My babies. Look who's come all this way to surprise you. Well, aren't you gonna come and kiss your old momma?"

Kenann's mind flew into action. She turned to Pierre and rolled her eyes with feigned impatience. Turning back to Mrs. Gage she groaned, "Mother, why did you come here. This was supposed to be *my* time."

"Oh now, darling, don't be mad. I just wanted to see my babies. What's wrong with that? Come here Danny and give your Momma a hug and a peck on the cheek."

He complied, and she palmed him the two way as slick as an Atlantic City grifter. He spoke kindly but firmly as if he had been doing it for many years. "Mother, go on back to the hotel. I will make arrangements with the Concierge to schedule you on some tours of the city. Since you are this close, go see the Pyramids at Giza. You'll enjoy that."

Mrs. Gage puckered up her face and whined, "All right Daniel but are you sure you and Kenann can't come with me?"

"No, Mother. Pierre has graciously opened his home to us and we have additional business with him. Kenann is helping me. Now go on back to the Hotel. You can charge your expenses to my account but please go lightly on the gambling and drinking. You know how you get when you've had too much to drink."

"Now Daniel, don't scold me. I'll be good. You kids finish up your business here and we'll have a nice little vacation together. Okay, sugar?"

Kenann turned to Pierre and rolled her eyes again. He smothered a laugh. She went to Mrs. Gage and put her arm around her escorting her to the door. "We will see you in a few days, Mother." Kenann's hands trembled slightly as she hugged Mrs. Gage, but she willed her eyes to remain dry and her voice calm as she said her final good byes on the front portico. Danny Mac hailed a taxi for her and as he helped her in, he spoke softly, "Well done, *Mother*." She smiled and blew him a kiss as the taxi drew away into the traffic.

*   *   *

Andy helped Judy into the surveillance van. For the moment they were alone. Andy fitted the ear piece into his ear and heaved a very heavy sigh.

"I guess I should apologize for being so hard on you."

"It's all right." But she did not meet his eyes. Andy was amazed at the difference in her demeanor from the woman he knew in Memphis. Something was terribly off.

"What gives, Judy?"

"What do you mean?" She looked at him then.

"You. You act like a whipped pup."

She felt a shudder go through her body but reigned it in. "I'm just tired. I guess the strain is getting to me."

Before he thought, he blurted out, "Why did you let me ramble on like an idiot about you?"

"It was sweet."

"Sweet? Oh, that's just great. Let me let you in on something here.

Don't use sweet or sensitive in any context when referring to me. And for the love of all things holy, *don't* talk like that in front of my men."

He was rewarded with the smile he had been going for. Man, but she was beautiful. He smiled back and then concentrated on the conversation coming over the wire. He laughed heartily at the exchange occurring in the villa. He put it on speaker, so Judy could enjoy Mrs. Gage's performance too. He saw her shoulders relax as their laughter mingled.

*   *   *

"What do you mean they are leaving?"

"Just what I said and I'm hitching a ride on the second chopper with Pierre's men."

Angelo had called Katerina on his cell phone from the villa. Andy's men monitored the conversation via the listening device planted by Mrs. James.

"That Bastard, I was scheduled to leave with him myself in two days. What is he up to?"

"I don't know but I am sticking with Danny and Kenann." He didn't mention the appearance of their delightful 'mother'. He had recognized her as the screwy lady from Memphis and then he made the connection as to why that kid had looked so familiar. He decided to stand back and see what happened.

*   *   *

The helicopters were riding low over the desert. Danny Mac was trying to get a bearing on their course and calling on his limited knowledge of the terrain, he estimated they were flying somewhere between the Baharia and the Siwa Oases. This left a considerable amount of barren landscape to get lost in. He had managed to give a full report to Andy before they departed on the helicopter. He complimented him on using Mrs. Gage for the transfer of the two-way but wasn't surprised to learn it was all her idea. They parted with a sincere wish on both their parts that they would be speaking again soon. He hoped Andy was getting at least some of their in-flight conversation. Pierre was still trying to play the cordial host and was explaining that he was anxious to show them the site of the ceremony. He assured them they would find the accommodations very comfortable.

Blade sat next to Kenann peering out the windows with wide eyed astonishment. The two helicopters finally set down near a stony outcropping. There was nothing but rocks and sand as far as the eye could see. Pierre jumped from the helicopter with the air of a child eager to show his new trick. He motioned for Danny and Kenann to follow. He ignored Blade as if he were not there. Kenann kept him close to her side. They followed Pierre to a cluster of scrubby pines near a large rocky prominence. He turned and beamed at them. With a flourish he pulled down on one of the branches and in a single fluid motion the entire section moved as one unit to expose a large ornate door.

Kenann stole a glance at Danny Mac and reached out and took his hand. She suddenly felt very afraid. He squeezed her hand and offered a prayer for all of them. Pierre led them through the doorway into the darkness beyond. He turned on a battery-operated hand torch and the area directly around them was suffused in faint light. He led them down a flight of steps to an area below ground level. No one spoke. Pierre turned and beckoned them to follow him. Kenann put Blade between her and Danny Mac as they followed Pierre. They walked for only a few minutes when Pierre stopped and told them to wait. He stepped away a few paces and suddenly their eyes were assaulted by light. They found themselves standing on a stone balcony of some type. Pierre motioned them toward the balustrade. When they reached the edge Kenann let out an involuntary gasp. Danny Mac gripped the railing. Blade whistled. Pierre had achieved the reaction he desired.

Before and below them stretched a panorama of unbelievable proportions. In this underground cavern was housed a pyramid to rival those at Giza. Far below them, they saw giant statuary and pillared buildings at the base of the pyramid forming a village with wide brick paved avenues.

Surrounding the entire tableaux was a honeycomb of balconied rooms overlooking the village below. Kenann turned to Pierre.

"I am speechless, Pierre. How long has this been here?"

"Legend has it that it has been here since the Pyramids. I cannot verify that. The rooms for our members have been modernized over the years and are quite luxurious. I think you will be more than pleased with your suite of rooms. Yours will be next to mine."

"But remember I am to remain in the company of Daniel and our young friend at all times until the ceremony."

"But Your Highness, you are completely safe here. I had hoped you and I could have some time to discuss the future of our Society before The Night of the Lion ceremony begins."

"We shall, Pierre. But it will jeopardize the fulfillment of the prophecy if I am separated from Daniel or B ... the boy," she faltered. Pierre was giddy with hope at her assurance to spend private time with him. His senses were clouded by his belief that the power of the entire world was within his grasp. His eyes took on a faraway look as he turned and gazed out over the panorama before them. Kenann looked at Danny Mac and raised her eyebrows in question. The slight shrug of his shoulder did little to quell the anxiety she felt building. Pierre was deteriorating mentally. She couldn't help the growing fear that things were soon to spiral out of control.

CHAPTER TWENTY NINE

A ngelo was experiencing a similar foreboding. He stepped up and lightly touched Pierre on the arm. Pierre turned and looked at him without really seeing him. Angelo spoke softly, "Pierre, I will take them to their quarters now."

Pierre nodded, "Yes, yes. Please do. Then come to me. We have much to do. Much to do." He turned back to gaze out over the underground landscape. Angelo turned to Danny.

"Come with me."

The other men who had come on the second helicopter positioned themselves in a semi-circle a few feet behind Pierre and waited.

Angelo led them around the circular balcony until he came to an ornate door. When Angelo opened it to reveal an elevator, it looked hopelessly incongruent in that setting. They entered without speaking and began their descent to the base of the cavernous structure.

"What is Pierre up to, Angelo?"

"I'm not sure. He's a wild card now. Katerina was confident of his alliance with her and counted on him naming her as his apprentice for succession to the leadership.

"He is slipping into a delusional state." Kenann spoke. The men turned to her.

Danny Mac asked, "What is that?"

"Basically, what it says. It's a form of psychosis in which a person believes a lie or delusion as undisputed fact. They can become dangerous if their delusion is challenged."

"Pierre is dangerous with or without his delusion being challenged." Angelo offered.

When they arrived at their destination and the door opened, Kenann felt she had been transported back in time. They entered a wide avenue paved with beautiful bricks and mosaics. She expected any minute to see the streets teeming with dark skinned people clothed in soft cotton.

"Angelo, have you been here before?" Kenann asked.

"A few times. The Society holds regular meetings here. The helicopters bring everyone in flying under the radar and drop them off. They are invisible to satellite surveillance once they enter the cavern."

Kenann realized she was still holding tight to Blade's hand. She looked down and gave him a reassuring smile. He hadn't uttered a word since they entered the underground complex.

"Are you doing all right, buddy?"

He only nodded. She pulled him close and put an arm around him.

"That's the kid from your neighborhood, isn't it?"

No one spoke.

"And mother dear is that rich lady who owns the mansion where you went to the party."

Danny Mac spoke, "Are you going to tell Katerina?"

"I'm not sure. Everything is off balance and Katerina is about as crazed as Pierre right now."

"Angelo," Kenann spoke softly, "We could not have predicted Pierre's delusion about me when Katerina put this in motion. I am very afraid this will turn into a blood bath if it does not go the way Pierre wants. We need your help to avert that."

"What could I do?"

"I'm not sure but it would be very reassuring if we knew we could count on you when the time comes."

"Are you asking me to betray Katerina?"

"Katerina is in as much danger as we are at this point."

Angelo threw up his hand. "Stop with all this talk. You are trying to confuse me. I work for Katerina, not you." He stopped in front of a large pillared structure. They followed him up several stone steps and into a large foyer whose walls were covered in mural paintings.

"Here are your quarters. I will be back after I check in with Pierre."

The three of them simply stood and watched him walk down the steps into the wide thoroughfare. Danny Mac sensed them looking to him for guidance. He gave them both his signature smile and spread his arms wide taking in the panorama.

"Well, let's check things out." Kenann tapped her ear and gave him a questioning look. He shook his head. He was getting no transmission from Andy. He was not surprised considering how far out into the desert they had come not to mention their depth under the sand. It was doubtful the vague description he had gleaned from the scrolls regarding the site of the ceremony would help Andy track them. He could only hope the GPS was still functioning adequately to pinpoint their location.

He moved further into the dwelling with Blade and Kenann following close behind. They entered the next room through an arch. It was a large circular common area with rooms exiting off in different directions. There were low divans and even lower tables. The room was sumptuously appointed. Pillows were scattered throughout, and luxurious tapestries lined the walls. Kenann was reminded of her childhood picture book of the Arabian Nights. There were bowls of fruit and a tray with cheeses, nuts and dates displayed on a large central table as well as earthen jugs which appeared to hold something to drink. Blade went over and began nibbling on some of the food. He peered into the jug and grabbed a cup to pour some out.

"Hang on there, pal. Let me make sure that's not wine."

"Hey, I'm entitled to a last meal ain't I?"

"Stop that!" Kenann turned on him. "That is not funny."

His big brown eyes grew large with tears and threatened to spill over. Kenann was immediately remorseful and dropped to her knees in front of him.

"Oh, I'm so sorry, Blade. My nerves are shot, and I shouldn't be taking it out on you."

"Oh, that's all right. I'm getting a little scared too."

She wrapped him into her arms and rocked him back and forth. "Danny Mac will get us through this, baby." She felt his shoulders give a shudder and heard a loud sniff before he straightened and stepped back. He gave her a beautiful bright smile that nearly undid her. But she smiled back and stood up.

Danny Mac had watched this with a fist gripping his heart. These two were counting on him to protect them and see them out of this alive. In his former way of life, he had trusted only in his own physical strength and cunning to get him out of jams. Now he also had the wisdom of the universe and the might of a legion of angels at his disposal.

"Come here you two." They approached him slowly. Danny Mac took their hands and led them to a low round table and motioned them to sit down on the plush pillows. He joined them and held his hands out in invitation. They joined hands and looked at him expectantly. Danny Mac closed his eyes and lifted his face to heaven.

"Holy Father and protector of your children, we claim your power. The same power that raised Jesus from the dead lives in us and we proclaim it now. Father we need your guidance and the protection of your mighty warrior angels. We do not know what to do but we trust you and believe that you will make all things right. We pray for your will to be done, Lord. Give us strength. Take away our fear and make us wise. We love you, Lord. Stay nearby. It is through the name of Jesus I pray these things and amen."

He looked up and clapped his hands together. "Now let's check out this food and drink."

*　　　　*　　　　*

"I've narrowed down their location to an area in the south east Sahara but it's going to take several hours, maybe days, to get clearance to go into that area to get them out." Andy was running his hands through his auburn hair causing it to spike up.

"I may have some other options." All eyes turned to Mrs. Gage.

Andy smiled patronizingly, "Now, what can you do that the US government can't?"

"Let me make a few phone calls. May I borrow those coordinates? Thank you." She left the room with a determined look on her well-defined face.

No one spoke. They were all pondering what kind of ace Mrs. G might have up her sleeve this time. She returned beaming.

"Ladies and gentlemen, we are in luck. Or as I am sure Jake will assure us, the Lord is blessing our efforts."

"By all means Mrs. G, don't keep us in suspense." Andy was a little peeved at the resources available to her.

"Andrew, how many men do you have at your disposal?"

"Counting the men under my direct command, I have 5. I could commandeer more if need be."

"No, that will be sufficient. A small recon force is what is called for I believe."

"Excuse me?" Andy gaped at her.

Jake draped his arm around Andy's shoulder. "Don't argue, son. It will only prolong the inevitable."

*   *   *

The food was top notch and the drink was some sort of fruit juice. It refreshed them sufficiently to begin developing a strategy. Danny Mac did not want to ask Kenann to meet with Pierre, so he was relieved when she volunteered. She seemed to have regained some of her fighting spirit. They found a phone in one of the bedroom areas and dialed 0. A man answered and Kenann straightened her backbone and adopted the tone she had come to call her goddess voice.

"Send Pierre to me." She raised her eyebrows and hung up the phone.

"They said he was indisposed but they would send him as soon as he was available. Let's go exploring, shall we?"

They stepped out onto the large thoroughfare and looked around and up. The pyramid loomed in front of them. The lighting in the large cavern made the street look like late afternoon or early evening. They walked toward the pyramid and up the wide ramp that ended in front of two gargantuan wooden doors. Danny Mac looked around for a mechanism to open them.

"We need to find a way to get in there."

Blade walked over and began pushing on stones beside the door frame. Kenann and Danny Mac smiled at each other in amusement until they heard an audible click and the huge doors began to move inward. Kenann and Danny Mac stared in stunned disbelief. Blade grinned.

"That's how they did it in my video game."

They walked into the great hall and were amazed to see that it looked very much like a medieval church inside – all stone and intricate carvings. The layout was just as it had been described in the scrolls. There was a large central aisle culminating in a platform staging area in the front. The side aisles were filled with rows of bleacher like seating as were the balcony areas above. A lone table stood at the foot of the stage area reminding Danny Mac of the communion table in his church building at home and then its ominous purpose struck him. He made no comment but guided them up the steps and said, "Let's see if there are any back ways out of here."

*   *   *

"Do you mean to tell me that you just *happen* to know a desert sheik who lives in the same area as the GPS coordinates where we last tracked Danny and Kenann?"

"That is exactly the case, Andrew." Mrs. Gage was making a valiant effort to hold her temper. "I have met a great many people in my lifetime. I left my home in Hungary as a young woman due to Communist persecution and spent the next several years traveling and enjoying a variety of adventures. These adventures brought me into contact with some very helpful people. Leo D. Poynter is one of them. He is an English gentleman who stayed in Africa after the Second World War and was adopted into a Bedouin tribe. He leads the tribe now and is willing to help us. Now do you want to stand here and argue about it?"

Andy met her steely gaze for several seconds and then finally heaved a sigh.

"How about I just shut up and let you outline your plan?"

He offered an endearing grin. She responded immediately with an answering smile and took in a deep breath.

"That sounds like a lovely idea, my dear. Now Leo says we can fly into his camp and he will outfit us with camels to go in search of our friends. Andrew has done a lovely job narrowing our search field using the limited information at his disposal. Leo will accompany us along with other men from his tribe to legitimize our disguise and provide additional firepower if needed. And since there can be only one field commander, I defer all other decisions to you, Andrew."

"I have been humbled by your abilities, Mrs. G., which begs the question of how you came to have so much experience in this espionage game." She simply smiled demurely and offered no comment.

He continued, "So I would be honored if you would become my second in command. Sorry Sir." He looked at Jake sheepishly.

"Not to worry, son. I know when I am out manned."

"That is a lovely offer, dear. I would be happy to assist you in any way I can. Oh, by the way, we fly out in the morning for Leo's camp."

CHAPTER THIRTY

Danny Mac, Kenann and Blade had found a sliding panel at the back of the dais and had gone into a small chamber with spiral stairs leading up to another level. Blade ran up the stairs with ease and called down to them.

"Hey come up here. This is cool."

Danny Mac and Kenann joined him on the upper level and were stunned to see a bed chamber that looked straight out of Scheherazade. Kenann felt her skin begin to grow cold. She sat down suddenly on the floor. Blade ran to her.

"What's wrong Kenann?"

Danny Mac knelt beside her and took her hand in his surreptitiously taking her pulse. It was slow and thready.

"Kenann, look at me." She did. "What are you feeling?"

"I'm sick- sort of faint." She didn't add but Danny Mac could see it in her eyes. She was also scared out of her wits.

"Blade, see if you can find a cup and bring me some water." He waited until Blade was across the room. "I won't let him hurt you, Kenann."

She looked at the bed and felt her skin crawl at the thought of Pierre touching her. She looked up into Danny Mac's eyes. Blade came back with a cup of ice-cold water and she sipped it until her head and stomach settled.

"Sorry, guys. I guess I'm a girly girl."

Blade laughed. "Naw, you're one of the guys, huh, Danny Mac?'

"Sure, just one of the guys," he responded absently and rubbed her hands until warmth returned to them.

"I meant what I said, Kenann," and before he gave it a conscious thought, leaned in and caressed her lips with his. It was such a tender gesture. She looked into his eyes trying to read his thoughts but was swamped by her own intense feelings of fear mixed with longing.

"Can we get out of here?"

"Sure thing. Come on, Blade, let's keep looking for that back door."

They descended the stairs again into the small antechamber and stood back to back staring at the walls. Danny Mac shifted slightly, and the others followed suit until they were turning slowly in a clockwise direction.

Suddenly Danny Mac exclaimed, "There!" and pointed at a section of wall. Kenann did not see anything out of the ordinary where he was pointing. He broke ranks and walked up to within a few inches of the cut stone surface running his hands along a seam recognized only by him. He looked down at his feet and pushed against the stone with the toe of his boot. The wall pivoted inward revealing a stone staircase descending into increasing darkness. He pushed in again at the threshold of the opening and the door pivoted closed again. He glanced over his shoulder at the other two.

"Now that's interesting. What do you say we find some flashlights and come back later to investigate? But we had better leave now before they come looking for us."

CHAPTER THIRTY ONE

Jake and Mrs. Gage were sitting on the veranda sipping tea and watching the evening sun play on the water of the Mediterranean. Both seemed content with the silence between them. It had lingered for several minutes when Jake spoke.

"Gabrielle, are you happy?"

Mrs. Gage turned slowly and looked at him. Her expression was unreadable. She cleared her throat.

"Well, I suppose I haven't spent a lot of time thinking about that."

"Why not?"

She turned her head away and looked out over the water. She shook her head and spoke softly. "I don't know. I guess I thought I could never be happy again, so I just went on living."

"Doing what?"

"It is not my intention to be mysterious, Jacob. I have others to consider so I have to weigh any revelations I make very carefully."

"Don't you trust me?"

"Oh, Jacob, of course I do but this is not about me and you."

"But it is safe to say, you are not what you seem."

"I'm not sure I like how that sounds."

"It is hard for me to know what to think when you withhold so much of yourself from me."

"I've never been in a relationship that required complete honesty."

"Not even in your marriage?"

"Especially in my marriage. Let's just say he valued other things. He was much older than me and considered me a trophy wife. Imagine me as a trophy wife." She laughed humorlessly. She went on as if to herself. "He met me in Istanbul. I was young and had adopted a complete disregard for life. He found that oddly appealing and pursued me until I decided to take advantage of what he was offering me."

"And what was that?"

"Extensive wealth to finance my personal endeavors."

"And he wanted?"

She looked away, "To fulfill his appetites."

"Why did you stay with him?"

"I had taken a vow." She answered simply. "I have done many things in my life that I would not want anyone to post on a billboard. But I do take my promises very seriously."

"How long has he been gone?"

"It has been almost 40 years and, God forgive me, I never shed a tear or grieved one day of his passing."

"Has there been anyone else?"

"I have had many lovers, Jacob."

"That's not what I am talking about."

She sighed, "I had one love. We joined the resistance movement against the Communists in Hungary. We were both so young and determined to fight for our right to freedom. When they opened fire on us in Liberty Square, he shielded me with his body. He was so full of life and hope, I never felt right being fully alive ever again."

"But Gabrielle, you are the most vibrant person I have ever met."

"I have been so many people for so many reasons and put on my face for so many years, I'm not sure if I'm even in there anymore." Her eyes glistened with unshed tears.

"I'm sorry, Gabrielle. I'm probing where I have no business."

She shook her head as if shaking off something unpleasant.

"Oh, Jacob, you really are a dear and decent man. I don't deserve your friendship."

"Of course, you do, and you shall have it no matter what. No strings attached."

She smiled a sad little smile. "Thank you."

She left Jake a few minutes later to turn in. As she passed the sitting room, she was delighted to hear Judy's deep, throaty laughter drift out to her. Andy was feigning indignation over something. He had obviously taken Jake's warning to heart and was treating Judy gently. She fervently hoped they had the opportunity after this was over to explore their feelings. She paused on the landing and gripped the railing. They were heading right into the lion's den. This adversary was larger and more organized than any she had ever faced and when she thought of those who would be going into this battle with her, she realized she had so much to lose. Her knuckles were white.

"Please God watch over and protect us."

Chapter Thirty Two

They had just returned to the main thoroughfare when they saw Pierre and his entourage hurrying toward them.

"There you are your Highness. We were getting alarmed."

"There is nothing to fear, Pierre. We were surveying our surroundings. Very impressive, I might add."

He beamed under her praise. "Your Highness may I have a few minutes of your time in private?" His hesitant attitude gave Kenann courage to go ahead with their plan.

"That will be permissible. Daniel, I will need you to familiarize yourself with the temple area in preparation. Pierre, provide Daniel with the ceremonial tools at this time along with torches."

"Torches, Your Highness?"

"Pierre, I will ignore your impertinence to question me. The ceremony will be conducted by firelight. Daniel will need to prepare himself accordingly. Provide what I have asked."

"Yes, Your Highness." He turned and ordered his men to bring the items to the temple area. Danny Mac took the opportunity when others were distracted, to wink at Kenann. Oh, how he loved this woman. She smiled quickly back at him and squared her shoulders for another performance of Her Highness Princess Inanna, Goddess of Ancient Sumeria, cradle of civilization, blah blah blah blah blah. She would be glad when this was over.

Pierre took a chance and extended his elbow, "Shall we?"

She stiffened at the thought of the contact but forced herself to take his arm. She paused long enough to say to Danny Mac, "I will meet you back at our quarters shortly."

"Yes, Your Highness."

"Your Highness, there are so many things I want to discuss with you. I have dreamed of this since my initiation into the Society. Have you always known who you were?"

"Actually, Daniel awakened my knowledge." She felt Pierre stiffen beside her and was reminded of his earlier jealous reaction to Danny Mac. She wasn't sure if she should encourage this. She knew she needed to keep him off balance in order to keep the upper hand, but this could potentially put Danny Mac at risk. She decided to follow Pierre's lead. She could feel him wrestle for control.

He finally asked, "Are you and Daniel intimate?"

Ancient Goddess or not she was offended by his boldness. The ice in her tone was very real. "Pierre, I will not even grace that question with an answer. If you continue to treat me in an impertinent manner, I will be forced to take action."

Pierre stammered an apology and then begged her forgiveness. He was making a muck of this. If he did not win her affection by the Night of the Lion his dreams would be lost. He stiffened his spine. He would not be defeated. He had come too far. A thought struck him. Yes! If she did not respond to him, he knew a way to control her. This realization renewed his confidence. One way or another he would be victorious.

Kenann did not like at all the wicked gleam she saw in Pierre's eyes. She much preferred him fawning and nervous around her. She remained silent as he led her up a set of stairs. The room they entered was much the same as she and Danny Mac occupied except for an area off the main foyer that housed elaborate electronic equipment. It appeared to be Command Central for this complex. Pierre gestured for her to sit down in a chair near the fire pit. He went to a sideboard and prepared drinks. She took hers and tried to maintain an air of superiority. He sat next to her with a sigh of satisfaction.

"Now, Your Highness, it is time for me to reveal the final chapter in the prophecy."

"And what is that Pierre?" Kenann was suddenly terrified but schooled her face into a mask of indifference.

"A new world order is ready to be realized. You are one component of that process, but I am the other, Your Highness." He spoke with renewed authority. She took a sip of her drink to steady herself and did not respond. She was painfully aware that she was completely out of her element. She prayed she wasn't blowing it. She concentrated on her breathing. She was surprised but pleased to begin feeling very mellow. She took another sip as she considered her options.

"Go ahead Pierre, I'm listening."

He leaned in and made intense eye contact with Kenann. She found she couldn't look away. When he spoke, his voice was soft and evenly modulated. He spoke quietly about inconsequential things until he sensed she was ready to receive his instructions.

"When you take your place on the dais you will hear the pealing of a gong to mark the opening of the ceremony. At that time, you will turn and reach out your hand for me to take my place beside you. You will make the pronouncement that I am to be your Royal Consort. Do you understand?" She nodded. Pierre leaned closer and whispered into her ear. She continued to stare straight ahead. He caressed her cheek with his lips- his breath hot in her ear. He leaned back in his chair with a smug smile playing across his face. He took a moment to revel in the apparent success of this scheme and then clapped his hands together.

"All right, shall we return to your quarters?" Kenann nodded again and allowed him to bring her to her feet. She walked with him back down the brick paved thoroughfare taking in the scenes from millennium past. She was oddly disoriented and had to keep reminding herself that she was a girl from West Virginia and not that goddess she was pretending to be.

Pierre saw her to the entrance of her quarters and bid her a restful night. When she entered the main area, Danny Mac looked up and smiled. "We hit the jackpot with our exploration. How about you?" He rose from his seat and came to her.

"Are you all right, Kenann? Did something happen?" He took her by the shoulders and ducked his head to get a better look into her eyes. She looked back at him steadily.

"No, nothing happened. He just wanted to talk about the ceremony and go over the details. I just feel overwhelmingly tired suddenly."

"That's understandable. Blade fell asleep out here and I carried him to bed a few minutes ago. Are you positive nothing happened to upset you?" He pulled her into his arms and held her for a few moments before letting her go.

"I love you, Kenann. And I will take care of you."

She shook her head imperceptibly to clear her mind and became aware of Danny Mac's large hands massaging her shoulders.

She suddenly felt desolate and so confused. She didn't know what to believe. He was only saying these things because of their situation and not because he was in love with her. There would never be anything between them. And she would be alone. She might as well join this stupid society. Pierre may be right. She belonged here with him."

He gave her a brisk kiss on the lips before stepping away. "So, I think I will get my mind off those lovely lips of yours and do something constructive. Come sit down and I'll tell you about what we discovered."

She complied and sat beside Danny Mac as he finished a sketch he had been working on when she came in.

"Here," he pointed with his pencil, "Is the secret entrance we discovered earlier. The stairs descend a very long way with passages leading off here and down here. I was about to give up and turn back when we hit bottom. I feared we had been gone too long at that point, so I couldn't explore as much as I'd have liked but I am convinced the passage is a way out of this place. And unless we want to fight our way out against an unknown number of foes, I think we had better explore this option further."

"How do you know the way out wasn't by those passages coming off the stairway on the way down?"

"There was no fresh air flow. Even if there is an exit door that is sealed tight, outside air will get in. A place this big pulls a huge draft. The only place I felt the fresh air was along the single corridor at the bottom."

Kenann felt like she was looking at him through a filmy veil. She was trying to remember something. Oh, yes. She told Danny Mac where Pierre's quarters were and then described the electronic equipment she saw there. Danny was thoughtful for a few moments.

"That could be very useful information, Kenann. Pierre must trust you implicitly to have allowed you to see that. Did he give any new information about the ceremony?"

Kenann seemed to wilt. Danny Mac brushed the hair back from her face, "What's the matter, baby?"

His endearment crumbled her defenses and she began to cry. He took her in his arms, stroking her hair. The fear that had been hovering near the surface for days rose up and swamped her. She clung to Danny Mac with all her strength. She was so confused. And scared beyond belief. Danny Mac drew her more firmly into his embrace. She was trembling all over as she muffled her sobs against his chest.

"Danny Mac, I don't want Pierre to touch me." Her words came out between sobs. "He cannot be my first."

"If I have anything to say about it, I plan on being the only one. Are you telling me you have never been with a man?"

She buried her face into his chest. "I never wanted anyone that close before."

"Kenann, I will protect you with my life. And I will be your one and only. I promise." He pulled her back so he could see her face. "Kenann, look at me. I promise."

She met his gaze and prayed he really could protect her from this devil who would stop at nothing to get what he wanted.

Danny Mac picked her up and carried her to her bed. He set her down and reached over to hand her a cotton gown lying at the foot of the bed.

"Here, put this on. You will be more comfortable. You need to sleep."

"Don't leave me, Danny Mac."

"I won't. Here I'll just turn my back." And he did.

She said, "Okay," and he turned back to her. He sat down on the bed and pulled the covers up over her shoulder. He could still feel the tremors that racked her body. He didn't know how to comfort her further.

"Lay with me, Danny Mac. I need you here with me. Please."

He stretched out beside her. He brought his arms around her shoulders and drew her to him, tucking her head under his chin.

"Go to sleep, baby. I will protect you."

Kenann slept.

CHAPTER THIRTY THREE

As usual Mrs. Gage had been able to outfit the entire entourage with proper attire for a foray into the desert. Light weight, light colored, loose fitting clothing was the order of the day. Andy entered the room where everyone waited.

"Well, that was fun." referring to his phone call with Carter to brief him on their strategy. "Mrs. G, Jake? Carter has requested the honor of your presence for the debriefing when this is all over. Prepare yourself for the grilling." He shook his head trying to assimilate the entire situation he found himself in since making that trip to Memphis.

He sat next to Judy who was looking more like herself. Her blond hair pulled back into a simple pony tail, she looked like a girl ready for an outing in the park. Her color was back, and she had lost that haunted look she gave him when she had first been discovered. He was glad. She was such a strong woman. It grieved him to see her looking so defeated. When this was over, he was determined to discover what had created that well of unhappiness and fear in her.

"So, Carter was in agreement with our current course of action?" Mrs. Gage asked.

"He thinks it is ingenious, actually. But of course, you understand if anything goes wrong, he will disavow any knowledge of it."

"Of course. Well, if everyone is ready, I think we can depart. The van is waiting to take us to the airport and our helicopter. Leo is expecting us shortly."

They rose as one, including the men assigned to Andy, and filed out to the paved courtyard where the van sat running. They were 7 in all. Andy had discussed it with Jake and they had agreed to have a few of the men remain in reserve in Alexandria. They had tried to convince Mrs. James to remain, as well, but she had simply crossed her arms and shook her head.

The flight to Leo's camp was uneventful, if not a little bumpy at times with frequent updrafts of dry desert wind. They sat down several yards from the oasis camp and waited until the props had stilled before disembarking. In no time, they were surrounded by native people in traditional garb. Andy spotted Leo immediately. Not because he did not look the part of a native Bedouin with his long flowing robes, tanned face and hawk nose, but when he strode toward Mrs. G and spoke, he was British through and through. She made her own brand of introductions.

"Leo, this is my dear friend, Jacob. He has been a rock of strength for all of us. And this lovely woman is Judy. She is a nurse and the very best friend of Kenann. Mrs. James," she reached over and patted her hand, "Is Kenann's grandmother and a remarkable woman in her own right. Andrew, here, is a friend of Danny Mac as well as an agent of my adopted government. The gentlemen standing back there are Johnson and Whitaker and they are with Andrew."

"Right Ho, Gabbie old girl. Welcome all. Come with me and we will have a bit of lunch and a spot of tea." The facial reactions did not escape him.

"Being a Bedouin does not require complete sacrifice." He laughed heartily and was joined by the members of his tribe standing round him. They obviously loved him.

He turned and strode away, leaving everyone to troupe along behind him. The camp was laid out in a circle around a small body of water in the middle of the small oasis. They all followed him into the interior of the largest tent. It was obviously the common area for the tribe. He motioned for Mrs. Gage.

"Gabbie, the ladies can make themselves at home to my right and the gentlemen will find their accommodations across the way to the left. Now let's relax over a cuppa, while your things are brought in." It became clear that Mrs. Gage and Leo had known each other for many years. Neither gave anything away as to the details or circumstances of their relationship during the conversation. After a light lunch of bread, cheeses and dates and the promised English tea, Leo explained that it was the custom of their tribe to lie down during the hottest part of the day and dismissed everyone to their respective couches. They each were shown the segregated facilities before retiring. When the women entered their quarters, they were struck by how cool the dark colored material kept the interior of the tent. They each stretched out and were napping in no time. They were awakened by a gentle touch and giggles from the young girls sent to fetch them. They were provided water with which to freshen up and brought back out to the common area where they found the men standing in a circle deep in conversation. Leo looked up and beamed at Mrs. Gage.

"Gabbie, we are about to dine. and I want you at my right hand. And Jacob, my new friend, come here on my left." Everyone assumed seats on generous comfy cushions and Leo clapped his hands. Young men with biceps bulging, carried trays laden with delicacies. Roasted meats and root vegetables, warm bread and pudding with fermented fruit. Conversation flowed genially. Judy was surprised that everyone spoke English, but this was a natural outgrowth, she supposed, from having an aristocratic Brit as their adopted pasha.

Andy leaned into Judy and whispered, "I wonder if we'll have jelled monkey brains for dessert?" She snorted and then covered it with a cough. She didn't tell him she had been thinking of the same scene from the Indiana Jones movie. They need not worry. They were served Turkish Delight and strong coffee. When everyone was thoroughly sated, Leo called for attention.

"Here is our plan. Tomorrow we will head toward the destination determined by the location Gabbie called to me yesterday. It is near enough to a major trading route that it will not seem unusual for us to be there. The area is riddled with stony outcroppings, so we should also be able to find shelter to use for observation if needed. I assume everyone has ridden a camel." His blue eyes twinkled as he threw his head back with booming laughter.

"Not to worry. They are wonderful creatures." And he laughed again.

CHAPTER THIRTY FOUR

D anny Mac had fallen asleep on top of the coverlet beside Kenann. He was unaware when she began to moan and whimper but when she started to fight out against the constraints of her covers, he awoke. He raised up and touched her shoulder.

"Hey Kenann, it's all right. You're dreaming."

She jerked awake, her eyes wild. Grabbing Danny Mac's shirt front with both hands, she pleaded, "Danny Mac don't let him take me. Please. He can't finish this."

He sat and pulled her into his arms trying to console her. The more he tried to convince her she was dreaming the more frantic she became.

"Danny Mac, you don't understand. If he does this, we cannot go back. Nothing will be the same."

"Kenann, what happened when you went with Pierre? Did he touch you?"

"No…no… He said things to me though. Disgusting things."

Danny Mac went rigid with suppressed rage. He would deal with Pierre. But first they had to get free.

"We will beat him, Kenann. He will not fulfill his stupid prophecy and I will take you home." He continued to speak soothingly until her breathing evened out and he felt her body relax in sleep.

He was so proud of her and the way she had conducted herself throughout this whole ordeal. She seemed naive and sweet, and she was, but he could see now that there was an iron strength in her as well. Even though she was afraid, she pressed on. He loved her with all his heart and prayed for a lifetime to prove it to her.

Blade came in the next morning and stood staring down at them. Neither Danny Mac or Kenann moved. Blade shrugged and walked away. He decided to do a little exploring of his own. Couldn't hurt. He wandered out into the thoroughfare and looked both right and left. He and Danny Mac had explored the pyramid temple last night when Kenann went with that Pierre guy, so he turned right and wandered down the first side alley he found. He checked for unlocked doors. Finally, he found one open and went in. It was obviously a back room cluttered and in disarray. There were boxes of old brown robes and long-stemmed torches. Blade heard footsteps. He dove for cover grabbing some robes to hide under and made himself as small as possible. Two men came in and started picking up the boxes of robes and putting them on a cart. They worked without speaking and Blade felt like his breathing was the loudest thing in the room. When they had finished stacking all the boxes of robes they could fit on their cart, they turned and maneuvered it out of the room. Blade breathed a quiet sigh of relief. Even though he knew they would probably just run him off or take him back to Danny Mac, these people gave him the creeps.

Everyone acted like he wasn't even there. He was nothing to them. He didn't trust anyone but Danny Mac. Well, Kenann too, but it was Danny Mac who was going to take care of everything. He figured he had better get back. Adults got freaked out when you weren't where they thought you were going to be. After a parting thought, he rolled up some robes and put them under his arm. He then grabbed a couple of interesting looking canisters off the shelf and slipped them into his deep pants pockets and left through the back.

He was right. When he walked up the steps to their rooms, he heard Danny Mac hollering for him. He sounded scared. Blade broke into a run and slid into the main room just as Kenann came in from her bedroom looking sleepy.

Danny Mac rounded on Blade, "Where have you been?'

"I was out looking around. I was careful," he added because Danny Mac now looked really mad.

"Don't *ever* go off by yourself like that again. Do you understand me?"

"Uh huh. Sorry, man, but you guys were asleep, and I thought I could find out some stuff. I did find a room filled with boxes of old brown robes. These two guys came in and carried some of them away on a cart."

Danny thought about this for a few seconds and then remembered he was supposed to be mad at Blade. "Well, just remember what I said. Stay with one of us all the time, okay Buddy?'

"Okay."

Danny Mac realized Kenann had come in and sat down. She was hollow eyed and pale. "Feeling better?"

"I'll manage."

"Hey, boy wonder here, despite disobeying me by going out alone -"

"You never said I couldn't."

"Don't split hairs. Anyway, he found a storage room filled with boxes of brown robes. Want to bet that's the dress code for tonight's ceremony? It could work to our advantage for everyone to be dressed alike especially when we make our escape."

Blade produced the robes with an impish grin.

"Good job, Buddy." Kenann smiled at him too.

"What's the plan?"

"If we can manage to make our way to the underground passage without being seen we can maybe make it to the outside before we are apprehended. And then hopefully Andy will be able to pick up our signal again. Then our only job will be to stay alive until the cavalry comes."

Blade's eyes lit up. "Do you really think they will bring in the cavalry?"

Danny Mac tosseled Blade's hair. "With Mrs. Gage on the case, I would not be at all surprised." Danny Mac turned back to Kenann.

"Kenann, you're starting to concern me. Do you think you are coming down with something?"

"I don't know. I feel really weird."

"Do you hurt anywhere?

"No. It's my head. It feels like cotton wool. I keep trying to clear it but then the fog rolls in."

A voice from the doorway responded, "I will have our physician come immediately to examine you."

Kenann jumped. Her hand went to her throat in a nervous, defensive gesture.

"There is no need, Pierre. I am sure I will be fine."

"No, I insist. He will be here within the hour."

Danny Mac wondered how long he had been listening at the door. He gave no indication he had heard their discussion about escaping but it was a solid reminder to be more careful. Pierre came over and touched Kenann's hair. She flinched imperceptibly. He smiled at her with a new air of propriety that Danny Mac did not like. Danny Mac took Kenann's hands in his and coaxed her to her feet.

"Come along Your Highness, you need to lie down. Excuse us, Pierre."

"Of course." His hooded eyes followed them as they left the room looking like that of a King Cobra ready to strike.

CHAPTER THIRTY FIVE

Judy was relieved that her camel docilely followed the one in front of her. She had finally become adjusted to the rhythmic jerk and sway of the camel's gait, but she doubted she would be able to steer the thing. Their caravan appeared nondescript in traditional black robes. Leo estimated it would take them a better part of the day to reach their destination. Judy settled in and tried to take her mind off the heat and smell of their hairy conveyances. Mrs. Gage turned occasionally to inquire how she was fairing. Judy hoped to maintain her relationship with Mrs. Gage after all this was over. She truly fascinated her. She allowed her mind to replay the events of the last several days. How was it possible that so much could change in such a short period of time? She couldn't wait to lay eyes on Kenann again. Without knowing it, Kenann had been her lifeline since they had met their freshman year of college. With her gentle, goofy ways she had soothed and comforted Judy and made her feel safe. A wave of murderous rage rose up in her as she thought of Kenann getting hurt. Her hands fisted, and she clenched every part of her body at the thought. She would rip the head off anyone who stood in her way to get to Kenann. Her camel turned its head and grunted at her. She realized she was digging her nails and knees sharply into its skin. She laughed and said, "Sorry."

"Excuse me, dear. Were you speaking to me?" Mrs. Gage had turned.

"No, to my camel."

"My, the heat is getting to you," and laughed. "We should be stopping soon for midday repast. Can you manage?"

"I'm fine Mrs. G. I was just thinking of what I planned to do to those people who were holding Kenann and I guess I was taking it out on my ride here."

Mrs. Gage nodded and turned back in her seat. She certainly understood hatred and a need for revenge. Those sentiments had controlled her life for many years.

*   *   *

The witch doctor, as Kenann considered him, came to examine her in the promised few minutes. He and Pierre insisted that Danny Mac leave during the examination. He took one look at Kenann's face and crossed his arms over his considerable chest and refused, daring them to try to throw him out. Something was happening with Kenann and he felt powerless to know what it was or how to stop it. He prayed silently, ignoring Pierre who sat waiting by the bedroom door. He called upon the protection and power of the Lord and felt strength, not of his own, fill his heart and was encouraged.

'Thank you. Lord,' he silently said.

After the doctor took her temperature and poked around on her awhile, he proclaimed, "She is fine. Just very tired. She must rest all day to be ready for the ceremony tonight. Give her this to drink in her juice." He produced a packet of powdered substance.

"What is in it?" Danny Mac was suspicions.

"It is only a mild sedative. She appears nervous about the ceremony. It is understandable. But she must rest so please make sure she takes it."

"All right."

Pierre motioned for the doctor to follow him outside. "Well?"

"It is as you wish. Her temperature is elevated, and her abdomen is tender when palpated. She is ripe with fertility on this day. You must implant her with your seed tonight."

*   *   *

Their caravan stopped at midday. They were getting into rockier terrain and found some shade on the lee side of a large outcropping. After eating and conversing, they all settled back to rest their eyes. Johnson and Whitaker never spoke to anyone except Andy. They sat off to themselves at the fringes of the group but kept vigilant watch. When Judy woke from her refreshing nap, they were still alert and on guard. Where do they get these guys? But she couldn't help but be glad they were on their side.

They remounted and continued. They reached the last known GPS coordinates before sundown. They saw nothing out of the ordinary and were deflated. They had no other leads.

The men remaining back in Alexandria were monitoring Katarina's conversations but were gleaning nothing useful. Danny Mac and Kenann could be anywhere now. Mrs. James had said very little for days, content to listen and observe. She cleared her throat, and everyone turned her way.

Speaking with a quiet confidence she said, "Can we move on and come back to watch this area after dark?" No one questioned her reasoning. They had no other course of action so this one seemed as good as any. When darkness fell, they tethered the camels, leaving them with Leo's men, and walked the mile or so back on foot to the area. The desert is a cold place at night and Judy was eternally grateful for the long, concealing robe for covering. Luckily there was little moon or starlight visible through the clouds. With all but their eyes covered in black, they were virtually undetectable as they walked silently along. Andy, wearing night vision goggles, was able to keep them on course and avoid pitfalls in the rocky terrain. He heard the sound first and halted the group. He motioned for them to crouch down and hug their bodies to the base of the nearest rock. It did not take long for the rest of them to hear it too. A helicopter was making its way toward them and landed not fifty yards from where they crouched. Eight people disembarked and walked up to a rock face. The helicopter immediately rose and flew away into the night.

Andy watched intently as one of the parties, pulled on what appeared to be a viney protuberance and a dark opening appeared in the rock face. The party entered, and the dark cleft filled in again.

"Well, I'll be ..." Andy whispered. It appeared they had found what they were looking for. In a few minutes another helicopter was heard approaching and the same scene was played out. Andy had a plan. He quickly outlined it to the group. No one argued with him but waited silently as they heard him make his way over to the cliff face that housed the secret opening. Johnson and Whitaker also had the night vision goggles. In deference to his experience and rank, Johnson gave his set to Jake. Jake acknowledged them with a nod and placed them on. He could see Andy in position but well out of sight of the now concealed opening. When the next load of people made their way to the rock face, he could see Andy making ready and as they began filing into the doorway, he silently joined the back of the group and was swallowed up into the darkness beyond. Jake realized he had been holding his breath and let it out in a sigh.

"Well, now we wait and pray." And he did.

Chapter Thirty Six

Kenann was being attended by young, dark skinned women sent to her loaded with white diaphanous material, jewels and perfumed lotion. She moved as in a dream while the women bathed and rubbed her with the lotion. The gown they draped over her head felt soft and luxurious against her skin. She wore nothing under it. They wound her hair into intricate braids around her head. Tendrils of hair curled around her face. They placed large golden intricately engraved bracelets on her upper arms bent in place with light pressure. They stood back and surveyed the result. Satisfied with her simple elegance, the women left as quietly as they came. Kenann stood motionless in the center of the room. Danny Mac found her this way several minutes later. Dressed in his own white robed material, he tried to keep his voice light.

"Kenann, are you ready for our command performance?'

She turned slightly and looked at him. His dark skin and hair looked exotic against the white material of the flowing robe. She was once again struck by the rugged beauty of his face. Her thoughts returned to the night ahead.

"What are we going to do about Blade?"

"We have it all figured out. Don't worry about it."

"Are you sure?'

"Yes. You just need to wow the crowd with your beautiful reincarnated self. Kenann, you are beautiful. Do you know that?"

"No."

"Well, trust me, you are. And I am proud of you." He walked over and took her face in his hands. She smiled up at him and he was undone by her honesty and vulnerability. He managed to smile back and then lightly kissed her on the lips.

"Listen, when this is over, we *are* going to talk."

Kenann could not respond. She was still concerned that Danny Mac was being affected by their situation and was not really in love with her. He had the power to destroy her heart and she was so scared to take that chance. She changed the subject.

"How much time do we have?"

He didn't push her for a response. "About half an hour."

"Where is Blade?"

"He's getting things ready."

"What do you two have up your sleeve?"

"An ingenious bit of trickery. We need to be watching for a way to get the three of us into the back without being followed."

*   *   *

It seemed like hours since Andy was swallowed up in the black hole of the rock face. Several contingents came and entered before they saw Andy appear at the entrance and motion with his arm for them to come quickly. They didn't hesitate. Andy grabbed each person as they came to the doorway and shoved them into a dark alcove near the opening. He motioned for them to be silent. In the next moment they saw a man appear and wait at the main entrance. It opened to the next group of arrivals and the man ushered them to an area half way down the hallway, where they were handed something before continuing. In a few moments, the area was quiet again.

Andy whispered, "Those people are being issued brown robes with hoods. I've been able to grab a few and watch what's going on. They are taking them down to the end of this passage and then someone else is taking charge of the group and leading them off somewhere to the left."

He grew silent again and they waited. The process repeated itself many times. They used the lull between groups to don the robes and make careful exploration. They discovered several deep alcoves along the corridor and slowly and systematically made their way toward the end. Johnson and Whitaker were amazed at the ability of this civilian group to move with such stealth. They were in the last alcove when they heard one of the men say, "That's the lot of them. Let's head down to the bottom level and watch the show."

"Shouldn't we keep watch up here?"

"Nah, I've engaged the locking mechanism. No one is coming through that door. Besides I heard they've got some dame claiming to be a reincarnated goddess. I've got to see this."

The men left, and no one moved. They looked at each other and waited for Andy's direction. He was at the front of the dark alcove on the alert, listening for any sign of movement. He pulled the cowl up over his head and ventured into the passage. He waited and then moved over to the balustrade. They saw him falter. When he returned to them, he was shaking his head.

"This place is beyond belief." He briefly described what he saw. The others shared his amazement.

"I'm going to do a bit more exploring. Johnson, you're with me. Whitaker, you and Jake stay here as the rear guard. We'll be back as soon as we have a feel for the layout." And they were gone. Andy was in his zone and completely focused on getting Danny Mac, Kenann and Blade back safely.

He spoke quietly into his mike. "Danny, we're in."

There were several moments of silence when a whispered voice echoed in Andy's ear.

"Where?"

"We are on the highest most balcony."

"How many men do you have?"

Andy chuckled and whispered, "We've got five men and three very extraordinary women."

"Why am I not surprised?"

"Where are you?"

"We are here together waiting the start of the ceremony." Danny Mac gave Andy instructions on how to help them now that they had arrived. Andy listened intently and indicated his understanding. He and Johnson made their way to the bottom level to comply with Danny Mac's orders.

The others were getting restless waiting on their comrades' return when Andy appeared in the entrance to their alcove. Johnson was not with him.

"Put your hooded cowl's low over your faces and walk with me. Talk quietly among yourselves as we go along. Be casual. If we are stopped keep talking unconcerned. I'll deal with anyone we meet."

Mrs. James spoke. "Have you seen the kids?"

"No, but I've spoken to Danny and they are all fine." He touched her hand.

Mrs. James smiled sweetly at Andy. He was a good boy.

They moved out into the dimly lit balcony and acted as Andy had instructed. They passed other groups of dark-robed figures moving about, making their way to the bottom floor. Andy jerked to a sudden stop throwing the others off momentarily. Jake gripped Andy by the elbow.

"What is it, son?"

"I just recognized a man from our own State Department."

They had gathered around Andy trying to maintain a casual stance. Everyone reacted in their own way to this news. Johnson and Whitaker cursed, Jake invoked the Lord and Mrs. Gage indicated she was not surprised.

Jake spoke, "We have to stop this operation somehow."

"That's the plan, Sir."

They continued their descent using the open stairway. Andy feared the small confines of the elevator would open them up for possible detection. They found Johnson on the main thoroughfare.

"Are we good?"

"Yes, sir."

CHAPTER THIRTY SEVEN

The central hall was dark except for the light from numerous torches burning along the walls and on stands near the pillars. Shadows danced along the cut stone walls. The bleachers were filled with hooded figures watching expectantly for the ceremony to begin. From somewhere distant came the sound of a ram's horn and the curtain at the back of the platform parted.

Danny Mac escorted Kenann onto the platform holding her hand out in front of them. They made a dazzling pair. Pierre was not concerned. It would make his triumph all the sweeter in the end. As leader of the Society, he intoned the beginning of their annual gathering. He reminded them that this was a very special event in that the Night of the Lion only occurred every five hundred years. He introduced Kenann and Danny Mac, who sat on raised platforms like royalty, as if it was the most natural thing in the world to have a reincarnated goddess and her high priest in residence. Just then Blade was brought in by two guards and placed face down at Danny Mac's feet. His hands were tied behind his back. It took great restraint for both Danny Mac and Kenann to remain impassive.

Danny Mac noticed there was no one else on the dais with them. The guards had retreated to stand just off the side on ground level. He could barely make out the forms of Katerina and Angelo sitting in a small boxed area just off to his right. All other participants were several feet away. The room had grown eerily silent. Something was off. Pierre was altering the planned ceremony. He nodded to someone in the shadows and then came the rich melodious sound of a gong.

Danny Mac started as Kenann rose from her chair. She glided to the front of the platform and stood erect and motionless for several seconds. He waited and wondered if she had suddenly had an idea to initiate their escape.

When she spoke, her voice had a strange ethereal quality. "Sojourners and brethren. I come to you from across the centuries. I have come many times but have not been known. Now is the time. The fulfillment of the prophecies will begin tonight. You will all know your part when the time comes. You have done well to name Pierre as your leader. He has now been chosen to fulfill the prophecy." There was a murmur in the crowd.

"Pierre," she turned and held out her hand to him. He stepped forward and came to her side. "I claim you as my consort. The gods have chosen you."

Pierre smiled and bowed slightly to Kenann. Danny Mac didn't like this. He wished he could see Kenann's face. If this were part of some plan she had hatched, he wanted to know what was next. She made no sign of communicating with him at all. Blade still trussed at his feet looked up with a question on his face. Danny Mac made an imperceptible lift of his shoulder. He was as much in the dark as Blade.

Pierre spoke in a commanding voice, "It is time for our future to be sanctioned with blood. The Fates have sent us whom they have chosen. Let it begin." He led Kenann to the back of the platform. Her face was still in shadow. She did not glance at Danny Mac as she passed. Danny Mac slowly rose to his feet. According to the ritual instructions he had memorized, he raised his arms and recited the required incantation. Then bending, he lifted Blade into his arms and walked toward the sacrificial altar. He was not aware when Pierre guided Kenann through the curtains at their back. Katerina slipped out of her seat as well. Angelo lifted a quizzical eyebrow, but she waved him aside as she followed Pierre from a distance.

Danny Mac laid Blade down on his back and releasing his bonds placed his hands in front of him. He recited the remainder of the recitation. He laid his hands on Blade as in a final blessing, making sure everything was in place. They had practiced this several times over the last two days. Danny Mac's hands were rock steady as he raised the razor-sharp dagger. As it was held suspended over his head, he heard a muffled cry.

Kenann! Angelo heard it too. He was on his feet. No one else had been close enough to distinguish the sound. Danny Mac stood frozen. He looked down at Blade. He whispered, "Hey, kid, can you handle things out here by yourself?" He had no idea where the others were at this moment. Blade would be on his own.

"Go for it."

Danny Mac plunged the dagger into Blade's chest. He used sufficient force to puncture the taut plastic bag filled with a red concoction they designed without stabbing Blade. It was tricky. Blade squeezed the makeshift pumping mechanism they had devised for maximum effect. Blood squirted from the boy's chest. The crowd gasped, and Danny Mac ran from the stage. The crowd sat stunned, unsure what was happening. No one moved for several seconds and then murmurs began. Blade had an idea.

He leaped to his feet to the horror of the crowd. He began swaying and chanting unintelligible sounds. He pointed at various sections of the spectators and suppressed a smile when they shrank back as one. He wasn't sure how long he could keep this up.

His heart sank when he saw a group of the hooded figures step out of the crowd and make their way slowly toward him.

*   *   *

Danny Mac and Angelo made it to the back area and were confronted by Katerina standing at the base of the spiral stairs holding a semi-automatic weapon cradled in her arms. The sound of a fierce struggle emanated from the room above. Angelo looked at Danny Mac. "May I?"

Danny Mac responded, "Please."

Moving with lightening speed Angelo punched Katerina square in the face and snatched her weapon as she dropped to the floor. Danny Mac was already running up the stairs and entering the room above.

Roaring in rage, Danny Mac grabbed Pierre who was attempting to pin Kenann beneath him on the bed. He shook him like a rat and tossed him head first into the stone wall. He ran to him and began pounding his face with his fists. The red haze faded slowly from his eyes and he stopped. Pierre lay as lifeless as a rag doll, his neck obviously broken. Danny Mac ran to Kenann. Her gown was torn in shreds as if clawed by a wild animal. He took her in his arms and they held on to each other as if their life depended on it.

Angelo moved into the room and stood guard a discreet distance from them. Danny Mac wrapped Kenann in the sheet. He turned from her to talk to Angelo and saw Katerina poised in the doorway holding the pistol she had pulled from her ankle holster. Murderous rage distorted her face.

"Angelo, you idiot. You ruined everything. Pierre told me tonight when he bedded that thing, he was naming me his Lieutenant. I'll kill you," and raised the gun to fire. Angelo had no time to react. Danny Mac made a powerful leap and was propelled back against Angelo by the impact of the bullet.

For a few seconds no one moved. A guttural cry escaped Kenann. She catapulted herself at Katerina, dislodging the gun with a swift downward chop of her hand. She drove her elbow into Katerina's windpipe and grabbing her by the hair, head butted her. Finally, she doubled up her fist and drove it into her already bruising face. The impact sent her reeling back and over the railing of the staircase.

*   *   *

Blade was poised to run from the figures moving menacingly toward him. One of the people raised their head and allowed the cowl to slip. It was Jake! He winked and smiled reassuringly. Blade stood his ground as the group divided and moved up the steps on either side of him. They paused on the platform.

Mrs. Gage whispered to Jake, "Get him out of here. I'll handle this crowd and join you in a moment."

The figures surrounded Blade and moved him toward the back of the dais. Mrs. Gage raised her arms and bowed her head as if invoking the gods. She waited a few more beats to give her friends the extra time they needed, and then she raised her face to the crowd. She greeted them in Russian, Greek and Dutch. She instructed them in English to stay in their seats until the goddess returned to give each of them a special assignment. They would be richly rewarded for their obedience. She lowered her arms and turning, forced herself to walk slowly to the back of the platform. She expected at any moment to hear a cry from one of the guards for her to halt.

Andy came through to the back area in time to see a female plummet to the stone pavement. Judy and Mrs. James outdistanced all the others to the crumpled form. Turning her over, Judy turned a quizzical gaze to Andy.

"It's Katerina," he said.

Judy examined her. "She's dead."

Blade ran over and stood by the panel that held the opening to the underground passage. He promised Danny Mac that he would get Kenann to safety no matter what. Not leaving his post he motioned to Jake.

"Hey guys, check up there." He pointed to the room at the top of the stairs.

Andy turned to the group. "Whitaker with me." They took the steps two at a time. Taking out their weapons, they instinctively took up positions on either side of the doorway but swiftly entered upon seeing what was being enacted before them. Angelo was cradling Danny Mac's head in the crook of his arms. Kenann was ripping material from an already tattered garment to staunch the flow of blood from the wound on Danny Mac's upper chest. Kenann turned at the sound at the door.

"Oh, Andy, he's been shot." Andy knelt beside them.

"He took a bullet for me. He stood in front of me." Angelo appeared to be in shock.

Andy turned to Whitaker, "Get Judy up here."

With swift efficiency she examined the wound, and applied a pressure dressing over the material already in place from Kenann's gown.

"Nothing vital appears to be affected. The blood loss is our biggest concern. We have to keep him from going into shock. Get me that bed comforter." Angelo continued to cradle Danny Mac with tender care. Danny Mac's eyes fluttered once and then opened.

"Hey." Danny Mac's voice was weak, but he grinned.

Angelo whispered, "Why? Why did you do that?"

"What?" Danny Mac croaked.

"Why did you take that bullet for me?"

"Someone died for me," His face grimaced with the effort to speak, "Once, a long time ago."

They swaddled him into the comforter and using ornamental spears hanging on the wall with the rest of the bed linen, they fashioned a litter. Judy gave Kenann her brown robe to cover her tattered gown. Andy said, "Let's get out of here." No one questioned Angelo's right to carry the head of the litter as they descended the stairs. Kenann didn't look at Pierre lying crumpled near the wall, his head at an unnatural angle.

Just then Kenan saw Granny James. Granny reached up and framed her face in her work worn palms. Here was all the love and security she needed. They grinned at each other and Granny stepped back to let her pass.

The group made their way to the opening that Blade had proudly produced. Once everyone was through, he maneuvered the mechanism that closed it behind them. Kenann directed them to make their way to the bottom and turn right in the passage. A few of them carried torches to light the way but the narrow steps required careful concentration to maintain their footing. As Danny Mac had predicted, the passage led to a back entrance. After a few minutes' perusal, the latch was discovered, and they were soon standing under the desert stars.

The band took a moment to orient themselves to the fact that they were free of the underground cavern. Andy instructed everyone to follow Leo who would lead them back to the tethered camels and their only means of escape.

Kenann pondered her rescuers as they made their way through the desert night– the adopted sheik, the government agent, the commander turned shepherd, the assassin turned minister and his enemy turned friend, the nurse, the boy, the Irish grandma and the international woman of mystery. As Kenann marveled at them and her part in it all, she tried to wrap her mind around the fact that she had killed someone tonight with her bare hands. She wasn't sure how she felt about that but knew she would do it all over again. She walked beside the litter and watched Danny Mac's unconscious form. His skin was pale under a sheen of sweat. He was looking worse. She cried out to the Lord in her heart to spare him and kept on walking through the night.

Chapter Thirty Eight

As usual Mrs. Gage had a few surprises up her sleeve. She revealed to them after leaving the subterranean cavern that there would be a private transport helicopter waiting on them near the tethered camels. She had contacted yet another "friend" before they had gone in with Andy and given them strict orders not to intervene but simply wait on them with the helicopter. They were all relieved to know that transportation was just over the next rise, when shots rang out behind them. They ran for cover behind those ever-present rocks and waited. Angelo ended up beside Jake.

"It's the guards from the temple. They're trained killers. They'll not let anyone escape. Let me go to them. Maybe I can stop them."

"Angelo, they'll just kill you and come after us."

"I need to do this." He stepped out from behind the rock and called out in Arabic.

"Brothers. It is Angelo. Let me come to you." A shot flying close to his head was the only answer. He stood frozen when he heard a cry from one of the guards. He glanced over his shoulder to see that Kenann had taken off her brown robe and was walking haltingly toward him with her arms outstretched in front of her, her tattered white gown billowing behind her in the moonlight. Angelo could hear the murmured cries of the men trying to decide who or what she was.

Angelo looked over his shoulder and smiled. The boy had joined the

Little Lion. With his blood-soaked garments, he moaned and waved his arms and looked the very picture of a zombie walking stiff legged at them. Blade then reached into his pants and pulled out the canisters he had secured. Pulling the pressurized tops, he dropped them at his feet producing the white smoke Danny Mac had assured him would work.

"Effrits," the armed men cried but still they stood their ground behind the wall of white smoke. By the time it had dissipated there was no one there. The armed men stood looking at their leader who was not sure himself what to do.

The group had hurried to the waiting helicopter saying swift farewells to Leo and his men who were mounted and ready to escape through a wadi that boasted a hidden cave. They secured Danny Mac into the long jump seat, and Angelo and Kenann took up posts on either side with a watchful eye from Judy. No one saw Blade stick out his tongue at the men raising their rifles to fire at the retreating helicopter.

EPILOGUE

Kenann sat curled up on her couch under her favorite afghan. She was desolate with misery. All the people she loved were gone. Life was not fair. She dropped her head onto the pillow she clutched to her chest and sighed.

Just because she had a stupid head cold with a fever, they wouldn't let her go with them to the hospital to bring Danny Mac home. It had been three very long weeks since they had come back to the States and a week before that getting Danny Mac stable enough to fly home. Rather than make them go to DC, Andy had arranged to have them interviewed and debriefed here in Memphis. She supposed this had more to do with Danny Mac than anything. Jake had his Medical Power of Attorney and he refused to let Danny Mac recuperate anywhere but Memphis much to Carter's extreme frustration.

Judy had taken a leave of absence and went home to be with her parents. She said she had a lot of catching up to do. She had not left Kenann's side while they were in Alexandria. Kenann wasn't sure if it was entirely for her, or to avoid dealing with what lay between her and Andy. Andy decided to give her the space she needed. He was not known to be a patient man, but some things were worth waiting for. He stayed in Danny Mac's apartment while the debriefings were conducted. Kenann found Carter to be a very interesting fellow. He was a small, compact man but powerful in personality. She could see how he intimidated even men as strong and brave as Danny Mac and Andy. There was a very wary respect between Carter and Jake. There is a story there, thought Kenann.

Angelo had mysteriously disappeared after a few days in Alexandria. Carter had been furious that he had been allowed to escape. But he was mollified with the extensive computer data that Johnson had been able to download from Pierre's quarters as Danny Mac had commanded. It would take years to track down and destroy this organization completely. Carter hoped to God they could. He knew that Andy had let Angelo go. He had no heartburn with that, really. Angelo had cooperated fully and was a different man since Danny Mac had taken that bullet for him. When the time was right, he might become an important asset.

Mrs. Gage and Jake remained inseparable, but they seemed a little guarded with each other. Neither wanted to let go, but they were not sure how to move forward. Granny James had returned to West Virginia after making sure Danny Mac was on the mend. A strong bond had forged between them since first meeting in the subterranean cavern.

Kenann could hear someone coming into the foyer. She heard Danny Mac's deep voice saying something and then the door to his apartment closed. She buried her face under the afghan feeling lost and confused. She had her arms up over her head and did not hear the door to her own apartment open. She became aware of someone standing over her and peeked out from underneath her cocoon. Danny Mac stood solemn above her. They continued to stare at each other for what seemed an eternity.

"You've been avoiding me."

"I have not."

"Kenann, you're a rotten liar."

"I haven't. There is always an army of people around you. If it's not church people, it's all those government guys. How would you know if I was avoiding you or not?"

"Because you're the only one I wanted to see."

She stopped breathing. She wasn't sure she would ever breathe again. She waited.

"Kenann, what do you want?"

"What do you mean?"

"You know what I mean."

"Don't do this, Danny Mac. I may puke if you make me talk about this."

"Well, that's flattering." He gave in and sat down on the coffee table facing her.

"I'm scared out of my wits," she whispered.

"You think I'm not?" He paused and then spoke softly, "Don't you want me?" It was Danny Mac's turn to stop breathing.

"How can you say that? Who wouldn't want you?"

"That's not what I asked. Do *you* want me?" She couldn't speak but only nodded. Despite his best efforts he couldn't stop the grin.

"Danny Mac, I don't get any of this. It doesn't make any sense to me. You are well... you and ... you know what I'm like. I am goofy and disorganized and unpredictable, and I'll never be as pretty as you are." At this he shoved her head back with the palm of his hand.

"Seriously, Danny Mac, why would you want me?"

"Kenann, I love you for all those reasons and then some. I can't explain it. I just know with all my heart, I do."

When she saw the look on his face, she wanted desperately to believe him but couldn't help herself from asking, "Are you sure?"

"Yep."

"I'm still scared." She paused, "Can we date?"

"Kenann, you're killing me here."

Her eyes implored. He caved. "Oh, all right, we'll date for a while, but one way or another you *are* going to marry me. Is that clear?"

"Crystal," and leaped into his arms knocking him backwards onto the floor. His grunt of pain was lost in the joy he felt.

*   *   *

Several moments later, Danny Mac finished trailing his lips up her neck. Nibbling on her ear lobe, he whispered, "Carter offered you a job."

/

CPSIA information can be obtained
at www.ICGtesting.com
Printed in the USA
LVHW040719140521
687395LV00007B/98